The Curious Cases of

Sherlock Holmes

Volume 1

By

Stephen Herczeg

Paperback ISBN 978-1-78705-758-6
ePub ISBN 978-1-78705-759-3
PDF ISBN 978-1-78705-760-9

Published by MX Publishing
335 Princess Park Manor, Royal Drive,
London, N11 3GX
www.mxpublishing.co.uk

Cover design by Brian Belanger

To Carol

for always being my muse

Contents

Copyright Notices

Foreword
by David Marcum

Sometimes over the last few years – and especially during the tumultuous events of 2020 (and now 2021) – I've thought about connections that we all have now that simply didn't previously exist. For many of us, not that long ago, our world was very small – family and co-workers and the people we saw in our towns. But with the connections of social media – for good or bad – we now have links to people all over the world that we would have never known otherwise. If the COVID pandemic had hit just a few years ago, I personally wouldn't have had any specific concerns about people outside of my own local sphere – it would have been horrible, but nameless and faceless. Now, by way of connections through mutual admiration of Sherlock Holmes, I "know" many people from around the world – even if we've never met in person (yet) – and my concern over their well-being and safety, and my joy at their triumphs and good news, exists in a way that wouldn't have been possible before.

One such person that I'm very glad to now "know" in this modern sense is Stephen Herczeg, Author.

I first became acquainted with Steve while editing a book of sequels to the original Sherlock Holmes stories. He had previously written a Holmes tale that was included in the Belanger Books collection Sherlock Holmes: Adventures in the Realms of H.G. Wells (2017), and now he wanted to write a sequel to "The Engineer's Thumb". As a diligent editor, I'm always happy to receive new stories, and I'm always hoping that the author will be good – which means to me that the stories are written in the mold of the original Canon in the voice of Dr. John H. Watson – and also that the author will become a reliable repeat contributor. Steve is both of these.

His enthusiasm is notable and always welcome. He always wants to join the party. When he doesn't know something about The Canon, he's always very happy to learn, and he's great to work with. Whenever I've been involved in editing a new Sherlock Holmes anthology – for either Belanger Books or MX Publishing – Steve always steps up, with stories that are Watsonian and uniquely interesting. When I also began editing new Solar Pons anthologies, he wanted to be part of those as well.

Like many of us Sherlock Holmes pasticheurs, Steve isn't in it to get rich. (In the case of the MX anthologies, he – along with the rest of us – donates his royalties to the Stepping Stones School for special needs children at Undershaw, one of Sir Arthur Conan Doyle's former homes. So far, the nearly two-hundred contributors from around the world have raised over $75,000 for the school, and no end in sight!) We write because we enjoy it – as painful as the process is sometimes – and also to add to the Great Holmes Tapestry. Another benefit of writing for these various Holmes anthologies is that they give us opportunities to produce more stories that we otherwise might not attempt, and after a while, we step back and see that we've written a good many of them.

And that's what has happened for Steve: After being in so many Holmes anthologies, he now has a plethora of adventures with his name on them, ready to be collected into his own book. I'm personally thrilled that this volume now exists, and that people who possibly didn't have a chance to read these stories when they originally appeared in various anthologies can now enjoy them collected in one place. I very much hope that this book will be followed by Volumes II and III and so on . . . .

I'm very glad, in this time of worldwide worry, to know Steve, and to have enjoyed his stories. Sit back and dive in – and let the present fade away for a while as Watson tells us another excellent adventure of his friend, Sherlock Holmes . . . .

David Marcum
February 2021

Foreword
by Derrick Belanger

It was on July 12, 2017 when I was first introduced to the talented Sherlockian author Stephen Herczeg via email. Mr. Herczeg wrote to me, starting off as he always does with a friendly "Gidday!" and asked if I'd consider including his story "The Curious Case of the Sleeper" in my anthology Sherlock Holmes: Adventures in the Realms of H.G. Wells. I read his story, and replied with a strong YES! "The Curious Case of the Sleeper" does a remarkable job of blending the writing of H.G. Wells with that of Dr. Watson's adventures. Add in a touch of Dickens with the ending, and you have a wonderfully imaginative mystery.

That was the first of many stories by Mr. Herczeg which I'm proud to have published. What amazes me with Herczeg's work is how he is able to create an excellent Sherlock Holmes pastiche no matter if he is working in the boundaries of Doyle's traditional Victorian England or if he is pushing those boundaries and incorporating elements of science fiction, horror, or steampunk. Take for example his excellent, "The Body at the Ritz". In this story, Holmes is called in to solve the mystery of a body found in an alley outside the Ritz hotel. The plot follows a traditional Holmesian narrative where Holmes and Watson are their 19th century selves; however, it also has them living in a steam powered world of horseless carriage lined streets and dirigibles covering the skies.

While this anthology focuses specifically on Herczeg's works around Sherlock Holmes, I would be remiss if I didn't also give a shout out to his wonderful writings of the other Sherlock Holmes, the one that resides in Praed Street, Mr. Solar Pons. Herczeg's Pontine works featured in The New Adventures of Solar Pons have Sherlock Holmes's successor with his partner, Dr. Parker, solving crimes in the early twentieth century, just as August Derleth intended. As Herczeg does with his Sherlock Holmes writing, sometimes he bends the rules a bit with his Pons stories. In "The Rondure of Cthulhu," his piece in

The Necronomicon of Solar Pons, the Praed street sleuth is pitted against the monsters from the world of H.P. Lovecraft. The story is an excellent piece of detective and weird fiction. I highly recommend seeking out Herczeg's Pontine work which is just as good as his Holmes writings.

One last point I'd like to make about Mr. Herczeg is how willing he is to push himself to keep writing new pastiches. Whenever I send out a call for new Sherlock Holmes fiction, Mr. Herczeg is always the first to respond, eagerly taking on the challenge of adding more stories to his personal Holmes canon. I'm sure this anthology will be the first of many.

Keep visiting 221 B Baker Street, Mr. Herczeg. We look forward to more thrilling adventures!

Derrick Belanger
February, 2021

The Curious Case of the Sleeper

I am fairly certain that if I had not been along at that precise moment then neither myself nor Sherlock Holmes would have ever heard of Thomas Graham or as he became known to the two of us, the Sleeper.

It was a bright day in July. A mid-summer heatwave was pummeling London with an unbearable ferocity. Even in my light frock coat, I could feel the pools of perspiration under my arms and the intermittent stream as rivulets ran down my side. I would have much preferred to have been home with my beloved, but Sherlock had called upon me to come with great haste.

As I walked briskly down Baker Street, I noticed a group milling around the entrance to 221b, my destination.

Mrs. Hudson was on the doorstep, attempting to convince the group to move away. I increased my pace to help out my dear colleague's housekeeper.

"I say, what seems to be the problem, Mrs. Hudson," I said.

She looked at me; hope crossing her face, then indicated the rabble before her.

"It's this lot Doctor Watson," she said.

I finally took in the members of the group. There were four young street urchins and an older man of about forty years. He was marginally taller than the children and likewise dressed in dirty rags and bare feet. I addressed him directly.

"What is the meaning of this Sir?"

He did not seem to hear. One of the urchins turned to face me. I recognised him. Tommy Bones he was called. He was one of the Baker Street Irregulars, Sherlock Holmes' personal network of spies and aides.

"Sir, this man, sir. 'e was down at the river bank. 'e don't make no sense. We thought that Mr. 'olmes might be interested in 'im".

I looked down my nose at Tommy.

"Is that all?"

Tommy's eyes roved around before sheepishly returning to gaze into mine.

"We thought there might be a couple o' coppers in it for us".

"That's more likely," I said.

I looked the man up and down. His eyes were slightly glazed and he stared off into the distance, vaguely taking anything in. He was certainly a mess. His clothes were rags that threatened to disintegrate if the slightest breeze were to touch them.

"He'd be better off at the hospital if you ask me," said Mrs. Hudson.

"I tend to agree with you there," I said.

I reached into my pocket and pulled out tuppence. I handed it to Tommy Bones.

"Run along now Tommy. We'll take this gentleman off your hands".

Tommy looked into his hand, his eyes lit up. He showed the other children then ran away yelling back over his shoulder "Thank you, Mr. Watson".

"It's Doctor Watson," I almost yelled, then thought better of it. I turned back to the dishevelled specimen before me.

"What should we do with you then?" I pondered out loud.

"Send him on his way I reckon," said Mrs. Hudson.

"I don't think he's quite right in the head. I'd like to examine him first and then he may need to go to the Hospital. I'll just take him inside," I said.

Mrs. Hudson looked terrified.

"Mind my floors then, I've just washed them. You can take him upstairs into the parlour. His nibs won't mind. He doesn't care how dirty the floors are," she said.

I helped the poor fellow up the stairs and brought him into Sherlock's parlour. It was empty. I assumed the great detective was out, which annoyed me more as he was the one who had sent for me.

I helped the distressed fellow sit down on the settee and began to give him the once over. His gaze continued to focus on distant objects, his eyes steady and unmoving. His clothing was very odd. A collarless, cuffed shirt. A pair of knee-length knickerbockers and no shoes. His feet were caked with mud. His right hand was covered in something black like soot, his left with dirt and blood from various scratches. He was unshaven and his hair was unfashionably long and matted with dirt.

I checked his pulse. Strong. Constant. His temperature. Fine. His breathing. Steady. I pulled out my stethoscope and listened to his heart. I gave him a cursory check for wounds, bumps and abrasions, but he was whole and unmarked. Within a couple of minutes, I had come to the conclusion that this man was perfectly healthy.

Mrs. Hudson came into the parlour. She carried a small glass half-filled with amber liquid. She looked at me and smiled.

"I thought a small brandy might help your friend here," she said.

She bustled over to the man and held the glass beneath his nose. His hand rose, grabbed the glass and downed it in one swallow. He continued to stare into space, but his head shivered slightly as the alcohol hit his stomach.

"Well I thought it would do more than that," said Mrs. Hudson. She shrugged, took the glass and wandered off.

I watched her go then turned back to my patient. It seemed to me that this man had lost his mind. He was beyond my help and would need another sort of professional. My train of thought was broken by a voice behind me.

"What the devil do you have here Watson?"

I turned. Sherlock stood in the doorway, dressed in a smoking jacket and eyeing us both with a slight expression of bemusement.

"One of your boys, Tommy Bones, brought this man to your doorstep. Mrs. Hudson wanted to turn him away. I wouldn't have it. The man seemed to be outside of his own mind. I wanted to examine him to make sure he was not injured or suffering some ailment that I could fix, but he is fine. What bothers him is beyond me, Holmes".

At the mention of my friend's name, the dishevelled gentleman's face snapped towards my voice. His eyes focused on us and uttered the first words he had spoken.

"Holmes?" he asked.

I stepped back in surprise. The man turned his head towards Sherlock. His eyes locked on my compatriot's face and examined him for a moment.

"Siger Holmes?"

The man stood slowly to rigid attention. His hand came up in a salute.

"Captain Siger Holmes?"

Sherlock's eyebrows rose. He returned the man's salute.

"At ease," said Holmes.

The other man dropped his hand and sat down once more. His eyes drifted off again.

"What in God's name was that all about?" I asked.

"Watson, I'm shocked to say that have no idea," said Holmes.

"Who is Siger Holmes?" I asked.

"That's a name I have not heard in a long time. Captain Siger Holmes was my great grandfather. He commanded a small naval vessel and died during the fourth Anglo-Dutch war in the late 18th century".

"How would this man know that?"

Sherlock studied the man carefully. After a moment a small grin crossed his face.

"Very clever. Very clever".

"What do you mean, Holmes?"

"Well Watson, we have here an unidentified man. He wears a shirt with no collar and long sleeves with the remnants of a ruff on the cuffs. This type of shirt would be worn with a cravat or similar, under a frock coat with a vest. His hair is long and untidy. If clean it would be worn swept back and tied. I would think it could lend itself to being powdered. He has a scraggly beard, uneven as though left to grow naturally rather than being trained into any particular style. He wears knickerbockers without any socks or shoes. What do those fashion choices indicate to you?"

"Very out of date?"

"Yes. Well done Watson. Then couple that with his knowledge of my great grandfather who died over a hundred years ago".

"Okay. But what does it mean?"

Sherlock shook his head.

"Watson, Watson, you do disappoint me sometimes," he said.

Sherlock moved in front of the man and came to attention.

"What is your name sailor?" he said in a commanding voice.

The man stood bolt upright and saluted.

"Lieutenant Thomas Graham, sir," he said.

"Who is King?" Sherlock asked.

"King George the third, sir," Graham said.

"What?" I blurted out.

Sherlock held up a finger to silence me.

"What year is it?"

An expression crossed the man's face, indicating in his mind that it was indeed Sherlock Holmes that was the mad man.

"Well it is 1790, sir," he said.

"Indeed," said Holmes "at ease again Sailor".

The man dropped his hand and sat. He seemed a little more aware of himself now and looked around the room instead of straight ahead.

I sidled up to Holmes and said, "What in the blazes is going on? Is he mad? Should we get him to a sanatorium?"

Holmes smiled.

"Watson. What we have here is one of two things. Either it is a man who has prepared himself to carry on in the persona of someone from the late eighteenth century".

"Or?"

"Or he is indeed a man from the late eighteenth century".

"That's impossible," I blurted out once more.

"Well that is for us to discover, isn't it?"

That smile still played on his lips.

"This could be a most satisfying mystery. I thank you for bringing it into my home," he said.

I started to say something but Holmes turned his attention back to the man.

"My dear fellow. What is the last thing you remember before my young compatriots found you and escorted you here?"

The man started to rise. Holmes held out a hand to stay his ascent. The man looked up at Holmes instead.

"I remember waking up. In a dark room. I was on a small cot. I found a door and staggered out into a long tunnel. It was so musty and dark. I don't know why I was there. I managed to find some light and headed towards it. I came out at the river. It was very strange. There were boats and buildings that I've never seen the like of before in my life. I tripped and fell into the mud. I must have passed out because when I awoke, that young rapscallion was kneeling next to me. I thought he was going for my purse. I barked at him to get away and tried to stand, but I fell to my knees again. Tommy talked to me and convinced me to come to you," he said.

"Good advice, I think. What's the last thing you remember before waking up?"

"I," he started, then stopped, closed his eyes urging his mind to remember.

"I had been sick. A fever. It had been days since I had slept. I took a sleeping draft and went to my bed," he continued.

He looked up at Holmes and said "and then I woke up in that accursed room".

Holmes' face remained stoic. He has never been one for emotion has our Sherlock Holmes.

"You said that you went to your bed. Where? What address do you live at?"

The man said, "I live above my shop, at number 5 Moorgate. Just south of the last remnants of the London Wall".

I'd had enough "what the Devil is he talking about? London Wall? That was demolished well over ..."

Holmes put a finger to my lips. Turned to face me. "Shhh. Let the man continue. Do you not see a pattern forming?"

Confused, I resigned myself to stay silent and grumpy. Once again Holmes was keeping me in the dark.

Holmes prompted him again "describe your home to us; it might help us locate it".

"I was a simple blacksmith before I served in the Navy. When I returned I used woodworking skills I'd picked up to expand the business and become a wainwright. One of London's best. We repair the coaches and wagons that frequented London. Business is very good and we are about to expand our premises. I had meetings with a financier today as I recall. I must return to my abode".

He started to rise. Holmes went to him and gently pushed him down again.

"I think Mr. Graham that you should take some time to recover. You must be famished and thirsty".

Graham nodded.

"Come to think of it yes. I am," he said.

Holmes said, "Watson can you get Mrs. Hudson to organise some food and drink for our friend here".

I moved away but Holmes called out again.

"Oh and a suitable change of clothes as well".

I nodded and moved away.

When I returned, Holmes was standing before Mr. Graham dressed and ready to leave. I was a little taken aback as I'd only been gone a few minutes.

"Well I'm glad you can move when you want to," I remarked.

"I'm intrigued Watson. I want to believe that Mr. Graham here is actually from the eighteenth century. I know that is highly improbable, but there is a chance and that excites me".

***

We arrived at the bank of the River Thames within the hour. The sun was still high and biting. Again, I was a streaming bath of sweat. Holmes, as usual, showed no impediment from the heat. His concentration was solely on the job ahead.

On our way, we made two stops. One to purchase two paraffin lanterns, the other to find Tommy Bones. It was he who now led the way.

"We found him down here," Tommy said as he led us down the stone steps.

Even from above, I could make out a small indentation in the drying mud of the riverbed. Holmes moved up to the depression and stooped down to investigate. He searched all around, examining every minutia. Finally, his eye fell on that which he sought.

He stood up and moved towards a small concealed opening in the wall beneath the street above.

"Give Tommy a couple of coppers will you Watson," he said as he moved off.

Grumbling, I reached into my pocket and once again paid the young street urchin.

He doffed a make-believe hat and said "thank you, Mr. Watson," and scurried away.

"Doctor," I shouted then turned to follow Holmes.

He stood at the entrance of a small passage; his lantern lit and held out to light the way. He turned and looked towards the depression then slowly scanned the ground back to the entrance.

"What is it, Holmes?" I asked.

"Do you not see Watson?" he asked me back.

I looked closer. Lit my own lantern and stooped down to examine the floor of the passage. Immediately I could see a set of footprints in the soft dirt covering the floor.

"Well that should make things easier," I said.

"Indeed Watson," said Holmes and bolted into the passage. I followed along behind through the cramped confines.

Several times I brushed the walls and my coat caught on the rough surface. I grumbled my annoyance prompting a reproach from Holmes.

"Yes, the coarseness of the brickwork explains the scratches on Mr. Graham's hands doesn't it," he remarked.

I'm sure he could see the expression on my face as realisation hit. I kept quiet not wanting to give him any further ammunition against me. It was a lot cooler in the corridor than outside. I gave silent thanks.

Holmes kept up a tremendous pace, but finally, he stopped before a wooden door set into the side of the passage. The door was shut. Holmes held up his lantern to examine the structure. He leant up against it and listened.

I started to speak but he held up a finger for silence. After a moment he pulled away from the door and grasped the handle, squeezed it and pushed the door open.

"What the devil was that about?" I asked.

"Well Watson, our Mr. Graham left this room in a bit of a daze, so you should ask yourself, why would the door be shut? It would seem improbable that he would have closed it, doesn't it?" he said.

I thought for a moment. Was about to say something but realised Holmes had already entered the room and kept it to myself. I followed him in.

The room was very Spartan with a dry, dusty, dirt floor. A small cot lay in one corner. The sheets were askew and filthy. There were footprints in the dirt near the bed, they overlaid each other in a messy pattern, but a single set led away towards the doorway. A cloying smell emanated from a small bowl on a stand near the head of the bed.

I moved towards it to have a closer look.

Holmes spoke from across the room "I wouldn't go too close to that if I were you Watson. Unless of course, you'd like to take the place of our Mr. Graham".

"What do you mean Holmes?" I asked.

"Those herbs are what was keeping our sleeper in a state of perpetual slumber," he said, "a distant cousin to the European valerian, procured from South America I would say. I smelt it as soon as we entered".

I backed away from the herbs, it was then I noticed the cold. I couldn't believe it. I looked around and noticed several boxes that held large blocks of ice. I breathed out. A cloud formed before my face.

"Makes you wonder why a sleeping man would need it to be so cold doesn't it Watson?" asked Holmes "possibly to keep his vital signs low and to avoid any stimulation".

I looked towards his voice and found Holmes stooped down on the other side of the room. He held the lantern before him. I could make out a faint set of shoe prints.

Mr. Graham had indeed had a visitor.

I looked back at the doorway. There was a trail of shoe prints leading out of the room, but not into it. I looked back towards Holmes and found him staring at me.

"Well done Watson," he said, "notice anything else?"

He started to examine the wall next to him. I looked back at the shoe prints and finally found what he was talking about. A heavier set of prints had been made near the wall, but with the heel closest to the wall, as if someone had stepped out of the wall and into the dirt-floored room. A trail of shoe prints led across the floor to the doorway where they exited the room.

The wall itself was fairly barren. It was plain stone brick with a single candle holder to one side. Some of the bricks were cracked and chipped, and a lot of mortar had fallen out over time. I guessed that this room was a few hundred years old, probably made when the original foundations of this part of London were laid.

"Ah-ha," said Holmes, pushing his finger into a gap in the mortar.

A loud click rang out in the silence and a section of brickwork, as tall as a man, pushed out from the wall. Holmes moved up to this new feature and prized the brickwork away from the wall. It formed a door and swung easily away from the wall. He looked back at me with a wry smile on his face.

"And that's how a man can walk out of a wall," he said.

Before I could answer Holmes had disappeared into the hidden corridor. I followed along in his wake. A short entrance led to a stairway that rose for about twenty feet and alighted at a corridor that was tight and very dark, our lanterns emitted a feeble glow that illuminated very little.

Suddenly, Holmes stopped. I pulled up short almost crashing into him and setting him on fire with my lantern. He turned when he felt the heat on his back.

"Look out Watson. I think I have enough light of my own thank you very much," he said.

He turned away and I heard a soft click. Then the corridor was flooded with light. I brought my hand up to shield my eyes. As they adjusted, I realised Holmes had found another hidden door. He pushed it open and stepped through.

I entered and found him standing before another door at the end of a wood-panelled corridor. He listened intently. I moved up to him and started to say something. His finger came up to silence me.

He turned his attention back to the sounds from the other side of the door, then without warning twisted the doorknob, pushed it open and walked through.

I heard a gasp from the room beyond and Holmes say, "Ah, Mr. Miller, I presume".

Another voice said, "who the Devil are you?"

I bustled into the room to find a portly man standing behind a desk staring at Holmes with a look of total surprise on his face. His jacket was draped over a nearby chair, his vest was open and sweat stains marred the pure white of his dress shirt.

Holmes had assumed a posture of complete arrogance near the centre of the room. He faced Miller, but his eyes roamed the room taking in every minute detail.

Miller moved out from behind the desk affronted at the arrival of two strangers in his study.

"I ask again Sir, who are you? What are you doing in my study?" he said.

I realised it was time to step in.

"I apologise, Sir, for this inconvenience. On behalf of my friend here, let me introduce ourselves. I am Dr. John Watson. This is Mr. Sherlock Holmes," I said.

Miller's face showed shock at the mention of Holmes' name. He stuttered before responding.

"Sh...Sherlock Holmes," he said, "why would you be coming from that corridor. Please explain yourself, Sir." His voice didn't seem to have the conviction of his words.

Holmes smiled.

"I think you know exactly why we've come through that doorway Mr. Miller," he said.

"I ... I don't know what you mean," he blustered.

"Your shoes seem to say something else," said Holmes.

I looked down at the large man's shoes. The soles had a small patina of brown dirt on them. Miller didn't even bother to look down, just tried to gather his thoughts.

"My shoes are dirty. It's not a crime," he said.

"No that's true. It is not a crime," said Holmes "but I think the authorities would look dimly at someone that confines a person against their will, uses their identity to forge corporate documents and takes over their company".

"What? Lies nothing but lies," he said.

Holmes walked to the desk and reached across to a pile of papers. It was then I noticed the nameplate with "Charles Miller" engraved on it. Holmes pulled a paper from the pile, studied it for a moment then held it up. It was on letterhead for a company called Graham Coach Builders. At the bottom was a series of black smudges that I recognised as fingerprints.

"I think you'll find these fingerprints belong to a man that once resided in the small room at the end of the passageway beyond the corridor from which we entered. A man who has rested in slumber in that room for quite a number of years. A man who is the original owner of the company that you represent Mr. Miller," Holmes said.

Miller blustered "what man? There is no man downstairs. I".

He thought for a moment. Smiled.

"Yes. I use that room for somewhere quiet to rest and escape the trials of the day. I find it very serene," he said, "in fact, I have just returned from a mid-afternoon nap".

Holmes smiled.

"I think not Mr. Miller," he said "the sweat stains beneath your armpits belie that fact. It would seem strange that anyone, even someone of your girth, could raise a sweat in that cold room".

Holmes shifted and moved closer to the desk.

"I put it to you, Mr. Miller. You were in that room earlier, but you found it empty. In your panic, you went into the adjoining passage and came out at the river. From there you searched high and low before returning to this office. That explains your sweaty underarms and the dirt on your shoes".

"Rubbish," said Miller "absolute rubbish".

Holmes continued "I will also put it to you that the man who normally resides in that room is none other than Mr. Thomas Graham. The founder of this company. That man".

Holmes pointed to his left. Miller's head, and mine, swivelled in that direction. On the wall above the fireplace was a large portrait of a man that had a strong resemblance to our dishevelled guest.

I gasped. Miller shuffled slightly forward. His hand went to the desk for support. He laughed.

"That man has been dead for a hundred years," he said, "you must be insane my dear Sir".

"I don't think so. In fact, I know so. Mr. Graham is at this moment sitting in my parlour. Very confused, but very alive," he said "I think he would be very interested to know that the great-grandson of his business partner has been keeping him alive and running the business in his stead".

Miller's face turned red with rage.

"This is an insane accusation. How dare you?" he said.

"Admit it, Charles. Your family has been running these Coachworks for a hundred years, haven't they? In the name of Mr. Thomas Graham's family, but his family does not exist does it?" he said.

"What do you mean Holmes?" I asked.

"Thomas Graham brought in a partner in 1785 by the name of George Miller. They built the company up but Miller remained as a silent partner, not a co-owner. George Miller gave Graham a concoction that caused him to slip into a deep sleep. One that has lasted for a hundred years. During that time, they have sown the tale of a reclusive Thomas Graham and family," he reached for the paper again and held it up "and used his fingerprints in lieu of a signature for all official and legal documents".

He placed the document down and turned to Miller.

"Is that not correct Mr. Miller?" he asked.

Miller's face had turned purple. He snatched up a letter opener and launched himself at Holmes.

Holmes, well versed in various styles of fighting, simply stepped to the side, threw a hand out and flipped poor Mr. Miller onto his back. The letter opener went clattering across the floor.

At that precise moment, the doorbell rang.

"Ah, a most opportune moment, I believe," said Holmes.

Within a few moments, Inspector Lestrade led a newly attired Thomas Graham into the office. Lestrade looked at Miller then at Holmes.

"What have you been up to Holmes?" he asked.

Holmes held out his hand towards Miller.

"This is Mr. Charles Miller. I'm sure he will have an interesting tale to tell you about our Mr. Thomas Graham, who is the true owner of Graham Coach Builders," he said.

Graham looked around the room. His eyes spied his portrait. He moved closer.

"I remember when this was painted. It was three years ago," he said.

"I think you'll find it was a hundred and three years ago," Holmes said.

Graham turned and looked at Holmes as if he was mad.

"What do you mean?" he asked.

I walked over to Graham and led him to a settee.

"I think you might want to sit down for this," I said. We both sat.

"Mr. Graham, this man is Charles Miller. I think you knew his great grandfather George," Holmes said.

"Yes. George. My good friend," he looked around "where is he?"

"I'm afraid he's been dead for about eighty years," said Holmes "but I don't think he was really your friend. Do you remember his giving you a draught to help you sleep?"

Graham smiled "yes, yes, he was worried I was a little tired and worn out. He prepared me a draught to help me sleep".

"Well you did sleep," said Holmes, pausing for effect "for a hundred years".

"What?" Graham gasped.

"Beneath this building. You slept. Kept cold and safe but in a perpetual slumber thanks to some South American herbs. While George and his heirs managed the company and built it up to quite a large enterprise, but they never had full control because you had never signed any part of the company over to George. They lived well off of your company. Used your fingerprints instead of your signature to keep control. There is a legend they spread that you had retired to the country and your family remain there," he said.

Lestrade spoke up "I've heard of Thomas Graham and his family".

"Very good Inspector," said Holmes, his condescending voice lit large for all to hear "and now you've met him".

Lestrade's face dropped. Confusion reigned.

"What?" he asked.

Holmes turned and held a hand out towards Graham.

"This is Thomas Graham. Alive and in the flesh. Confused and a century out of place, but he is here," Holmes said.

Lestrade stepped forward. Looked at Graham. Turned and looked up at the painting. Looked back at Graham. Shook his head.

"Can't be," he said, "that's impossible".

"It does sound highly incredible," I added.

"And I would say the same thing if the evidence was not mounting up before me," Holmes said, "but let's ask those involved".

He stepped over to Mr. Miller.

"Would you mind getting up Mr. Miller? It's a little bothersome having to look down at you like this," he said.

Miller slowly rose to his feet. Lestrade sidled up next to him. Stopping any chance of his escape.

"Now Mr. Miller. Can you verify what I've said so far?"

Miller still steamed. He looked at Holmes with a stare that could wither an oak tree. Holmes noticed and simply smiled.

"What was that?" asked Holmes.

Miller's eyes narrowed, but a certain swagger grew within him.

"I said nothing, but everything you've said Mr. Holmes is to be expected from someone that many think insane. Your crazy story has no basis in fact. You present some unknown man. Claiming him to be the long-lost owner of this company and concoct a tale about kidnapping, drugging and fraud," he said.

He turned to Lestrade.

"My dear Policeman, I think you should remove these gentlemen from my premises before I ask you to lay charges against them. I have a mind to seek legal representation as I feel you have besmirched my good name," he said, his chest puffed out in faux irritation.

"Really," said Holmes. His hand moved to his pocket. He stepped towards Miller and pulled his hand out. It was now full of something.

"I picked up a handful of the herbs that we found in the room downstairs," he said as he raised his hand "if you deny my accusations then you have no problems taking a deep sniff of them". He stepped towards Miller and shoved his hand in the portly man's face.

"No, keep that away from me," Miller said as he recoiled in abject horror and stepped backwards, tripped over a small ottoman and fell heavily on his immense rump.

Holmes stood over the man, looked down and smiled.

"I assume that you are now happy to corroborate my story then?" he said.

Miller dropped his head.

"Yes. Yes. My great grandfather started this whole mess," he said. He turned and pointed at Graham. "It was his fault," he continued "he denied my ancestor his share. He wouldn't bring him into the business as an equal partner".

Graham looked surprised.

"What are you talking about Sir? I always treated George with the utmost respect. We have always been equal in everything," he said.

"But you wouldn't make him a partner," Miller retorted.

"We have been in negotiations for many weeks. George has been ...," he stopped for a moment, looked over at the portrait then back to Miller "had been seeking financial aid to buy half of the business off of me. I had been patient and wanted to bring him along with me".

He stood up and walked to the portrait.

"I can only think that George had come to his wits' end and couldn't raise the capital," he said. He turned back towards Miller.

"If he had only come to me. I would have worked with him. I'm not an unreasonable man. Never have been. George knew I'd raised all the capital myself and brought him in when the business was growing quite well. He worked hard but didn't have any money behind him. I paid him half of all the profits in the hope he could buy-in," he continued.

He walked forward shaking his head.

"But poor old George. He couldn't save a penny. Spent everything he earnt I'm afraid. I assume your Great Grandmother played a large part in it," he said.

"Here, watch what you say, Sir," said Miller.

Graham held up a hand to stop his protest.

"I apologise, she was a remarkable woman. Gloriously handsome and very strong-willed. A fine woman, but very ambitious I'm afraid. This whole thing was probably her idea, not George's," he said.

"What would you have us do with Mr. Miller here?" asked Holmes.

Graham turned to face Holmes.

"That is an interesting question, Mr. Holmes. I have spent the best part of this day confused and a little lost. You and Dr. Watson here have convinced me that I was asleep for a hundred years, an incredible slumber, but in my mind, I have only awakened from a single night's sleep. In all normality I would have been in this office," he looked around once more then continued "well in an office a bit less salubrious than this one, going about my work".

He walked back towards Miller.

"Instead, I find myself with a company that appears to have grown to a level of grandeur that I could only have dreamed of".

He pointed at Miller.

"Because of this man's ancestors. My good friend and his progeny, in my absence. I can no less take that away from them and claim it as my own as I could let them continue without me," he said.

"Does that mean you wish to form a partnership with Mr. Miller here?" asked Holmes.

"I think it does, dear Sir," said Graham. He turned back to Miller and placed a hand on the man's shoulder. "What do you think Charles? Want to take on an apprentice and teach him the ways of this newfangled company you've grown?"

Miller was taken aback for a moment. Then he asked "As a partner? A full partner? No more sneaking around with fingerprints?"

Graham nodded.

"I think your great Grandfather would be proud if you did," he said. Graham held out his hand. Miller looked at it for a moment then took it in his own.

Lestrade piped up "hold on, does that mean there has been no crime? A man was drugged and held captive against his will for a hundred years and now nobody is to be charged".

Holmes nodded his head.

"As strange as it seems Inspector, that seems to be correct," said Holmes "in fact, I think we three can leave these two gentlemen to their future partnership".

Lestrade looked dumbfounded. He stood in a huff, grabbed up his hat and thrust it on his head.

"Take heart Inspector, your journey was not a total loss. You brought Mr. Graham here as I asked and were on hand in case things went against my initial expectations and Mr. Miller here became a source of concern. As it is all has worked out well and peace has been accorded," Holmes said.

Lestrade didn't look convinced.

"Fine," he said then doffed his hat to Graham and Miller "I bid you gentlemen goodbye, but I will make a note of this for future reference".

Graham walked over and held out his hand to Lestrade. "Thank you, Inspector. I'm sorry you didn't find the crime that you wanted, but you have been instrumental in helping me none the less," he said. Lestrade shook his hand, eyed Miller one more time then turned and left.

Holmes walked over to Graham, took his hand and shook it.

"I'm glad we could help in your restoration, Mr. Graham. When originally presented with a case as curious as yours, I was a little perplexed, but once all the evidence was collected and the illogical removed, it was fairly obvious what had occurred. One would be remiss with not acknowledging the bizarre nature of your story but I would hope that your future will be less so," he said.

"Thank you, Mr. Holmes," said Graham. He leant towards me and grabbed my hand "and thank you Dr. Watson. Without your charity I would have wandered these strange streets and fallen afoul of its denizens".

"My pleasure Sir," I said.

Holmes piped up "we should be going Watson. Mrs. Hudson will wonder what has become of us".

He turned and moved off. I doffed my hat to Miller and Graham once more and followed.

Back in the bright sunshine, Holmes began to fill his pipe with the contents of his pocket.

I was dumbstruck but managed to say, "isn't that from the basement room?"

Holmes smiled. "Don't be foolish Watson. This is pipe tobacco, always was. I must admit that I have taken Mr. Miller's herb in the past. Left me unconscious for three days. I wasn't going to touch it again and obviously neither was Mr. Miller".

We walked along for a while, basking in the sunshine until I broke the silence.

"What do you think will happen with Messrs. Miller and Graham?" I asked.

"Well, Watson. Mr. Graham left a small local wainwright one day, returned to one of London's largest carriage makers the next. With developments in such things as the internal combustion engine and two astute businessmen joining forces, I can only imagine good things to come for them," Holmes said.

"I can see the name Graham and Miller coachbuilders, or maybe Miller and Graham?" I said.

"A bit of a mouthful, perhaps they'll just use the first letters?" Holmes said.

"Mmmm, MG does have a certain ring to it," I said.

The Adventure in Nancy

. . . wherein Victor Hatherley of "The Engineer's Thumb"

finds himself in new danger . . .

Though it had been many months since I witnessed the most unfortunate series of events that led to the demise of my true friend, Sherlock Holmes, my grief had started to dissipate and I could finally begin to expound on and document several adventures that occurred in the months preceding his plunge into the Reichenbach Falls whilst wrestling with that dastardly villain, Professor Moriarty.

As with many of the more intriguing of Holmes's cases, it all started with the simplest of requests but continued with the two of us sent off to the wilds of France and Germany, dragged into a world of espionage and conflict of an almost global nature.

Our adventure started one bright spring morning. I was seeing patients whilst Mary was away in the country visiting with the children and family for whom she was once governess. Although I missed her dearly, I was kept busy with the somewhat trivial nature of my patients' maladies.

Upon hearing an urgent pounding at my door, I almost bowled over the person who was next in line for my services in my hurry to answer. Standing diligently on my doorstep, I found a young postman holding a message for me. I took the envelope and thanked the man, sending him away in my haste to have at the contents.

As I turned and opened the message, I noticed several sets of eyes staring back at me. After I read the message, all thoughts of doctoring vanished.

I apologised profusely to the people in my waiting room and bade them goodbye. I told them that a family emergency had arisen and that I had been called away from London. I would post a note on the door when I returned to active duty. There were many grumbles, but quite a few sympathetic murmurs as my patients left. A small part of me retained a deep level of regret and worry, but I read the message again to re-energise myself.

The message was, of course, from my good friend Sherlock Holmes. He wished me to meet him in the Stranger's Room at the Diogenes Club at two o'clock that very afternoon. The club was an interesting place and one that Holmes frequented occasionally, but usually in the company of his brother, Mycroft.

***

The hansom dropped me off at the entrance to the club. To the uninitiated, it could have been any manner of establishment. The small leather-clad double doors that served as the entrance were manned by Wilson, the club's affable footman.

I nodded to him as I climbed the short staircase and received a familiar nod in return. I don't think in all these years that I have ever heard Wilson speak. I've often thought that he holds to the traditions of the club with a vice-like grip, or he is in fact mute, and as such has found the perfect occupation.

Wilson opened the doors for me and I stepped into the dark womb of the club. Taking off my coat and hat, I left my accoutrements with Smythe at the cloakroom and continued down the silent hallway toward the Stranger's Room. I saw many an older gent sitting alone in the various rooms leading off from the hallway. Silence was their creed, every one of them. The club frowned on any form of verbal communication and instituted a policy whereby any member or visitor caught speaking would be given a notice of offence. Upon three offences, they would be brought before the committee and could find themselves banned.

The one place where this rule was relaxed was the Stranger's Room.

I came upon the entrance and stepped inside. As expected, I found Holmes. He sat in a chair facing towards the door and spoke in a sullen, quiet voice with a man, opposite him, who was hidden from view.

I moved up next to Holmes's chair and turned to face the hidden man. A smile came to my face as I recognised him.

"Hello, Doctor," Mycroft said as he looked up at me. "Please sit, won't you," he continued holding a hand out to indicate the vacant chair beside him. "I've already taken the initiative to order coffee and brandy," he finished.

"Thank you," I said as I took my seat.

It had been a while since I last laid eyes on Holmes's older brother. He had barely changed. He was what I could imagine Sherlock Holmes would look like with a couple of years of sedentary lifestyle and a hearty appetite to boot. Mycroft retained the Holmes's tall physique but encased in a soft, thick wrapping. Where Sherlock was wont to wander the streets in search of interesting subjects and puzzles to vex his mind, Mycroft simply sat, sipping coffee and brandy, and partaking of whatever fare was on the offering.

But they both had the sharpest minds that I would ever know in my lifetime. Mycroft's was a degree sharper and more encompassing than Sherlock's due to these simple lifestyle choices. Where Sherlock would expend intellectual and physical energy in the pursuit of answers, Mycroft would sit back and cogitate in comfort until the answer appeared in his mind.

I studied each of the Holmes brothers, in turn, mulling over in my mind what this meeting was all about. I was about to speak when a butler entered wheeling a trolley towards us. Mycroft immediately held up a finger to shush my question as it formed on my lips. I closed my mouth and watched as the butler served our coffee, brandy, and an assortment of cakes and scones.

Mycroft took a scone, slathered on jam and cream, and sat back to enjoy the delicacy. I had brandy, while Holmes simply poured himself a cup of coffee, adding two sugars and stirring it slowly until the butler turned about and left. He tapped his spoon against the side of the cup and gently placed it in the saucer. The tinkling of the chinaware in the quiet space was almost deafening.

After taking a sip and returning his cup to the saucer, Holmes leant forward and said, "Now that we are both here and have been served, would you like to tell us the reason for this meeting, dear brother?"

Mycroft finished his scone, wiped his mouth on a cloth napkin, and then sat back in his chair, steepling his fingers and looking across them at the both of us.

"I believe," he started, "That you are both familiar with a young Mr. Victor Hatherley."

My mind flashed and I blurted out, "The engineer. Lost a thumb, down Reading way. Was almost killed by a mad German."

"Yes, that would be him," Mycroft said.

Holmes simply smiled and considered Mycroft for a moment before he spoke.

"You've taken him into your service, haven't you?"

Mycroft looked slightly indignant.

"Well, not me personally – far too low level for me to be involved – but members of the government approached Mr. Hatherley to assist in certain matters," he said.

Holmes's smile increased as he noticed a note of discomfort in Mycroft's appearance and voice.

"What matters?" he asked, "Would they have anything to do with the remnants of the machine we found in Colonel Stark's house?"

Mycroft blanched at Holmes's quick appreciation of the situation.

"Why, yes they would. Again, I would remind you this has nothing to do with me. I only made the knowledge of the situation available to other members of my Department."

"And what Department would that be?" Holmes pressed a hint of a smile on his lips.

"Never mind about that," Mycroft retorted.

I was beginning to get lost in the conversation, so tried to bring it back to the obvious.

"What exactly is wrong with Mr. Hatherley?" I asked.

Mycroft turned his attention to me and away from the prying eyes of his brother. He regained his composure and smiled his little ingratiating smile towards me.

"Well, that is one of the main questions. My superiors are unsure what has happened to Mr. Hatherley. They haven't heard from him for a while, so it would seem he has disappeared."

"Where was he?" Holmes asked.

"Nancy, in the eastern Alsace province of France," Mycroft said.

"France?" I asked, "What the devil was Hatherley doing there?"

Sherlock Holmes smiled broadly and chuckled.

"I think you've nailed it, Watson," he said, "It was the Devil's work, wasn't it dear brother?"

Mycroft's face turned bright red with indignation as he said, "He wasn't working for me."

***

As is often the case with Sherlock Holmes, a whirlwind of action blows up around him and I find myself quite swept up in the torrential eddies that swirl in his wake.

Mycroft furnished Holmes with the details of a "safe house", as he called it, in a mostly rural part of the town of Nancy. He revealed that Nancy itself had been under siege from a torrent of refugees escaping the Prussian invasion of Alsace-Lorraine, beginning in 1870. What was once a tiny rural town had doubled in size over the past two decades.

I was unsure if it was the probable increase in the criminal population, as well as a proportional increase in good folk, that was the problem. Holmes was playing a quiet game within his own mind and would only divulge tiny details at any time.

I must admit I was becoming quite frustrated and almost contemplated staying in England and leaving Holmes to his quest, but I had grown to like Mr. Victor Hatherley during our brief encounter of some time before. If he had been placed in danger by Mycroft's compatriots, then I felt it was my duty to help in any way possible. Plus, if there had been foul play, a medical doctor's help might be at the top of the agenda.

Besides, Mycroft had mentioned that his superiors did not want to send any more agents to avoid any diplomatic embarrassment, which meant Hatherley was on his own.

After the Diogenes Club, Holmes and I parted ways to return to our respective homes and prepare for our journey to eastern France. I prepared a message for Mary and had a servant take it to the telegraph office to send it to her, letting her know that I expected to be gone at least a fortnight, if not longer.

I bade my servants goodbye and took a hansom to Baker Street to meet up with Holmes. He had taken Mrs. Hudson into his confidence and she was busy helping him pack – though her aid consisted mostly of suggesting items for Holmes to take and him shaking his head and removing them from consideration. Finally, she threw up her hands and went off to make some tea.

Holmes quickly threw some basic items into his carryall and closed it, cursing "Damnable woman," under his breath. He dropped the bag near the doorway and turned to me.

"All set, Watson?" he asked.

I nodded, "I would be more so if you would actually tell me what is going on."

Holmes chuckled, "All in good time, my dear Watson, all in good time."

I shrugged and slumped down on his settee, just as Mrs. Hudson returned with afternoon tea. She began pouring cups for each of us and then moved in closer to me.

"Do you know what's going on, Dr. Watson?" she asked.

I shook my head, "I know scant details of what is behind it all. But, I do know we are to head for the eastern part of France to investigate the disappearance of an old acquaintance."

"Oh," she said, "Well, please look after him. You know how bad he is amongst the English. The good Lord knows how the French will take to him." I chuckled at her comment. She turned to watch Holmes pottering about amongst his chemicals, tools, and books, shook her head sagely, and then left the room.

I continued to watch Holmes whilst sipping my tea. He filled a small bag with a few bottles of dry chemicals and a small cache of tools. I didn't catch what any of the items were but was mindful to check at a later date in case my old friend had snuck in any of his store of illicit chemicals.

Holmes moved to his carryall and slipped the bag into it. Then he retrieved his frock coat and deerstalker hat from a nearby rack. I took this as a signal for us to leave and placed my cup down.

Holmes was already gone before I gained my feet, so I hurried after him and onwards to whatever fate awaited us.

***

With a quick goodbye to Mrs. Hudson, who stood on the doorstep, we boarded a hansom cab and made our way to Victoria Station. Our progress through the busy station was eased by my tall friend's ability to scythe through the crowds of London, and we were quickly aboard our next mode of transport, the train to Crowley.

Although I love train journeys and would be most appreciative of reading a full narrative of the trip, I have decided to limit my account to just the relevant destinations. From Crowley, we changed trains for Dover and the English Channel. There, we boarded a steamer bound for Calais. It was whilst sharing a cabin that I became acquainted once more with my erstwhile companion's annoying habit of snoring. By morning he was well refreshed from a deep slumber, while my head was pounding with the continuous internal replay of Holmes's wood-sawing noise.

After a hearty breakfast in the steamer's buffet, we alighted on French soil and quickly made our way to the railway station. There our journey took us north to Lille to meet up with the Brussels-to-Paris line. Finally, we arrived at the Gare du Nord and found ourselves in the splendour that is Paris in the spring.

My elation was brief as Holmes bustled me off to a nearby hotel and reminded me that we were not here on holiday, but on important business. I was mindful to book two rooms, which amused Holmes, who quipped, "What would Mary say about the extra expense?"

I retorted, "I have the receipt and will send the final bill to Mycroft for complete recompense. In the meantime, I need my sleep."

Holmes merely smiled as we made our way to our allotted rooms.

Even though the room was small, the bed was wonderfully soft. I fell into a deep sleep and awoke to the bright sunshine streaming in through the parted curtains. A noise from the corner of the room grabbed my attention. I started in shock when I saw Holmes sitting in the chair in the corner.

"Oh, do pull yourself together Watson," he said.

I asked, "What in blazes are you doing in my room, Holmes?"

"Time was getting away from us while you slumbered. Now, come on. Time is wasting and we have far to go."

He turned on his heel and left.

***

I met up with Holmes a short while later in the café next to the hotel. We dined on croissants and *café au lait* before making our way back to the station to continue our journey east.

I must admit that I was a little disconsolate at being in the city of romance without my dearest Mary and any time to enjoy the place. However, I was thrilled to see the city's newest landmark as our train pulled out of the station and ran along the edge of the Seine towards the outskirts of the city.

I pointed out the *le Tour Eiffel* to Holmes. Surprisingly, it piqued his curiosity slightly. He studied it while it remained in sight. Once the scenery returned to the simple suburban landscape of any great city, Holmes sat back in his seat and resumed his private thoughts.

I withdrew a notepad from my bag to begin sorting through the notes from our many adventures when Holmes piped up.

"It is a pity that such a marvellous accomplishment will have such a short life," he said.

"How do you mean?" I asked.

"Monsieur Eiffel was only granted a permit for the tower to stand on that location for twenty years. They will be compelled to demolish it in 1909. A shame really," he said.

"I'm surprised that you would be so sentimental over such a thing," I replied.

"As we have seen on so many occasions, the ingenuity of the human mind is wasted on frivolous pursuits that make no genuine contribution to the pool of knowledge as a whole."

He waved a hand towards the disappearing tower and continued, "Monsieur Gustav Eiffel was commissioned to build a simple entrance to the World's Fair, but he chose to go beyond his brief and built a possible contender for one of the wonders of the modern world. And his marvel will be consigned to the scrap heap because of some simple-minded bureaucrat's insistence on the rules. I find such things a little depressing, Watson."

With that, he pulled his hat low over his eyes and resumed his recumbent posture. I took this as my dismissal and turned my attention to my notes, but Holmes's words played on my mind for much of the remainder of our trip.

Around noon, we arrived at Reims and were made to change trains to continue on to our destination. We took luncheon on the next train and stayed for coffee and a smoke, mostly to pass the time before resuming our seats.

The sun was starting to dip below the western horizon by the time we reached Nancy. We departed and were lucky to find a hotel near the station which could provide us with a pleasant, if not simple, meal along with our twin rooms. I still wasn't going to lose any more sleep to Holmes's snoring – not while I was secure in the knowledge that Mycroft would repatriate any expenses. I hoped.

***

The morning broke brilliant and glorious with a serene silence that one could rarely find amongst the hustle and bustle of London. Holmes and I made our way downstairs for our morning repast and found a small nearby café. We settled at a small table outside in the sunshine and broke our fast on croissants and coffee, a little habit I'm sure we would continue to develop before leaving France.

Holmes sat back and seemed to me to be enjoying the scenery and soaking up the ambience, but that was shattered when he spoke.

"Watson, we have much to do today. Our first port-of-call post-breakfast will be the address gifted to me by Mycroft. I am hoping that a local hansom can take us directly there, as it is a little way out of town."

He stood up so abruptly and looked down his aquiline nose at me a stern expression on his face.

"Well, don't dilly-dally. Time is wasting."

I quickly downed my coffee and proceeded to cough on the last dregs. Holmes wandered off to look for a hansom, I assumed, so I walked inside the café to pay for our breakfast.

At the counter was a large bearded man who looked at me with suspicious eyes. I asked for the bill in my best broken French. He continued to stare at me as if I had just insulted the President before replying, "English?"

I nodded.

"*Trois francs et quarante*," he said.

I handed over a five-franc piece. The bearded man kept his eyes on mine the whole time as he took my coin and slid a selection of coins back to me. I was mesmerised by his gaze and not a little perturbed. I picked up the coins without looking, pocketed them, and turned to leave. I walked to the doorway and quickly looked back. The man was gone. I stepped out into the sunshine and felt the coins jingle in my pocket. It was only then that I noticed the weight of them.

My knowledge of French currency was not up to date, but I was intrigued by the size of one of the coins. I withdrew it to have a look. It wasn't French, but a German 1 Mark coin. I thought about walking back into the café, but Holmes chose that moment to join me, looking down at my new acquisition.

"What have you there, Watson?"

I held it up for him to view. Its unblemished surface glistened in the sunlight.

"Ah," he said, "I think you have stumbled onto quite a find."

He turned on his heel and headed for a small open carriage drawn by a single chestnut horse. He seated himself in the rear and looked back at me. I pocketed my coin and hurried after him. He spoke fluent French to the driver, well beyond my capacity to understand, and the horse was whipped into action.

We cantered through a few winding village streets before the houses gave way to wide open fields. The blue sky above provided a wonderful counterpoint to the greenery below. I drank in the blissful sight again.

Within a few moments, however, we turned into a long tree-lined drive and emerged from the shadows before a small but picturesque farmhouse. The carriage pulled up and Holmes leapt out and hurried away, calling over his shoulder, "Pay the man, there's a good chap."

I stepped down, reached into my pocket and pulled out my coins. The driver perused the offering before him and reached for the Mark. He picked it up, turned it over in his hand before huffing and dropping it back in my hand. He proceeded to pick out a few francs then doffed his cap to me.

I said, "*Merci, Monsieur*," but received only a slight grunt before he flicked the reins and moved off.

"How rude," I thought to myself before hurrying over to where Holmes was studying the front door. I watched the driver disappear down the shadowed laneway before I spoke again.

"I get the idea that we aren't exactly welcome in this area," I said.

"Has any Englishman ever been welcome in France? Besides, the locals around here are probably a little more wary of the English since the denizens of this house moved in and then disappeared."

The lock suddenly clicked. I turned to see Holmes withdraw his lock picks and push the door open. He pocketed the tools and strode into the house.

***

The interior was dark but lacked the mustiness associated with long-abandoned houses. The only smell that greeted us was the strong tang of machine oil.

Holmes's shoes made a rather loud clopping noise as he strode down the main hall and into a reception room at the end. I followed closely behind and peered into the rooms that led off the corridor. Each was fairly Spartan, containing an unkempt bed made from a single mattress lying on the floor. There were three of these bedrooms. I stopped by the doorway of the last room and studied it for a moment.

At first, I believed that the bedding had been swept back by the man who had reposed within, but upon closer examination, I realised the bed had been searched. The blankets and sheets stripped back to show the mattress. In fact, the mattress in this room had been slashed open. The straw padding spilled out on to the floor as the intruder searched for something within.

I turned and hurried after Holmes to show him my find. I stepped out of the corridor and into the reception room itself. I had expected to find a cluttered room that would explain the goings-on, but it was devoid of all furniture and fittings, except for a fireplace with spent ashes along one wall, and an overturned wicker chair across the room from it.

Holmes was kneeling and examining some small rents in the wooden floor. I peered down near where I stood and saw similar marks. They consisted of holes with splintered edges and a large number of scratches radiating off and around them, looking as if someone had ripped a fixture out of the floor by twisting, pulling, and finally levering it out.

"Holmes," I began, only to be cut off when the target of my question looked up and put a finger to his lips. He stepped across to the middle of the room and gestured for me to accompany him. He kneeled again and withdrew a small glass bottle from his pocket. I could see some metal shavings on the floor before him but nothing else.

He poured some white powder from the bottle and blew it across the floor. As a result, the powder highlighted a series of faint white rings that I hadn't seen before.

"Watson, could you please pass me the 1 Mark coin that you were given today?" he said.

I quickly dug out the coin and put it in his outstretched hand. He bent down, placed it on the wooden floor, and slid it into one of the round grooves. It fit perfectly. He tried a few others nearby and showed them to be of the same size each time.

"What does that mean?" I asked.

"Come on. Surely you've picked up on the reason for us being here, or at least the reason for our Mr. Hatherley having been here, haven't you?"

"Refresh my memory again, if you will."

Holmes stood and handed the coin back to me. He walked to the far end of the room and pointed to the most splintered hole.

"Do you know what these holes with the splintered wood around them were for?" he asked me.

"I assume that something was secured to the floor and then removed in a rather rough way," I said.

Holmes smiled, "Well done. And the indentations?"

"Perhaps there was something heavy resting on some hidden coins," I answered.

"Would it not be more logical if the indentations were made by a machine as it was worked, rather than somebody trying to hide a few German Marks?" he said.

"Hatherley and that infernal machine that he was employed to investigate," I said. "The German was using it to press counterfeit English coins."

"Yes. But that machine was destroyed by the fire in the house at Eyford," he said. He scanned the room again and walked over to a pair of double French doors. Several deep scratches led to the door and appeared to extend beneath them. Holmes grabbed both handles and thrust the doors open. The scratches finished at the doorstop, but deep gouges were cut into the grass outside.

"This was a similar machine, wasn't it? But it stamped out German 1 Mark coins," I said.

"Exactly, my dear Watson, exactly. A much smaller version, but basically a hydraulic press for coining."

I pondered long and hard. There were many thoughts running through my head, but I think I managed to put it all together. I studied the floor, the grooves and the scratches, and then joined Holmes at the doorway and looked out across the grassed area beyond.

"Hatherley, an engineer, familiar with hydraulics – the only Englishman to have seen Stark's machine."

Holmes smiled his little sardonic smile and nodded slightly.

"You told Mycroft about Hatherley's adventure. Mycroft employed Hatherley to create a coin press identical to Stark's."

"Well, not Mycroft himself, but one of the other areas within the government."

"But why bring it here? Why the German Marks?"

"Ah, that was the bit that had embarrassed Mycroft, and why he wants to avoid any further involvement. Around two years ago, Germany installed a new Chancellor, Wilhelm II. As a commemoration of that event, a new currency was minted to replace the previous version."

I reached into my pocket and pulled out the extremely shiny and new 1 Mark coin. I flipped it over and studied both sides. It was the first time I had noticed that the minted date was from two years earlier.

"Yes. That's right Watson. Very shiny for its age, is it not?"

"I still don't understand, Holmes. Why would our government be minting fake German coins in France?"

"But Watson, we are only about five miles from the German border. The nearest large town would be Colmar, and further north is Strasbourg. With the change of Chancellor, the German economy is in a state of flux. The perfect time for a discreet form of sabotage to occur using fake currency. The counterfeit coins would be used in exchange for real currency, which would then be taken out of circulation. At some stage in the future, either the fraudulent currency would be found out, or a story would be leaked to the appropriate authorities. A scandal would ensue, and the populace would lose faith in the country's currency, thereby undermining the economy."

"How devilishly clever," I said. "But if this has happened, where is the machine? And the men?"

"That is the question that Mycroft has sent us to answer. There are only two solutions that I can see at this stage. One, the men felt the need to remove the machine and themselves to a safer location, or, two, they were removed by force. There is not enough evidence in here to conclude anything, so we must investigate further or wait for further clews to be presented."

With that, he strode out through the double doors and across the grass. I followed and noticed a small storage shed, possibly for wood, at the rear of the property, and a large unkempt area of long grass and overgrown foliage nearby.

I wandered over to the small shed as Holmes looked around the overgrown area. It was as I approached that I noticed the blackened chimney stack poking out of the roof, and to one side a large pile of coal. Intrigued, I tried the latch on the door, and to my delight, it opened, bathing the interior in light.

My questions were answered quickly, as inside the small shed was a blacksmith's forge with a large metal pot, spattered with solidified silver metal. A rolling press stood nearby. A tray lay before the pot, which would take the liquid metal and set it in strips ready for rolling or pressing into the appropriate thickness. From my rudimentary knowledge of metalworking, I assumed this was used to mix the alloy required for the coin press.

Excited at my discovery, I hurried out to find Holmes.

He was staring at something in the deep underbrush at the very rear of the property. I started towards him and began to speak as I approached.

"Holmes, I have found something rather marvellous," I said.

He held up a finger and stopped me in mid-sentence.

"What?" I asked.

"Listen," he said.

I did and could hear the sound of a horse trotting along at quite a pace. The clatter of a cart being pulled accompanied the horse.

"Quickly! They come, as I assumed they would," Holmes said. He then ducked into a long thicket of grass and lay prostrate in such a way as to keep an eye on the rear and one side of the house.

"How in blazes did you know?" I asked, joining him.

He brought out his pistol and checked that it was loaded and ready.

"Shh! If you must know, the two gentlemen behind us told me all I needed to know. I assume our friend who comes was signalled by either our driver or your friend in the café," he said.

"Gentlemen?" I asked then turned around to peer into the tangled growth behind us.

"My God!" I uttered as my eyes fell on the corpses of two poor, unfortunate men that lay hidden behind us. Both lay on their backs. They had suffered at the hand of a knifeman as their lifeblood had drained from the deep slashes across their neck. I studied them for a moment longer before the sound of the cart driving up before the house snapped my attention back.

"Neither one is Hatherley," said Holmes, "I assume they were the hired help or muscle, sent to assist him with the operation. They would not have known of the machine's workings, and therefore they were considered dispensable by our government's foe."

"Do you think Hatherley is still alive?" I asked, dreading the answer.

"I cannot be sure," he said, "As long as his skill is still required, then he should be alive, maybe even safe."

I looked once more at the two unfortunates behind me. Holmes noticed and, knowing my propensity for empathy, spoke again.

"We can mourn those two later, but at the moment we must concentrate on the possibility of finding Mr. Hatherley, and above all maintaining life ourselves."

The possibility of my own death hit home very quickly and realigned all my senses to the task at hand. I pulled my revolver out and ensured that it was fully loaded.

Through the still air of the countryside, we heard the cart driver open the front door and enter the house. Holmes got to his feet. I joined him, and we began a quick trek through the underbrush via the side of the house, circling round to the front.

"That's a stroke of luck," he whispered as we came around the front.

The cart stood all alone. The man hadn't brought any company. It had two seats up front for the driver and a passenger and a large flat-bed behind for transporting cargo. The entire rear was covered by a large canvas sheet. This was probably the same cart used to move Hatherley's machine.

Holmes moved along the side of the house, being careful to keep away from the gravel path and to only step on the grass and dirt area running along the building. I followed and arrived at the rear of the cart just a moment behind him.

He pulled up the canvas and climbed beneath. Again I followed and resumed a most uncomfortable position next to him.

"Now we wait," he said.

For what seemed like an eternity we lay in that stiflingly small area beneath the canvas sheet, listening intently, but only hearing our own breath and hearts beating.

Finally, the front door slammed shut and a key turned in the lock. The crunching of gravel indicated that the man was making his way to the cart. It lurched as he hopped back into his seat.

He mumbled under his breath, *"Niemand hier. Stark wird wütend sein. Dumme englische Männer."* – Roughly, "No one is here. Stark will be unhappy. Stupid Englishmen."

On hearing the name Stark, my eyes opened wider. I stared toward Holmes in the darkness, and could barely tell that his face was impassive. Again he put his finger to his lips.

The man said, "Hah!" and whipped the reins. With a whinny from the horse and steps upon the gravel, the cart pulled away from the house.

Holmes lay back and closed his eyes. I tried to do the same but my hands closed tighter around my pistol as my mind imagined what would come next.

***

We bumped along for well over an hour. The growling in my stomach was almost as loud as the clattering of the cart as it trundled along the roadway. I looked across at Holmes, still laying back in a supine pose. He snapped awake when the cart slowed and veered to the right. The sound of the wheels rolling across gravel followed.

Holmes pulled out his revolver and held it at the ready. I hadn't let mine go but had to admit my hand was feeling very numb and sore. We travelled along for another five minutes before the cart finally stopped.

We heard the driver drop-down from his seat and move away across the gravel. Holmes held up a finger until the noise died down and we appeared to be alone. When all was quiet, we slid across to the edge of the cart and peered out.

The world beyond the cart was an empty space devoid of any movement. I took this as a good sign and quickly escaped the cramped confines. Looking around, I now had a better view of our environs. We had found ourselves in the side courtyard of a large stone mansion, enclosed by a thick stone wall shielding the building from view.

Holmes joined me and motioned towards a small door nearby. We both hurried across the gravel expanse as quietly as possible. Luckily the door was unlocked and we scampered inside.

We found ourselves in the tradesmen's boot room. There were a number of well-worn and dirty pairs of boots and galoshes strewn about the place. Several slickers and coats hung up on a rack along one wall. Two doors led away, one near the entrance and one at the rear. I tried the near door and peered through.

"Kitchen," I whispered to Holmes. He nodded and indicated the rear door. I made my way there and found it led down into the cellar.

"Let us make our way downstairs for the moment until we formulate a plan," he murmured.

The journey downstairs was quite a desperate affair, as there was no light to guide us. Holmes pulled out a small box of matches and struck one. The feeble light allowed passage but little more, and soon we stood on the firm but damp cellar floor. Holmes looked around and found a candle on the near wall. Lighting it chased a bit of the darkness away and gave us more confidence.

"Where the devil are we, Holmes?" I asked.

"I don't know for certain, but from my calculations, I believe us to be in a country mansion in the Bezirk Lothringen Department in Alsace-Lorraine," he said.

"Germany?"

"Yes. Hence the driver's speech to himself."

"All right, I'm curious. How did you come by that judgement?"

"To begin with, the farmhouse in which we started was situated about five miles northeast of Nancy, not very far from the German border. Our driver cantered along at approximately ten to fifteen miles an hour. We travelled for just over an hour, so are now up to twenty miles from Nancy."

"And the direction?"

"Ah, you possibly observed me during our journey, did you not?"

"Yes. I thought you were reposing in contemplation, as you are want to do."

"Close, Watson, close. As we got undercover, I found a small tear in the canvas and situated myself below it. I made the tear a little larger and concentrated on the beam of light emitted by the hole. It shone onto my crossed hands and I watched the direction that the beam moved as the cart journeyed on. At this time of the year, the sun travels across the sky at about a sixty-degree angle, higher in summer, lower in winter. The spot from the sun was closer to my face than to my boots, which meant we were lying north to south and the cart was moving east, or slightly northeast. From my knowledge of the area, we would have passed into western Germany after about fifteen minutes, and are now well into the country."

"Extraordinary," I remarked.

Holmes smiled his laconic smile that usually accompanied one of his brilliant deductions.

"Thank you, Watson. Simple elucidation based on the evidence. Nothing more."

"Indeed," I said.

I found another candle, lit it, and walked around the cellar. It held bric-a-brac and other items useless to our endeavour and had just the one entrance.

"I would think this is an old disused root cellar. We will need to enter the kitchen or exit the building if we are to proceed," he said. I nodded my agreement.

Back in the boot room we sidled up to the kitchen door and listened for a moment. Silence. I unlatched the door and stepped into the deserted room. My stomach grumbled as I spied the makings of a decent lunch. Bread, cold meats, and pots of butter and jam sat upon the bench in the middle of the room.

"No time for that, Watson," said Holmes as he moved past and sidled up to the exit doorway. He listened intently and withdrew his revolver. I pulled mine out quickly and a small part of my mind became nervous with anticipation.

Suddenly, he waved at me to move to the other side of the doorway. I flattened myself as much as possible against the cupboards there. Holmes did the same on his side, hiding slightly behind the door.

A young scullery maid entered the room, singing a soft tune to herself and completely unaware of our presence. She placed the tray she carried down on the bench and began to put the luncheon makings onto it.

Holmes quietly closed the door and slid home the latch. I moved towards the young lass in expectation of her startled reaction.

"*Fräulein?*" said Holmes, not too loudly, but enough to be heard.

The young girl turned, spied Holmes and his gun, and opened her mouth to scream. I ducked towards her and put my hand across her mouth to stifle any noise. Holmes put his finger to his lips.

"*Sh, sei ruhig. Wir werden dich nicht verletzen. Ja?*" he said.

My rudimentary German translated this as, "Be quiet. We won't hurt you. Yes?" I'm not sure it worked that well, as the young girl's eyes were ready to pop out of her head in fear. I tried talking calmly to her.

"It's all right. We mean you no harm. We are looking for a friend of ours," I said in my most caring doctor's voice.

Either my words or expression seemed to work. She calmed down and tried to speak. I pulled my hand away, ready to slap it back in place if she cried for help.

"*Englisch?*" she asked.

We both nodded. My German at least extended that far.

Our confirmation seemed to fill her with either hope or confidence. She stood tall and continued to direct questions to Holmes, whom she figured was the best person with whom to speak.

"*Bist du hier für den Engländer? Meine herrin, sie kann helfen,*" she said. ("Are you here for the Englishman? My friend, she can help.")

"*Ist der Engländer am Leben? Warum sollte deine herrin helfen wollen?*" Holmes asked. ("Is the Englishman alive? Why would your mistress want to help?")

I was lost but assumed they were talking about Hatherley and another person. I tried to wrack my brain for details of Hatherley's original adventure with us. I remembered a woman and a portly man being involved.

"*Sie hat sich in ihn verliebt. Sie möchte mit ihm fliehen,*" she said. ("She fell in love with him. She wants to escape with him.")

Holmes chuckled at this last confession.

"What is it, Holmes?" I asked.

"It seems our Mr. Hatherley has won a young girl's heart during his imprisonment. That should prove useful to us, I think," he said.

"*Wie heißt deine herrin?*" he asked. ("What is your mistress' name?")

"Elise," she replied.

Immediately, I knew what was going on.

"Elise. The young girl that tried to convince Hatherley to escape Stark's clutches last time," I said.

"Yes, Watson. Funny how matters of the heart play out, isn't it?"

The girl sidled up next to the door. She quietly opened it and looked through. We stayed back but listened intently for any sound from beyond. She finally turned and motioned for us to follow her through. Holmes and I both made sure our revolvers were primed, just in case, and trailed after her.

The maid scurried down the hallway beyond the kitchen and stopped at the end. She waited while we caught up, then looked through before moving across the open foyer beyond. Holmes followed her to the foot of a staircase leading to the upper floors. I lagged behind slightly, searching for any evidence of others in the house. It was then that I heard the noise.

From deep within the bowels of the ground floor there came a whooshing noise, followed by the creak and groan of metal and finally a clanking noise. The whoosh became higher pitched and a tinkling of metal followed.

I started to move towards the noise when the scullery maid spoke.

"*Mein Herr! Nein!*" she said.

I turned to find the maid's face aghast with fear. Holmes stood beside her with a look of grave concern on his own. He nodded up the staircase and proceeded to climb. The maid turned and scuttled upwards herself. I shrugged and took one last look in the direction of the noise as it became louder once more. With no one to back me up, I decided discretion was the better part of valour and joined the other two in ascending the staircase.

***

In short time we came to a doorway at the far end of another corridor. The maid knocked once then let herself in. Holmes and I bundled our way in without waiting, rather be caught in an open room than an enclosed corridor.

A beautiful woman sat at a small dressing table in the middle of brushing her hair. At the sight of the three of us, her face dropped.

"*Mein Gott, Gertrude, was bedeutet das?*" she said. ("My God, Gertrude, what does that mean?")

"*Diese Engländer sind hier für herr Victor, meine dame,*" Gertrude replied. ("These Englishmen are here for Mr. Victor, my lady.")

Elise placed her hairbrush down and stood up to face us.

"English?" she asked with very little accent, "You are here to rescue Victor?"

Holmes stepped forward.

"Yes. I am Sherlock Holmes and this is my associate Dr. John Watson. We have been sent to locate Mr. Hatherley and bring him back to England. Do you know if he is safe, Madam?"

Elise sat down. Her eyes dropped to the floor. There was an obvious air of loss in her pose. I could take no more and stepped forward.

"He's dead, isn't he?" I asked.

Elise's face shot up. Her sad eyes locked onto mine. Tears welled in those eyes and threatened to pour down her cheeks. She shook her head from side to side.

"No. No, he is not dead. Death would be better than this. That monster has him caged downstairs. He makes him work that infernal machine from dawn till dusk. That noise is all I hear, apart from the occasional scream from my dear Victor."

She dropped her head into her hands and sobbed.

"And it's entirely my fault."

Gertrude moved across and put her hands on Elise's shoulders and cooed to her in a soothing voice.

"*Mach dir keine Vorwürfe, meine Lady. Du wusstest nicht, dass das passieren würde,*" she said.

Holmes provided a vague translation, possibly for my benefit. "'Do not blame yourself, my lady. You did not know that would happen.'"

"Now, now, my dear, do not blame yourself. Tell us what happened so that we may help solve this conundrum," he said.

She dried her eyes with a small kerchief hidden in her sleeve then looked up at us and told her story.

***

"A few weeks ago, Gertrude, myself, and Karl, our driver, went to Nancy. I was tired of being cooped up and wanted to peruse the local dress shops. Karl went off, so Gertrude and I wandered the high street. I looked around and spotted him. Victor Hatherley. The engineer I had saved in England. I could not believe it.

"I hurriedly wrote a note and tasked Gertrude with delivering it. Victor hurried over to me but said he needed to return to his dwellings and could we meet up again the next week.

"I agreed and we bid each other goodbye. My heart fluttered at our meeting. There had been something there since our first encounter, and it still remained.

"I didn't realise it at the time, but Karl had been sitting at a nearby café and saw the entire reunion. It was when he noticed Victor's disfigured hand that he remembered one of the Colonel's tales. He made enquiries and found out the location of Victor's home.

"As soon as Karl told the Colonel, he went mad and ranted about how the engineer had destroyed all his plans in England. I could hear him from my room and knew that no good would come from this.

"I cried myself to sleep, but when I awoke, the Colonel and his men were gone. I confided all to Gertrude, but neither of us knew what to do. I paced the house all day until late that night when they arrived back with a second cart containing something large under a canvas covering. I watched from my window and saw a fourth man, with a bag on his head, taken from the cart and into one of the large rooms at the rear of the house. The Colonel and his men worked into the early hours to move the covered item inside. I tried to watch and listen but finally fell asleep, waking with the sun streaming into my room.

"I crept my way downstairs and was greeted with the hiss and whir of some great engine. I approached the origins of the noise but found my way blocked by Karl. Innocently, I asked what all the commotion was about. He told me some fable about a new printing press that the Colonel was using to publish his memoirs. He pressed me with the urgency of the work and that the Colonel was not to be disturbed.

"I left knowing full well what those noises were. They mimicked the infernal machine that the Colonel had been using to press coins in England. I did not know the connection between the machine and Victor at that stage, but I was committed to finding out.

"Later that night, when all was quiet and I was sure the Colonel and his men had retired for the evening, I used the servants' passages to steal my way into the downstairs rooms where the machine had been positioned. There I found Victor, bound, gagged and chained to a wall. I was horrified and tried to unbind him, but the chains were beyond my strength. Victor was unconscious and had suffered from multiple blows to his back and chest.

"I stole away when I heard the main door open and returned to my room. I haven't been back since and fear the worse for Victor."

**

She began to sob again before saying, "I blame myself. If only I hadn't sent Gertrude after him on that day in Nancy."

Gertrude tutted and rubbed Nancy's shoulders again.

I looked across at Holmes. He stood quite rigid, cogitating on all we had heard. He peered at me. A small smile came to his lips and he winked.

"I do believe, Watson, that it is now that we shall find out our true mettle. I think our first course of action is to disarm and disable our enemies. Then we release the hostage and escape."

"Sounds simple when you say it like that, Holmes," I said. "Should we destroy the machine while we're at it?" I added sardonically.

"Of course we should." He turned his attention back to Elise.

"Now, Madam, can you show us to these internal passages so that we may confront this Colonel Stark."

43

Holmes, myself, Elise, and Gertrude made our way through the tight passages that wound through the house and kept the servants from the view of the gentry. We stopped outside of a small doorway. Holmes stayed, and the rest of us went on towards the lower levels where the machine and our unfortunate engineer were to be found.

From the account that Holmes told me later, I pieced together his encounter with the Colonel.

He opened the doorway with nary a sound and quietly stepped into the Colonel's study. Stark sat at his desk with his back to the small entrance.

Holmes stood stock still, withdrew his revolver, and pointed it at the Colonel. He started to speak but the Colonel beat him to it.

"So, Englander, you have come to rescue the disabled engineer?" he said in very good English.

Holmes was shocked and taken aback. He retained enough presence of mind to thumb back the hammer on his revolver.

"Yes, I have actually. If you would be so good to release him to me, we'll be on our way," he said, hoping that his bravado would destabilise the German.

"I can't let you take him. I need him to operate the machine," he continued without looking around.

"I'm sure the Kaiser would be interested in your continuing to mint counterfeit coins."

"True, just as much as he would dwell on the knowledge that another government was doing the same. *Your* government in fact. He may wish to talk to you about that."

"I am but a private citizen, and have only a loose connection to the forces of government."

Holmes sidled around the edge of the room to get a better look at Stark's face. He much preferred to debate face-to-face so he could study the untold language of his foe.

Stark looked up from his work and studied Holmes for a moment. A smile played on his face. A smile that disturbed Holmes more than he would have liked.

"What do you find so amusing?" Holmes asked.

"Oh, you are exactly as he described."

"Who described?"

"An old colleague of mine with whom I became reacquainted with during my stay in England. He warned me that our paths may cross if I pursued my goals. Interesting how it all came down to us meeting in the middle of Germany, rather than England. My friend will be most annoyed when I tell him how you were dispatched."

Holmes became confused.

Stark then yelled, "Karl!"

The driver burst into the room brandishing a large cleaver and headed straight for Holmes. He brought the gun around but it was knocked from his hand, with one sweep of the cleaver, and skittered away. Holmes ducked back and felt the wall behind him.

Karl brought the cleaver up and down in one sweep. Holmes ducked sideways and dropped to the floor. The cleaver struck the wall, splitting the wood and becoming wedged. Holmes lashed out with one foot and caught Karl in the knee. A loud crack drove him to the ground, where he howled in pain. Holmes gained his feet and stepped back towards the driver, smashing his fist into the side of the man's face. Karl's head slammed into the floor and his body dropped into an untidy heap and stopped moving.

Holmes retrieved his revolver and pointed it at Stark. The man looked more annoyed than frightened.

"*Hans, Ich brauche hilfe hier!*" he yelled. ("Hans, I need help here!")

The door opened again revealing a larger man than Karl. Hans held a small pistol in his meaty hand and pointed it at Holmes.

"*Erschieß ihn!*" Stark yelled. ("Shoot him!")

Hans smiled. Holmes ducked to one side as the sound of the gun retort echoed through the room. Hans' smile slowly faded from his face and a small dribble of blood ran from his mouth. He toppled and fell to the floor, revealing to Holmes my shocked self, standing behind him, holding a smoking gun.

"Watson, what fabulous timing."

Holmes quickly rose to his feet and turned to face Stark. The Colonel looked extremely annoyed. He stood up and opened a small desk drawer.

"Fine. I'll do it myself," he said and dragged a revolver from the drawer.

Holmes pre-empted Stark's actions and leapt forward, driving his right fist into the German's jaw and knocking him backwards. The Colonel crashed to the ground and lay still.

"My word!" I said as I walked up next to the desk.

Holmes looked down at what had preoccupied Stark's attention when he entered the room. A broad smile came to his face.

"Interesting."

***

Holmes and I sat across from Mycroft in the Stranger's Room once more. The fire burnt low, even though a bright summer's day reigned outside.

"Hatherley?"

"Safe and healthy."

"And this Stark – a habitual coiner, but not working for the Kaiser?" asked Mycroft.

"Correct. It was only luck that drew him to Hatherley's machine. With it, he planned to recoup his losses from his English experiment and set about undermining the new Kaiser himself – thereby doing your work for you."

"It wasn't my work, as I've said. But why did you stop him then?"

"There were innocents involved, and I have no care for the matters of government at large."

"And where are these innocents now?" I asked.

"Elise and Victor have been furnished with a country estate and an allowance," said Mycroft. "They will not pose a problem."

"And this Stark fellow?"

Sherlock Holmes smiled, "We left him and his driver secured by the chains near the machine. On our way to Nancy, we notified the local *Polizei* that they may be interested in the goings-on at a nearby mansion. I'm sure Stark is a problem to nobody by now."

"Good," said Mycroft, "This has been a very embarrassing affair, all told."

"Quite so. But I think that it still has the potential to become more than just embarrassing. If not investigated further from both of our perspectives, it threatens to endanger not just ourselves but the general populace as well."

"What makes you think that?"

Holmes reached into his jacket pocket and withdrew a letter he had taken from Stark's desk. He slid it across the table. Mycroft picked it up and opened it.

"It's not the contents you should worry about, just the seal at the bottom."

The red wax seal was indented with a stylishly curved capital "*M*".

Mycroft's expression changed to show slight worry and confusion.

"This is not my seal," he said.

"Correct. Think harder and you will understand the gravity of the situation."

Mycroft stared at the seal until the penny dropped. He looked back at Holmes, fear writ large on his face.

"*Moriarty!*" he said.

The Case of the Gila Monster

During my friendship with Sherlock Holmes, I have, on numerous occasions, found myself over-awed by the breadth of knowledge that resides behind those aquiline features, and also been humbled by his immense understanding of all things medical. At times I have been left mouth agape in surprise as some esoteric piece of information springs forth from that immense intelligence.

These incidents have been quite frequent and ego-shattering, but none so much as the time Holmes solved the mystery surrounding a death from the bite of a Gila Monster.

It was a wonderful spring day and I was enjoying a late afternoon cup of tea in the back garden behind my Kensington practice. I had seen numerous patients all day and rewarded myself with some peace and quiet. The serenity was sadly broken by the appearance of my beautiful wife, Mary, at the rear door.

"Sorry to bother you, John, but we've received a late patient. I suggested that she return in the morning, but her manner was ever so compelling that I thought it best if you see her now," she said.

I stood up and replied, "Quite alright, dear. It will probably be nothing, but I would rather quieten her fears now than allow any to develop further overnight."

I moved to the door, but Mary placed a hand upon my chest stopping me short. She glanced over her shoulder then leaned in close to me, whispering, "She's a formidable lady. If I was to have an opinion, I would think that her problems are all in her mind. But of course, you are the doctor."

I smiled and patted her on the shoulder. "I'm sure they are, but I've never met a patient that could pull the wool over my eyes."

Mary allowed me to pass and I stepped through into my consulting room. My patient spied me and immediately stood up to greet me.

My wife was right. The lady before me was an astounding specimen. She stood just short of six-foot-high and was quite rotund as well. She wore an extremely tight-fitting black tulip skirt and a matching black blouse wrenched over her enormous bosom and brought in tight at the waist. Her hair was pulled back into a high bun, giving her face a fierce expression, even at rest.

She had the look and presence of a private school governess. My only thought was pity for her students.

Her face split into a fierce smile and she said, "Dr. Watson, thank you so much for seeing me at such short notice. I have to apologise, but I didn't know where else to go."

I bade her to sit and took my seat behind my desk.

"What is it I can help you with Mrs, ah . . . ?"

"Bell," she answered, "Mr. Moira Bell. I live not far from here on the edge of Regents Park with my son."

It was then that this remarkable woman lost all composure and showed that underneath her gruff exterior was someone full of emotion and love. As soon as she mentioned her son, a torrent of tears poured forth from her eyes and she sobbed uncontrollably into her sleeve.

I jumped up, raced around the desk, pulled a clean kerchief from my breast pocket, and offered it to the distraught woman. She took it, wiped her eyes, and then blew her nose into it. As it was an inexpensive silk kerchief, I decided to let her keep it.

I quickly found Mary and asked her to brew some tea while I attended to Mrs. Bell.

The troubled woman finally calmed down once the offer of a cup of hot tea was made. She began to tell me her tale whilst sipping the brew.

She was a local resident who lived in a line of properties that edged onto a lovely part of Regents Park, not far from the London University College. Her family had possessed one of the three-storey Georgian houses for well over a hundred years, and she had inherited the lease on the passing of her father almost thirty years previously.

She lived alone with her grown son, Julius, as her husband had died in the Afghan war. I told her my own war tale and was able to provide a larger level of empathy towards her because of it.

She went on to explain that her son was a Professor of Zoology working at the University College. He possessed a rather large and exotic collection of snakes and reptiles, which he kept in a room on the second floor.

"A herpetologist?" I asked.

"If you insist," she answered, indicating to me that she had no real interest in her son's profession. "It was those damnable lizards that caused all this trouble."

I pushed her for more information and was finally told that her son had been arrested for manslaughter. A man named Hyram Shrubb had forced his way into their home and had died as a result of being bitten by one of her son's lizards, a Gila Monster from America.

I frowned internally at this revelation. Gila Monsters are venomous, but to my knowledge are rarely deadly. Most victims are usually left with horrid wounds caused by the strength of the jaws rather than from the venom.

At the remembrance of her son's current whereabouts, she began to sob all over again without revealing any other pertinent details. I quickly went to her aid to calm her once more and prescribed a relaxant to help her sleep that evening. I also suggested that a friend of mine might be able to shed more light on the facts of the case and help to unearth the true nature of this horrid affair. She then admitted that it was my friendship with Holmes that had led her across town to see me.

Once she was calm again, I helped her out of my rooms after securing her address and said that I would bring Holmes to her home at precisely eleven o'clock the next day.

Through a veil of drying tears, she agreed, thanked me for my service, and marched off home.

As I watched her go a small thrill went through me. I know that my good friend Holmes requires constant stimulation of his mind to keep the *ennui* at bay, but during these quiet times, I find myself in such a need as well.

This case also promised the need for a high level of medical knowledge, and there was hope that the depth of my experience would be of use to Holmes.

Sadly, that was not to be.

***

I arrived at the front doorstep of Mrs. Bell's home on Cumberland Terrace at a few minutes of eleven. The day was quite warm and I found that I had underestimated the walk and was awash with perspiration.

I had removed my hat and was mopping my brow with a fresh kerchief when I noticed Holmes walking towards me. He was elegantly dressed as always and tapped along with his cane. He had left his hat at home and showed no sign of being overheated.

"Good morning, Watson, and what a wonderful morning it is!" he said, admiring the building before us. "Poisoning by venomous lizard. Not a regular occurrence in London, one would think."

"Indeed."

We both studied the house before us. It was part of a long series of terraces flanking this side of the park.

"I took the liberty of walking around the back of the houses. There's an alleyway running along the buildings used by the night soil men and a gate through which one can access the park. Very convenient for a quiet evening stroll or for accessing the rear doorway unseen," he said.

I nodded in agreement, unsure of what he meant.

We turned to mount the steps to the front door but were disturbed by a commotion next door. Two men were struggling to manhandle a settee down the steps and into a large cart parked by the roadway.

I turned and watched their antics just as the lead man slipped off a step and tumbled to the pavement below, bellowing in pain. By the time I reached him, he was sitting up and holding his right ankle.

"I'm a doctor. I can help if you like," I said.

"Ow! It's my ankle! I nearly broke it!" he cried.

I gently pulled his hands away from his foot and straightened his leg out. The ankle was certainly swollen. I moved the foot about, which elicited more howls of pain. To stop his moaning, I lowered his foot and spoke to him.

"I don't think it's broken," I said as I reached into my pocket for a card, "but you certainly won't be doing any more furniture moving today. I suggest you make your way home, rest, and put some ice on it to take away the swelling,"

He took the card and I continued. "Come and see me tomorrow – or better yet, the next day. I'll be able to tell how badly damaged it is by then. Meanwhile, stay off it."

"I'll 'elp 'im get 'ome," his friend offered.

Another man emerged from the doorway with an angry expression on his face.

"Here, what's all this laying about then?" he asked.

I stood up and addressed him.

"I'm afraid your man has had a rather nasty tumble. He's sprained his ankle or worse. I'm a doctor, and I've told him to rest up for a couple of days before coming to see me about it."

The man was indignant.

"I can't wait up for him to get better. I need this place emptied today," he said.

He pointed to the man on the ground, "Get up, Harry, or you're fired!"

Harry's eyes lit up in fear. He tried to pull himself up but screamed in pain as he put weight on his leg and collapsed again.

"I think that answers that question, then," said Holmes.

The angry man turned to face the detective.

"And what do you care?" he asked.

"Nothing, really. I'm just a casual observer, but anyone can see that if this man is not fit to work, then the work will not get done."

The angry man turned back to Harry, ready to blast him again.

"And why are you in such a hurry?" asked Holmes.

The angry man turned once more, "What's it to you?" he said.

"Just a casual observer," repeated Holmes evenly.

"Well, if you have to know, this whole place," he indicated the line of terraced houses, "Is going to be pulled down and replaced by nice, new, modern houses."

I was horrified.

"Why destroy these wonderful buildings? Who would do such a thing?" I asked.

"I think the answer to that, Watson, is pretty much under your nose," said Holmes.

I looked at him and saw that he was staring at the wagon behind me. I turned and read the sideboard of the cart. *Shrubb Brothers*.

"I've never heard of them," I said.

Holmes smiled at me, that smile I had seen far too often for my own liking. I'd missed something again.

"I think you'll find, Watson, that one of those brothers is exactly why we are here."

I once again urged the injured man to rest, much to the annoyance of his employer, and then joined Holmes on the neighbouring doorstep. Holmes smiled at me and indicated the door.

"Well, it's your case so far, Doctor," he said.

I stepped up and lifted the heavy knocker. I rapped only once before the door was unlocked and opened. It revealed a sallow-faced young maid. She looked at us wide-eyed through the crack in the door.

"Can I 'elp you, sirs?" she asked.

"Yes. Dr. Watson and Mr. Sherlock Holmes, to see Mrs. Bell. We are expected," I said.

"Oh, yes, sirs. Please come in," she said as she backed away and opened the door for us to enter.

We stepped into a small entry hall that proved a little too tight for both Holmes and I together. The maid squeezed past us, locked the door, and withdrew the heavy iron key. She moved to a nearby wall stand and hung the key on a hook next to its twin. A third hook remained empty, so I placed my hat upon it. The maid once again moved past and motioned for us to follow her into a room off to the right.

"Does that key unlock the rear door as well?" Holmes asked.

The maid was surprised by the question and shrank back slightly. "Yes. Yes, it does," she said.

Holmes simply nodded.

We entered the small reception room and found Mrs. Bell sitting by the window, reading the day's newspapers. She looked up and brightened when she saw me, and then eyed Holmes with a curious lift of her eyebrow.

"Mrs. Bell, I'd like to introduce my good friend, Mr. Sherlock Holmes. I've described the scant details of your son's case to him, and he is very interested in hearing more to see if he can indeed provide help."

Mrs. Bell began to rise from her seat. Holmes gallantly tried to stop her with a gesture but was too slow. He was taken aback when she rose to full height and met him almost eye-to-eye, something that happens rarely for Holmes, especially with women.

Mrs. Bell held out her hand and said, "Mr. Holmes, I am very pleased to meet you. I am Moira, but I do prefer Mrs. Bell in deference to my late husband."

A small grin came to Holmes's mouth as he shook hands with the dominating presence that was Mrs. Moira Bell.

"Please tell me all about your son's troubles, Mrs. Bell," he said, indicating her chair. Holmes and I took seats on the small settee nearby. My friend sat back and steepled his hands before his face, his standard pose when absorbing facts provided to him.

Mrs. Bell began her tale.

"My son has been charged with the manslaughter of a very nasty man, Mr. Hyram Shrubb. My son, Julius, lives here with me and is a Professor of Zoology at the University College, just down the road. He specialises in the study of lizards and snakes."

"Herpetology," Holmes said, "Yes, Dr. Watson informed me. To be honest, that was probably what piqued my interest the most. I have heard a lot about your son and would dearly love to meet him. I can assure you that I will do all I can to clear this little matter up for him."

Mrs. Bell continued, "Oh, thank you. Well, this Mr. Shrubb turned up on our doorstep one day and barged past my poor Milly uninvited."

"Your maid, I presume?" asked Holmes.

"Why, yes. I'm sorry. He stormed into this room and blurted out his introductions, and then laid out an offer to buy the lease on my house. I was far too perplexed at his gruff manner to even consider such a request unannounced. I sent him away without another word, but he didn't leave it there. He turned up several days in a row, but Milly, God bless her, held her ground and wouldn't let him in. After the seventh time, he arrived when Julius was home, so I agreed to meet him again and hear him out."

She took a deep breath before returning to her story.

"We met in here with tea and biscuits to present an amicable setting. Mr. Shrubb called himself a 'property developer'. He is purchasing all the houses along this street with the idea of demolishing them and building a new set of larger terraces to serve the officers of the nearby Regents Park barracks. Julius became very nervous at this talk. Our house has been in my family for over a hundred years. Julius was born here. He's never known another home. He's a good boy and would never hurt a fly. He needs this house, as it's near to the University which is his life, and he needs the space to store his collection."

Holmes sat forward, a slight glint in his eye, "I take that to be his collection of reptiles," he said.

"Yes," she continued, "My Julius has a large collection of reptiles upstairs, with some very rare breeds that even the London Zoo doesn't possess." She made a slightly disgusted face. "I never go in there myself. Dreadful things," she finished.

"And that's where the Gila Monster is housed," asked Holmes, sitting back and resuming his contemplative pose.

"Oh, yes. That's also where everything went wrong."

"Go on."

"Well, I told Mr. Shrubb that there was no way that I would even contemplate selling. Julius was much relieved. Mr. Shrubb tried to offer more money to persuade us, but my mind was made up. I don't need any money, as my poor unfortunate father, God bless him, was well invested. I shan't be in need for the rest of my life and neither will Julius. Mr. Shrubb left in quite an angry mood and I hoped that would be the last we saw of him."

"But it wasn't," I said.

"No. Not at all. That meeting was a fortnight ago. Earlier this week, I was at my bridge club, Milly was out at the grocer, and Julius came home early to feed his collection. He stepped in through the front door and heard screams coming from the second floor. He ran upstairs and found Mr. Shrubb lying on the floor with Julius' favourite – his Gila Monster – clinging to his arm. Julius went to his aid and managed to pry the lizard away from Mr. Shrubb's arm. He then put the reptile away, latched up the case, and then attended to Mr. Shrubb. My dear boy managed to bring the man down to this room just as Milly returned. They both helped to tend his wound and call him a hansom. He kept blubbing that he found the door unlocked and was looking for me. He stumbled into the reptile room and was attacked by the lizard. The last they saw was his slumped form in the seat of a hansom, taking him to Dr. Brown's surgery around the corner in Robert Street. Frankly, no one thought any more of it until the police came two days ago and took my poor boy away. Manslaughter, they said, caused by the lizard bite. They blamed Julius for leaving the cage open."

"Hmm," said Holmes, "I think I'd like to see this reptile room and then, Watson, I think we should pay a visit to Dr. Brown."

***

The reptile room was more crowded than I had presumed. It was located in what was a rather large second-floor bedroom, but it seemed to shrink when filled with a dozen or so large wooden framed enclosures with glass sides. Each had a glass lid and held a single specimen.

Holmes moved around the room, a look of delight on his face as he stared into each of the reptile tanks. He stopped by one and studied it.

"Ah," he said, "*Vipera berus*. The common adder. The kingdom's only venomous snake, but really quite shy and harmless."

He moved on to another that contained a brown snake lying on a flat rock.

"*Naja haje*, the Egyptian Cobra, also known as the Asp. It was this snake that was thought to have been used by Cleopatra to commit suicide. Very good, very good."

He moved on and stopped by another enclosure.

"Ah, and here is our little mischief-maker himself."

Inside the glass cage was a fat, squat lizard with a pink and brown mottled body and black face.

"*Heloderma suspectum*, the Gila Monster. Native to the southwestern United States and northern Mexico. I'm not sure if I'm more impressed in seeing it, or the fact that Professor Bell managed to find one and keep it alive."

He studied the cage and unlatched two slide bolts near the top which caused the front to fold down. The lizard hardly moved with the door open and simply looked at Holmes for a moment before falling back to sleep.

"Hardly the vicious killer of legend, hey, Watson?"

"Is it still alive?" I asked.

Holmes chuckled and relatched the door.

Just then the room's door opened and Milly walked in with a tray of food scraps. She saw the two of us and a slightly shocked look came to her face.

"Oh, I'm sorry gentlemen. I can come back and feed these beasts later."

"Never mind that, Milly. Please ignore us, will you. Go about your chore," said Holmes.

Milly moved to the nearest cage and opened the top. She dropped some scraps inside and the resident lizard wandered over to eat. She replaced the lid and repeated the exercise with the next few tanks.

Holmes watched with interest.

"Milly," he asked.

The young maid almost dropped the tray in shock. She turned sheepishly to face the detective.

"Yes, sir?"

"I assume that Professor Bell usually feeds the reptiles."

She nodded.

"Since he's indisposed you've taken up the challenge."

Again she nodded.

"I noticed that you only feed them through the top of the enclosure. Do you ever need to open the front?"

"Oh, no, sir. Julius, er, the *professor* always uses the top. 'E would only open the front if 'e was moving the animal to another enclosure, and then 'e would use those."

She pointed at a pair of thick leather gloves hanging from a peg on the wall.

Holmes studied the gloves, looked back at the Gila Monster sitting on its rock, and then turned to me.

"Watson, it's time to visit Dr. Brown."

***

We were shown into Dr. Brown's room just as his last patient before lunch left.

Behind the desk sat a man of about sixty years of age with a ramrod-straight posture. He was quite bald but possessing of a luxuriant grey moustache and a monocle held in with his right eyebrow.

A quick look around his room showed the standard paraphernalia of a modern doctor. A full-sized human skeleton hung from a frame in one corner. A gurney sat against one wall with a curtained area for undressing next to it. On the wall behind the desk was a small but marvellous collection of artefacts from the east.

A Ghurkha knife stood on a stand in the middle of a mantlepiece that framed the grate of a small fireplace. On the wall to either side were framed copies of the doctor's professional certificates and a letter with the seal of Her Majesty. I strained to read the letter, but only made out a comment about service to the Crown. It looked very similar to the one that I had received.

"Let me introduce ourselves, Dr. Brown. I am Dr. John Watson, and this is Mr. Sherlock Holmes," I said. I pointed to the Ghurka knife and asked, "You served in India?"

He looked around for a moment and turned back with a smile of fond remembrance, "Yes," he said, "I was an officer in the Indian Army for more than twenty years." He studied me for a moment, "And yourself? You have the air of a military man as well."

I nodded with a slight bow. "In Afghanistan, until I was injured."

He looked at Holmes, taking in my tall companion's presence for a moment before directing his enquiry at the detective.

"Sherlock Holmes. I have heard of you, sir, but never believed I would find myself in any need of your services, so forgive me if I am surprised to find the reverse."

A small smile crossed Holmes's face. "Let us not take up too much of your time," he said, "A couple of days ago, you received an emergency patient by the name of Hyram Shrubb."

The doctor nodded, "Yes. Lizard bite. Very strange and nasty."

"I know it may constitute a breach of privacy, but could I enquire as to how you treated the bite?"

"Well, I don't wish to let out my secrets, as it wasn't something well known among British doctors."

"Could it have been with the administration of a weak mix of strychnine?"

The doctor looked aghast. "How in the blazes would you have known that?" he asked.

I was just as shocked. "Yes, Holmes. How?"

Holmes's face possessed that smile generally reserved for me when I've been surprised by one of his deductions. He took a deep breath and enlightened us.

"Dr. Brown, before you even spoke, your Ghurka knife told me that you lived in India. I presumed that you would have served as a doctor for most of that time."

"Yes," said Brown.

"Mr. Shrubb presented to you with a bite from a Gila Monster. He may not have known the actual species, but you would have seen fang marks and much damage caused by the bite. I expect that you would have treated him as if he had been bitten by a venomous animal."

"Well, yes. Once I treated any infection, I naturally took the precaution to treat for poison."

"And coming from India, where the standard procedure for cobra bite is to use strychnine, a treatment developed in Australia in the 1850s to care for bites from their local snake population, as it contains species far deadlier than the cobra of India."

"Yes. Correct again. Amazing. You got all that from a Ghurka knife?"

"You would be amazed what information Holmes can gather from the smallest of sources," I said.

"Thank you, Watson," Holmes said. "By the way, Dr. Brown. Do you know that your patient, Mr. Shrubb, died the very next day?"

Brown's face dropped in complete shock.

"What? That's impossible. Once I administered the strychnine and settled him down here for a little while, he was right as rain. I loaded him into a hansom and sent him home. I'm flabbergasted."

"Quite so, but I would have experienced the same reaction if I were in your place. I do give you my promise that we will return and explain what happened when I have solved it myself, which will be quite soon," said Holmes, "I thank you for your time, Doctor."

He spun on his heel and spoke to me.

"Watson, if you will, I think we should take a visit to Scotland Yard. We need to see the unfortunate Mr. Shrubb."

***

Martin, the young mortician, looked up as Holmes and I entered. He was just finishing his lunch and had probably expected a little peace and quiet. He stood up quickly and addressed us.

"Dr. Watson, Mr. 'Olmes. I wasn't expecting anybody today. What can I do for – "

He was cut off by the arrival of Inspector Lestrade, who seemed a bit flustered. He carried the small note from Holmes that had been passed to him by the desk Sergeant on the floor above.

"Ah, Inspector," said Holmes, "I believe you will find the following of interest."

"Why did you drag me away from my luncheon to come down to this God-awful place?" Lestrade asked.

Holmes ignored the question and instead addressed Martin.

"If you would be so kind to please direct us to the corpse of the unfortunate Mr. Hyram Shrubb, Martin."

Martin put his sandwich down and pulled the napkin from his collar before skirting a few gurneys and stopping before one covering a large bloated body.

"'E's a big 'un," he said, before pulling back the sheet to reveal the corpse below.

"Thank you," said Holmes. He bent forward and looked at the man's face, studying the mouth and nose while making small humming noises to himself – something to which I have long become accustomed when Holmes investigates. He pulled out his glass and had a closer look at the man's nose. I did find this particularly odd, as I could see the bite mark on the man's left forearm quite clearly.

Finally, Holmes moved away from the man's face and studied the bite. From where I stood, I could see that the flesh on the arm had been ravaged by multiple teeth marks. The lizard had latched on with considerable force and thrashed about before being pulled off. There were two larger holes on opposite sides of the bite which were deeper and more pronounced. I took these to be the venom-bearing teeth.

Holmes's examination of the bite was remarkably short as he moved away from the area and fixated on the man's upper forearm. I could see more puncture marks, which I presumed were from the injections administered by Dr. Brown.

Holmes rose and stood staring at Shrubb's corpse for a moment before turning back to Martin.

"The Coroner hasn't performed an autopsy," he said.

It was more a statement than a question.

Martin replied, "No. No, 'e 'asn't. 'E said that we know 'ow the man died, so no need to mess 'im up any more."

Holmes's face screwed up. I knew that he viewed such actions and sloppy, as they restricted the amount of information that could be gleaned.

"Why do you think that would be important?" Lestrade asked, "We know it was the lizard, and we know that this professor was the lizard's owner. Case closed."

A short flash of fury leapt to Holmes's face before he replaced it with calm. I believe that Lestrade barely missed a thorough lecture.

"Because, Inspector, this man is extremely obese. I dare say a good shock of any sort could have caused him to keel over. Also, do you not think it would be a good idea to ascertain the amount of venom in his system? I've seen the lizard in question. Unless it had friends working with it, then it wouldn't have been able to generate enough venom to kill a man of this size."

With that, he placed his lens back in his pocket and abruptly departed, speaking over his shoulder as he did.

"Thank you, Martin. Your help has been admirable. Inspector, I think you should meet Watson and me at the house of Mr. Hyram Shrubb and his brother in two hours. I will announce my findings there forthwith. Please bring Professor Bell, for he has nothing at all to do with this unfortunate event and you can release him afterwards."

I gave thanks and said my goodbyes before following after Holmes.

***

We took luncheon in The Rag nearby in Pall Mall. My status as an ex-serviceman held me good stead amongst the military folk that inhabited the place, and Holmes was always welcome once his identity was known, even though he'd never served Her Majesty in the armed services.

Throughout the meal, I kept prodding him about the solution to the case. His only answer was to smile, nod, and say, "All will become clear." A most infuriating affair it was. He seemed more intent on studying the diners at several other tables, most of whom wore very high-ranking insignia on their jackets.

"My word, this is a very prominent gathering for this time of day," I remarked.

"Yes," said Holmes, "One would almost imagine that we are centralising some of our garrisons in preparation for another campaign."

"I'm sure it's nothing to do with war, Holmes. Just a gathering of officers."

Holmes simply smiled.

***

At a little after two, we were the first to arrive. Holmes went straight to the door and knocked. It was opened by a pasty-faced doorman, who eyed us with slight suspicion.

"I am Sherlock Holmes and this is Dr. John Watson. We should be expected."

62

The doorman nodded and replied, "Yes, sirs. Mr. Shrubb was informed of your imminent arrival. He has seen fit to meet with you in the parlour."

He stepped back and allowed us to enter. The foyer was quite luxuriant with deep-grained woods and leather. The doorman led us down a short corridor and into a spectacular room lined along every wall with bookcases, each crammed with leather-bound volumes in nearly perfect condition, and a small number of display cases holding an assortment of bric-a-brac.

Both Holmes and I were quite taken aback by this room. Neither of us has any expectations of such a place in a house occupied by a pair of bachelor property developers.

It was then I noticed a man sitting in a high backed chair towards the far end of the room. He was the spitting image of his brother, but lacking most of the weight. For a split second, I imagined the Holmes brothers, with Mycroft lying in the Scotland Yard morgue and Sherlock sitting before me.

"Gentlemen," he began, "Welcome to my home."

He rose and stood a good two inches higher than Holmes. He made his way towards us and held out his hand to me first.

"I am Aubrey Shrubb," he said and took my hand.

"John Watson," I replied.

He turned to Holmes and repeated the action, remarking, "And you would be the famous Sherlock Holmes."

"I'm sorry about what happened to your brother," said Holmes, shaking and finally releasing Shrubb's hand.

"Yes, damnable strange way to die, that. Who would have thought such an intelligent man would allow his creatures to run free and attack any innocent person who happened upon them? Very negligent, it would seem."

"That is partly why we are here. Mrs. Bell has asked me to investigate a little further and determine just how your brother came into contact with the lizard, and what happened afterwards."

"I think the police have worked all that out, haven't they? He was bitten by a venomous lizard and it killed him. Case closed."

"Forgive my cynicism, but the police are likely to take the most obvious answer when investigating a strange case such as this. I much prefer to look at all the facts and evidence before jumping to conclusions."

The sound of the door knocker filtered in as the second group of guests arrived at the Shrubb residence.

"Ah, speaking of the police," said Holmes.

Moments later, the doorman showed a slightly aggrieved Lestrade and a very perplexed and dour-looking man, who I assumed was Professor Bell, into the parlour.

Shrubb took one look at Bell and asked, "What is *he* doing here?"

"I thought it best to have the professor here to provide any expert information concerning the Gila Monster, and to be on hand to defend himself if required," said Holmes.

"Hmm. I only agreed to this because your note said that you had new information that would shed light on Hyram's death. I was hoping that you would find something to convict this man with murder rather than manslaughter," Aubrey said, his contempt for Bell on show as he spat out the word man.

"Well, it could go either way," said Holmes, "To move things along, would it be possible to see your brother's rooms? My understanding is that he had a suite of apartments on the second floor and that he was found in his own drawing-room."

"Yes. The rooms are as he left them. I haven't had the heart to let the help tidy up yet."

***

The second floor was a large and sumptuous collection of rooms styled in a more minimalistic way than the parlour below. I assumed that they reflected the less austere tastes of the younger and larger of the Shrubb brothers.

The climb up the stairs also left me a little breathless and I wondered how a man of Hyram Shrubb's girth would have found the journey. It was later that I discovered there was a lift, which explained quite a lot.

Aubrey Shrubb led us down a short corridor and into a large but modestly decorated drawing-room. There was a sizeable wooden desk at one end, with a small collection of leather-bound volumes on a set of shelves behind it. I pulled a book down and looked closer. They were mostly books relating to the history of London's property transactions. It seemed this room doubled as Hyram Shrubb's office, or else his work was also his hobby.

I turned back from the shelf and found Aubrey directing Holmes to a large chair in the far corner. The elder Shrubb brother pointed to a stain on the carpet and spoke.

"My poor unfortunate brother was found face down here. His last act was to expel his luncheon – hence the stain. I did allow the maid to clean the results after the police allowed it."

Holmes turned to Lestrade and said, "Did your men take samples for examination?"

"Why?" Lestrade asked.

Holmes closed his eyes for a second, pursed his lips, and said, "Because it would have been a trivial exercise to determine the contents of his stomach, revealing how much venom was in his system, and also what else may have been ingested."

"Right," said Lestrade.

Holmes turned back to the scene and moved to a small table next to the sitting chair. Opening the drawer, he pulled out a bottle of white powder and a half-full syringe containing a clear liquid. Holmes picked up the bottle, uncorked it, and dabbed a small amount of the powder on his finger. He tasted it, nodded, and smiled. I questioned him as he put the bottle down.

"What is that?"

"My old friend – though a lot more concentrated than my favoured seven-per-cent solution," he said.

"Cocaine?" I remarked.

Aubrey piped up with a hint of offence. "What my brother did in his own house is none of your business!"

"Indeed," said Holmes. "But it must be taken into consideration with all the other evidence."

He turned and scanned the room, seeking out *minutiae*. His eyes fell on me, and then the desk. He strode over and stood behind it, opening the top drawers and rifling through them.

"Hello, what the blazes do you think you are doing?" yelled Aubrey, "That's Hyram's private business!"

He started to move towards Holmes but Lestrade placed a hand lightly on his shoulder.

"I'd let Mr. Holmes finish, sir. If there's something that we've missed, then he is most likely to find it. I'm sure he's not interested in any private affairs of your brother's."

With that, Holmes finished looking through one of the bottom drawers and stood up withholding his prize – a large iron key.

Professor Julius Bell yelled out in surprise, "That's our missing key! We thought that Milly had lost it. She got a right dressing down from Mother. No wonder she cried so much. I had to console her for hours."

Lestrade turned to look at the professor, who suddenly realised he'd said too much. A sheepish look came across his face.

"Well, she was very upset," he added.

All eyes slowly returned to Holmes, who placed the key in the middle of the vacant leather desk pad. He looked around all of the faces full of anticipation and smiled. "This, gentlemen, is the vital clew for which I have been searching."

"But what does it mean?" I asked.

He ignored me and turned towards Shrubb.

"Mr. Shrubb. You and your brother are highly successful property developers, a new occupation that takes the city's old and derelict districts and renews them for the next generation and in turn attracts a tidy profit. Is that not right?"

Shrubb nodded, "Yes, why?"

"Your brother wasn't used to failure, I think. He studied the city and chose the best locations for these developments – hence his detailed volumes of property transactions and locations in London. A well-versed man in that field, I would presume."

"Yes. He was the educated one. He found the properties and I organised the workmen and ran the operation."

"So, his latest venture was to revitalise parts of Regents Park, with the view of establishing residencies for the officers of the nearby

Regents Park Barracks and the new garrisons that will be moving there soon."

"We had already convinced most of the residents to depart, and were almost ready to demolish."

"But one held out."

"Yes. Mrs. Bell wouldn't sell. Even when we made a higher offer than to any other resident."

Holmes held up the iron key.

"And that's what drove your brother to purloin this key and gain access to the Bell residence when he believed all to be away."

"How dare you besmirch my brother's good name!" said Aubrey as he stepped towards Holmes.

Lestrade intercepted him and posed a question of Holmes. "How can you be sure that Shrubb took that key from the Bell residence?" he asked.

"When we arrived, we noticed that there were only two keys on the rack near the front door. Professor Bell has told us that there was a third which seems to have gone missing. Mr. Shrubb was found inside the house when all occupants had left. I would say that his claim that the door was unlocked was a fantasy. With this key, he could have entered from the front or back, as both doors use the same lock."

"Why did he break-in?" asked Lestrade.

"Ah, well, that's where I must presume a little, until of course more evidence is unearthed that proves me incorrect. The sticking point of the sale of the house was Professor Bell's residency at the University College. His mother would not have them move. The facts as they standpoint to Mr. Shrubb entering the house with the express purpose of removing one of the venomous reptiles and probably placing it in Mrs. Bell's bedroom."

"Preposterous!" said Aubrey.

"Possibly, but if Mr. Shrubb could cause a ruction between mother and son because of the reptile collection, then he may have thought he could convince Mrs. Bell to sell up."

"Yes, Mother is proud of my work, but she doesn't like my collection," said Julius.

"But that lizard bit him. It's obviously vicious and," Aubrey pointed at Julius, "*he* is responsible!"

The professor looked shocked at the accusation. "I would never – " he started before Holmes cut him off.

"You have no need to apologise, Professor Bell, I have seen the lizard in question and it is a somewhat sedentary beast. Can you explain to us how and why the Gila Monster in question would act the way it did?"

Julius Bell's posture changed completely as his professional stature was called upon.

"The Gila Monster, especially the male that I possess, is rather slow and sluggish. They generally don't attack unless provoked."

"If someone were to pick one up, would that be enough to elicit an attack?"

"Possibly, especially if it was handled roughly. A Gila Monster will bite and latch on for dear life then thrash around until they subdue their prey," Julius said, "That was how I found Mr. Shrubb. My lizard had bitten him on the wrist and clamped its mouth shut with some force. I had to remove it with a stick."

"But it wouldn't attack unless picked up or moved?"

"Yes, that's right."

I felt I had to step in and clarify things. "So, what you're saying is that Mr. Shrubb stole a key from the Bell's household, and then came back when they were away and tried to pick up a venomous lizard to put it in Mrs. Bell's bedroom, but was himself bitten."

"Precisely. We already heard from the maid that the cases are rarely opened fully, so the lizard had to be extricated from its confinement, which probably aggravated it enough to attack," said Holmes.

"That doesn't excuse this man!" said Aubrey Shrubb, pointing at the professor. "He kept dangerous reptiles in his house, waiting to leap on unsuspecting victims and kill them."

"Yes," said Lestrade, "Regardless of whether Mr. Shrubb entered illegally, he was still killed by the professor's lizard, which is manslaughter under the eyes of the law."

"Ah, but did the lizard kill him? What say you, Professor?"

"As I explained to the police, it's simply not possible for my Gila Monster to inject enough poison into a man of Mr. Shrubb's size to kill him. Even if he had ingested the entire poison sack, he would simply have been rendered prostrate for a matter of hours and lethargic for a good week."

"Quite so. That was also my estimation. If the neurotoxic poison of the lizard didn't kill him, we should then look at the treatment," Holmes turned and addressed me directly. "Watson, of the doctor's use of strychnine in treating the lizard's venom?"

Searching my memories, I stated, "Strychnine is itself a poison, but like many poisons when administered in small doses acts as a stimulant. I've never come across its use in this way, but I would assume it is used to stimulate the nervous system to counteract the retardation effect of the neurotoxin."

"Exactly. And what of cocaine?"

"Again, another stimulant. The two together would engender an extremely vigorous reaction from the heart and respiratory system." I clicked my fingers as the penny dropped. "By God, Holmes! I see where you are going."

Lestrade looked as lost, as always. "What are you suggesting?"

I continued, "The dual actions of the strychnine and cocaine on a man of Mr. Shrubb's size would have put such a strain on his heart that it would have seized, if not burst."

"And as I found out in the morgue, Mr. Hyram Shrubb was a very habitual cocaine user, with many injection marks in his left forearm."

Holmes pointed at the syringe.

"I'm sure that if we test the contents of that syringe, it will be a very highly concentrated dose of cocaine. I would presume that Mr. Shrubb was in intense pain from the lizard bite and mixed himself what he thought a heavy dose of pain relief, but to his poor luck, turned out to contain the seeds of his own demise."

Aubrey Shrubb stepped forward and said, "Are you saying that my brother accidentally did it all to himself?"

"Yes. Through his actions, your brother paid the ultimate price."

Holmes turned to Lestrade. "I would think that the death should be put down to misadventure. I'm sure that the Bells would be most happy to remain out of any further enquiries."

Lestrade nodded and gave Aubrey Shrubb a look of contempt which made the taller brother shrink back. "I'll do that, but I'll be making some notes about the practices of Shrubb Brothers for future reference."

He turned and stormed out.

Aubrey Shrubb looked apologetically at Professor Bell and tentatively held out his hand. The professor took it in his own and gave it a perfunctory shake.

"No hard feelings, I hope," said Shrubb, "I can only apologise for my brother's actions, but can assure you I knew nothing about them."

Julius eyed him with suspicion before begrudgingly nodding his acceptance and turning to leave.

"Professor," Holmes said.

Bell turned and saw Holmes holding the iron key.

"Yours, I believe," he said.

The professor walked over and took the key, saying, "Thank you, Mr. Holmes. I can't tell you how much that I'm in your debt. I'm sure my mother has made some recompense offer, but I would be prepared to increase whatever it was."

Holmes smiled, "No need for that. This has been a most interesting day and has broken the monotony with much verve. There is only one reward I would be most interested in seeking."

"Name it, sir, please."

"I would love to return to your reptile room and discuss all things herpetological with you, at your leisure."

The professor's face lit up with glee.

"Oh, any time, sir, any time! I would also be delighted for you to attend my lectures at the University College whenever you have the time. From what I've seen and heard today, I believe that there are things I can indeed learn from you."

"I'm sure we can both benefit," said Holmes, "I will check my calendar and take you up on your offer."

Still beaming, the professor pocketed the key, turned on his heel, gave one last desultory look at Shrubb, and exited.

Shrubb's face was aghast with all that had happened. He looked around his brother's room as if every artefact held a level of danger and betrayal in his mind. He finally stepped towards Holmes.

"I am in awe of your deductive skills, sir, and owe you an apology as well. I truly believed that young man meant ill to Hyram. I was possibly blinded by a brother's love, but now see what Hyram was up to. Sadly, his actions have left me with several terraced houses that serve no purpose in my business – business that I will need to re-examine in case there are other occurrences of this kind."

He turned, shoulders slumped and trudged out of the room. I watched his tall figure reduced by bereavement and betrayal and almost felt a touch of sympathy towards him. I told Holmes as much as we stood alone in the dead man's parlour.

"I wouldn't be too sad for him, Watson. His pride has been damaged more than anything else. I don't think the loss of his brother will affect him too much. It's more the damage to his reputation that worries him. With all that's happening in this city at the moment, I'm sure a person like Mr. Shrubb will recover and build an empire with a renewed vigour. I just hope he refrains from utilising the devious methods of his kin."

I leaned back and took down the great index volume to which he referred. Holmes balanced it on his knee, and his eyes moved slowly and lovingly over the record of old cases, mixed with the accumulated information of a lifetime. ". . . Venomous lizard or gila. Remarkable case, that!"

Dr. John H. Watson – "The Adventure of the Sussex Vampire"

The Adventure of the modern Guy Fawkes

Most of the adventures that involve my companion Sherlock Holmes are of a rather mundane nature, involving a cross-section of the folk who live the bulk of their simple lives within the great metropolis of London.

Sometimes, however, Holmes is called upon to decipher mysteries that involve the upper echelon of modern society, and on rare occasions, his investigations are tangled up with even the highest levels of Government. Such was the case when I opened the front door to the frantic tapping of a distraught young man dressed in a heavy woollen suit and bowler hat, the distinct attire of the civil service.

He handed me his card, which announced him to be *"Godfrey Jones, Under-secretary of the Committee of Imperial Defence"*. I held my hand out to shake his hand and introduce myself but was greeted with his coat and hat. Though slightly taken aback, I took it in good humour, as his distress seemed to overwhelm him.

"Thank you, my good man, I'm here on orders from the secretariat to seek out the services of Mr. Sherlock Holmes. Is he at home?" he asked.

I pointed to the stairs and said, "If you follow me, I'll take you to him." I backed away and allowed him entry.

We found Holmes reclining in his favourite chair, smoking a pipe and reading the daily paper. "This would be the man you are after," I said to Jones as I placed his coat and hat on a nearby chair. I extended my hand again and finally introduced myself.

"I am Doctor John Watson, Mr. Holmes's associate," I said and indicated Holmes, "This is Mr. Sherlock Holmes."

His face dropped a little and his cheeks flushed red with embarrassment. He held out his hand and took mine. "Oh, I am sorry, sir, I didn't realise."

I smiled and let go of his hand. "Never mind," I said and indicated a free chair. I handed Holmes the card and turned to leave to ask Mrs. Hudson for tea, but was greeted at the door by our landlady with a laden tray containing tea, three cups, and biscuits.

I smiled and remarked quietly, "You are a wonder, Mrs. Hudson."

She placed the tray on the side table and turned back towards me, a slight smile on her lips. "Yes, I am," she agreed as she moved past me.

While the tea steeped, I took a seat a little way from Jones and watched the proceedings.

Holmes carefully folded his paper and placed it to the side. I noticed that he had left a specific article on the top to continue reading later. I took note of the strange headline, "*Robbery at Woolwich Artillery Base*". He read the business card and then looked up and studied Jones for a moment, I presumed that he was gathering data and forming an opinion about the man. I smiled to myself as I also observed Jones's agitation at Holmes's silence.

Finally, Holmes looked up into the young man's eyes and spoke. "Well, Mr. Godfrey Jones of Her Majesty's Civil Service, it is a pleasure to make your acquaintance." He rose and shook the young man's hand. "If I'm not wrong, you are a clerk, having been in the service for some six years after leaving Rugby Public School at the requisite age of seventeen. You once played rugby as well, but since moving to London have relinquished your sport. You are also married with a small child."

Jones's mouth dropped open. "How? How?"

A smile developed on my face, I'd seen this time and time again but was a little perplexed at how Holmes had gleaned such details in such a short time. "Yes," I said. "How did you work all that out?"

"Quite simply, Watson." He indicated our guest. "Mr. Jones here is about twenty-two or twenty-three years of age. He sports a dark blue tie, with light blue-and-green diagonal stripes – the traditional colours of Rugby college. Plus I cheated. You are wearing your school's pin on your lapel."

Jones looked down at his lapel. Holmes smiled at the last remark, and I winced internally for missing that obvious detail.

"Mr. Jones here is also wearing a suit that is of a slightly out-of-date style, possibly purchased on his promotion from clerk two or three years ago. It is now heading towards retirement itself. He is quite well built, which suggests a history of sporting endeavours, but is sporting a slightly pronounced belly which indicates those days are over. He has a simple gold band on his left ring finger, and there is a small crusted stain on the right shoulder of his coat, which indicates spittle from an infant nestled there. Am I correct?"

Jones was still staggered in amazement.

"Yes. Yes, sir, you are correct on every detail. No wonder they wanted me to come and fetch you."

He sat down heavily, his brain whirring at a frantic rate, trying to take all of Holmes's abilities on board. I passed around cups of tea to break the tension.

Holmes sat back and sipped, his steely gaze still locked onto young Jones. "Who told you to come fetch me?" he asked.

Jones sipped his tea to steady his nerves and answered, "The Secretary, through his assistant, asked me to bring you immediately." He looked at the cup of tea in shock and placed it down a little unsteadily.

"He said immediately. I . . . I . . . must bring you back," he said standing up and taking us both a little by surprise.

Holmes smiled, "I'm sure it's not so urgent that we can't finish our tea."

Jones looked at the both of us and realised we weren't going to move. After a moment, he sat down again and picked up his cup.

"I – I have a hansom waiting outside," he said.

"Good, good. That will save time, and you can tell us all about why you are here," said Holmes.

Jones looked surprised again. "I'm sorry to say that I have been sworn to secrecy and was told to simply fetch you and bring you to the Houses of Parliament. Once there, all will become clear," he said.

Holmes's face showed a wide grin.

"Oh, really, how very intriguing. Someone was relying on your innocence to stir my curiosity. Very good," he said as he drained his cup and placed it on the side table. He stood. "Well Watson, shall we prepare ourselves and go with young Mr. Jones *here to see if there is* some game to be had in this little adventure?" He smiled to himself and added, "I feel that my brother is mixed up in this somewhere."

***

The hansom pulled up on Great George Street, about fifty yards from Westminster Bridge and across the road from the clock tower. Luckily for us, Big Ben was silent, as it was a good twenty minutes to the hour. The sound of that great bell is fixed in the minds of Londoners, but at that close distance, it tends to have a dire effect on one's hearing.

We followed Godfrey across the street towards the magnificent site that is the Houses of Parliament. I looked up and down Great George Street and was surprised by the number of uniformed constables milling about. Usually one would see the odd bobby walking near the houses, but on that day, I spied a good half-dozen.

I thought to myself, "Something must be afoot."

Jones led us around the lush grass of the Speaker's Green, below a small arch in the side of the building, and up to a wooden door set back from the pathway.

He rapped twice on the door and announced himself. A heavy lock was turned and a bolt drawn before the door swung back into the building. A large cloud of smoke blew out of the open doorway, causing all three of us to cough. It slowly dissipated, revealing a heavy-set man with a ruddy complexion who eyed all three of us suspiciously whilst chomping on his cigar.

"Ah, Mr. Parsons," said Jones, evidently aware of the man's identity, "This is Mr. Sherlock Holmes and his associate, Dr. John Watson. The Secretary asked me to fetch them to investigate the, ah, the little problem."

The ruddy-faced man looked Holmes and me up and down then drew on his cigar again before *harrumph*-ing and stepping back from the doorway to allow us passage. He peered out through the entrance once more before slamming the door behind us and bolting it shut.

"This is highly unusual, but I've orders from upstairs, so follow me, please," he said, letting the last word hang in the air before walking off along the long dark corridor leading away from the door.

I could detect a small grin on Holmes's face as he turned and followed Parsons, looking around from time to time to discern any details that might prove useful.

Jones walked next to me and spoke. "Please excuse Christopher. He was formerly in the Army and takes a lot of pride in maintaining the security here," he said.

"I was in the Army myself," I replied, "and I can quite understand. I can also see that he wouldn't like the idea of civilians simply waltzing in."

"Quite so," said Jones.

The corridor was a long, painted brick affair with no decorations of any kind. Every twenty yards or so, a small gaslight provided the only illumination. The barren nature told me that it was a service tunnel, used mostly by the cleaning staff or tradesmen who needed to access the underbelly of the Parliament buildings. Every so often we crossed another corridor and passed by dull, grey doors that were firmly shut. The only sounds were our footsteps on the ancient tiled floor.

Parsons stopped and opened one of the doors, revealing a set of stone stairs leading further down into the bowels under the building. A single gaslight shone on the ancient stone steps and allowed us to safely descend. The exit door led to another dimly lit passageway that headed off at a right angle to the one above.

We traversed this next narrow passage for about fifty yards before Parsons stopped, bent down, and picked up a small paraffin lamp. He lit it from his cigar and indicated an open archway leading into another passage perpendicular to the one in which we stood.

"I don't generally let civilians into this area," Parsons said. "Not within protocol, but . . . ."

Holmes finished his sentence for him, "You have your orders," and stepped through the arch.

We all followed and found a wide room with a doorway at the far end, along with a multitude of pipes running across the ceiling.

Parsons stepped up to a nearby gaslight and brought more illumination into the room by lighting it with his cigar. I noticed the pipes were a mix of dull brass and ceramic. I assumed they carried both water and sewage, and hoped they were watertight, as the thought of any leaks down here filled me with dread.

It was then I looked down and saw several small barrels, sitting in a neat pile, nestled against one wall.

Holmes spoke up, "I take it that this is either a storeroom or the source of your little problem."

"These appeared last night. One of the guards was doing a routine check, before I started, and found them. He reported to the duty clerk, then suddenly some shiny-bottom starts yelling 'Guy Fawkes!' and all hell breaks loose," said Parsons.

Holmes stepped up to the barrels and brought his lamp closer. Suddenly, he stepped back again and handed the lamp to me. "Keep this at a distance, will you Watson? I need to examine these barrels, but don't want the flame to get too close," he said. He turned to Parsons and said, "Do your protocols mention anything about smoking near explosives?"

Parsons looked sheepish and stepped back a couple of yards.

I approached Holmes and held the lamp at a suitable distance. Even from there, I could see traces of a black substance on the lid of one of the barrels. My rudimentary knowledge of explosives came to the fore.

"Is that - ?" I asked.

"I think so," Holmes answered.

He looked toward a brightly lit room through the door at the far end. He picked up a barrel and marched off towards the doorway. I started after him, but he held up a hand to stop me.

"No need for us both to be in danger, Watson," he said.

I stood, mouth agape, as he strode away.

"In danger?" I said to myself.

I watched from afar as Holmes placed the barrel on the ground just inside the room and pulled off the lid. He stared at the contents for a moment before dipping a hand into the barrel and bringing it out, full of black powder. He let it spill through his fingers and then rubbed two together with the remnants of the powder on their tips. I could see a smile play on his face and realised something was up. I hoped to be privy to it soon.

Holmes dipped his hand again, replaced the lid on the barrel and poured a small pile of the powder onto the lid. He picked up the barrel and turned back towards us.

Something just inside the other room grabbed his attention. He examined it for a moment before returning to us.

"Good news?" I asked.

"Interesting news, I think," he replied.

He placed the barrel on the floor, away from the others. I spied the small pile of black powder on top.

"Gunpowder, I presume," I said.

Holmes smiled and said, "That's what our perpetrator would lead us to believe."

He turned, plucked Parsons's cigar from his mouth, and rammed it into the little pile of powder.

We all reared back in terror.

The cigar simply sizzled slightly and let out a small stream of smoke. The powder remained inert.

"What in blazes?" said Parsons.

"It's sand. Fine, black sand, and ground-up charcoal with a small amount of black powder," Holmes said.

"Good Lord," said Jones.

"Why?" I asked.

"I'm not sure at this point," said Holmes. "But something of this nature would be to sew discontent and terror, or to distract attention from another act." He turned towards Parsons, who was fishing out another cigar. "As you have said, the public isn't allowed into this area, so who would have access?" he asked.

"Guards," he said. "Cleaners. Maintenance crew. Why?"

Holmes pointed to the next room and said, "There is a cleaners' trolley sitting in the adjoining room. There are traces of the same black powder, so I am assuming it was used to transport these barrels. You would also have noticed that there is no fuse leading away from the barrels."

All three of us looked at the base of the pile. I felt ashamed that I had missed such an obvious clew.

"The only way to ignite this lot would be to set fire to a barrel itself, which would leave no time for the perpetrator to escape," said Holmes. He looked to the ceiling and posed another question. "And the room above?"

"That would be the House of Commons," said Jones, who had been silent for quite some time. "It's the main reason this was elevated beyond internal security and kept on the quiet."

"So the whole Guy Fawkes analogy is quite within reason," I said.

Holmes grinned then stepped towards the wall at the end of the room. He looked to the ceiling and through the doorway, then paced out the distance between the wall and the barrels.

"Twenty paces," he said pointing at the wall behind the barrels, "And this wall would be in the centre of the room to provide support for the chamber floor above."

He pointed to the ceiling and continued, "I propose that whoever sits on the Government benches above this point is the subject of this plot."

***

We re-assembled in the chamber of the House of Commons, several feet above the barrels of weakened black powder we had examined minutes previously.

The House was luckily empty as Parliament wasn't sitting that week. Holmes stated that this fact indicated that the barrels were merely a distraction from the true nature of this conundrum.

Parsons stood near the entrance with his arms folded and a scowl on his face. "I don't know why you need to be in 'ere," he said. "It's very out of the ordinary for Johnny public to be allowed access to the chamber. But – "

I finished his sentence, more in desperation at the man's insistence on protocol than anything. "You have your orders."

He nodded, grim-faced. At least he had disposed of his foul-smelling cigar. I assumed even he wouldn't deign to smoke in the chamber – much to my relief.

Holmes was indifferent to Parsons's complaints. He was busy taking in the grandeur that is the chamber of the House of Commons.

He paced the floor of the room between the two rows of benches, stepping up to the beautiful wood-panelled walls at either end and examining them in detail. He knocked a couple of times, eliciting a shocked response from Parsons. "'Ere, what you doing?"

Holmes looked over at him and replied, "Ensuring that I'm correct in my assumption that the solid stone wall below us is in fact the same wall that this wood panelling hides from view."

Content in his deduction, he proceeded to pace out his measurements from below. He repeated the process a couple of times then turned to face the Government benches.

"Whoever sits in this area would have been the most affected by the blast from below," he said pointing at the green leather-upholstered bench, "*if* it were true gunpowder."

Godfrey Jones strode over and checked the location. He pointed to Holmes's right. "The Prime Minister sits there. To his left is the Chancellor," he said, pointing out each imprint in the leather as he turned. "Then the Foreign Secretary, the Home Secretary, and the Secretary for Defence,"

"Any of those last three," said Holmes, "could have been sitting directly above the bomb."

"But you said it wouldn't work," commented Parsons, "so it doesn't matter who it was,"

"As I said," added Holmes, "I think it is a distraction, aimed at sending a message, rather than inflicting any wholesale damage."

"Speaking of messages," interrupted Jones, "I think that brings us to the next piece of information that you should see."

Holmes and I both turned to look at him with slight surprise on our faces.

***

Jones brought us to the outer office of Sir Nigel Attleby, the Home Secretary. We entered and found a rather attractive woman sitting behind a desk looking extremely frazzled. She looked up as we entered, and her face dropped even further. "What is it now?" she asked.

Jones answered her with a calming voice, "I'm so sorry to disturb you, Miss Plumb, but these are the men that are helping us with the little problem downstairs. Sir Nigel also requested that they be brought to him when appropriate."

Her demeanour changed as she realised why we were there. "Ah, yes, I understand," she said, rising from her seat and stepping up to the padded leather door. "I'll see if he's free then," She knocked and waited until a muffled reply came from within. Opening the door, she entered and shut it before we could see inside.

Jones turned to us. "Please forgive Miss Plumb's mood. In addition to the barrels downstairs, we have a visit from King Alfonso of Spain next month, plus the Queen will be spending the summer at Balmoral. The Prime Minister has asked for an increase in security on both fronts due to this incident. Sir Nigel has been tasked with coordinating it all, which means it falls to Miss Plumb, his secretary."

I raised an eyebrow. It was quite unusual for a woman to hold such a position. Miss Plumb's reappearance broke me from my thoughts. She opened the door and stepped into her office, allowing us to file into the Secretary's room.

Holmes was at the end of the queue and stopped briefly next to the young lady. "Does your husband work in the Home Office as well?"

The woman's face dropped in shock. I turned in time to see it and assumed that my good friend had once again performed one of his miraculous observations.

"But, how – how could you know?" she stammered. "I've never seen you before in my life, sir."

Holmes simply smiled and nodded towards her hand. "You disguise it well, but your wedding bands have left a light mark on your ring finger. Perhaps you should leave them off for an extended time to allow the skin to darken in line with the rest of your hand," he said.

"I couldn't do that," she answered. "My husband would become enraged if he caught me without them. I only leave them off here to keep the peace amongst the other girls."

"I understand," he answered and tapped the side of his nose. "Your secret is safe with me."

"Thank you, sir. Sir Nigel signed a waiver for me when I married. David wanted me to resign, but then he left the Army and the money dried up, so I asked Sir Nigel if I could stay until David found employment. Really, I didn't think I'd be here this long. Poor David. He hasn't been himself since . . . ." Tears quickly formed in her eyes. She excused herself and fled from her office.

I walked over to a surprised Holmes and asked, "Something you said?"

"I think, perhaps, Watson, that there may be some deeper emotional strife within young Miss Plumb's marital circumstances," he said.

***

Inside Sir Nigel's office, the Home Secretary was a far different man than I had imagined. One tends to form an image of members of the upper levels of the civil service as stocky men tending to fat from their desk-bound lifestyle and with the ruddy complexion of those who indulge in the demon drink a little too much.

The man who stood up and moved out from behind his desk was nothing like my cerebral musings. Sir Nigel Attleby was an athletic man in his early fifties. He was tall – even taller than Holmes – with chiselled features that would have had many a young lady swooning from his attentive gaze. He raised his hand and thrust it towards Holmes. "Mr. Holmes, I presume. A pleasure to meet you. Your brother has spoken well of you on many occasions," he said. "He and members of his department have worked closely with my own people at numerous times over the years." He turned in my direction. "And you would be Doctor John Watson, yes?" he asked.

I took his hand and shook, letting go before replying, "Yes. That I am, Sir Nigel."

"I've heard that you're the chronicler of Mr. Holmes's cases," he said, smiling again. "I don't think you'll find much to write about from this little nuisance."

"Interestingly enough," I said, "it is usually the seemingly mundane adventures that prove to be the most fascinating."

"Well, let's hope this remains as mundane as it seems." He leaned back against his desk and held out a hand to the three chairs before him and then looked up Parsons. "You'll be fine standing, won't you?"

Parsons scowled at the suggestion but nodded his head. Holmes, Godfrey Jones, and I took the proffered seats.

Sir Nigel studied each of us in turn. "Now, I know that Parsons has shown you the little display downstairs."

We nodded, and I noted, "You seem to be very calm, given that there's a large pile of gunpowder-filled barrels sitting below the House of Commons as we speak."

His expression remained calm. "Yes, but no one will be in there for another two weeks. So whoever put it there either didn't realise or didn't care. There was no way the barrels would go unnoticed for that period of time, and if ignited, they wouldn't have hurt anyone and would have just been a nuisance. They're safe enough now until we determine what's going on. So, yes, I am calm."

I peered at Holmes, who was studying Sir Nigel. "And you are correct," said Holmes, "The bomb, as it has been called, is merely a diversion. The powder in the barrels is not explosive, and there was no method to detonate it anyway. I'm still trying to discern what the person's motivation was in planting the barrels."

"I may have a clew as to the motivation," Sir Nigel said. He reached behind him and picked up a small handwritten parchment from a pile of paperwork. He turned and handed it to Holmes, who quickly read it. I noticed his eyebrows raise and a wry smile cross his lips. He then handed the page to me. It read:

We, the members of the Sudanese Mahdist Revolutionary Army, demand the immediate full-scale withdrawal of all Anglo forces from our country. If our demands are not met, we will unleash terror and hell upon the Parliament of Great Britain the likes of which have never been seen."

It was signed "*Mahdi Muhammad Ahmed Bin Abd Allah*".

I turned towards Jones and offered the page to him. He waved it away which told me that he'd already seen it. I gave it back to Sir Nigel. "Is this real?" I asked.

Sir Nigel peered at the page whilst answering, "Her Majesty's troops are currently engaged with Egyptian, Italian, and Ethiopian forces in the Sudan, fighting against this Mahdi Muhammad Ahmed's army of militiamen."

"Would they have the resources to undertake an operation of this kind on British soil?" asked Holmes.

Sir Nigel thought for a moment then stared into Holmes's eyes, his expression had turned serious. "No, no, I don't think they would, but that's not to say that some other nation, or group of people, has provided them with the resources. I'm still not overly worried as I prefer to think that this – " He waved the page about. " – is another diversion, as you call it. But I don't know what the true objective is."

At that moment, Sir Nigel's now-composed secretary popped her head in through the connecting door and spoke. "Sorry to disturb you, sir, but the Prime Minister would like an update on the incident downstairs."

"Very good. I'll be with him shortly."

The woman withdrew and shut the door quietly. I noticed Sir Nigel's gaze lingered on the doorframe for a few moments before he turned back to us. I put it down to the stress of the situation, but I found out later that Holmes had other ideas which proved to be correct.

"I would think," Holmes said, "that you can assure the Prime Minister that the barrels are relatively inert and may be removed without incident. As to what is behind all of this, I will return to my rooms and cogitate upon it further. I believe that it will be a one or two pipe problem."

Sir Nigel looked a little perplexed by the last comment. "He simply means," I explained, "that he will need to sit back and smoke one or two pipes and think."

Sir Nigel's eyebrows raised. "Oh, an interesting way of approaching a problem."

"Quite so," I said.

"Well, gentlemen," he said as he ushered us out of his office and into the outer office, "I do hope to hear your solution quickly, but as you are aware, my presence has been requested, so I shall have to leave you."

He turned to his secretary. "Please give Mr. Holmes my home address, in case they have any information and need to contact me after hours. I'll be with the Prime Minister for a good while, but we will need to discuss the Balmoral arrangements when I return." The woman nodded and took down a small note to that effect. Sir Nigel then bid us *adieu* and left quickly.

I noticed the woman watch him leave, her gaze staying on the doorway in much the same as Sir Nigel's had earlier. I also observed that Holmes had seen the same thing.

We said thank you and goodbye and left her office. Parsons escorted us to a side door that led out onto Great George Street. As he started to leave, Holmes stopped him. "Mr. Parsons, if I might offer a suggestion." Parsons stopped and looked back a poorly hidden look of contempt on his face. "It might be worth your while to undertake an investigation of the residential premises of the Home and Foreign Secretaries, and anyone else that may have been in the supposed blast radius of the gunpowder bomb," he said.

Parson's expression relaxed slightly. "You think these idiots would try to get them at home?" he asked.

"If they have received local help, enough to get them into the Houses of Parliament, then they might be able to set up a similar bomb, or worse, a *real* bomb, at the home of one of our politicians,"

Parson's eyes grew wide. Holmes's suggestion had hit at the heart of his world. He disappeared quickly, leaving us alone with Godfrey Jones.

"Thank you, Mr. Holmes," he said. "I must admit that I am astounded at your ability to look at the simplest situation and determine so much detail. I can only hope to learn the art of deduction and follow in your footsteps. It would be much more interesting than a life in the civil service."

I smiled a little at this confession, and a wry grin crossed Holmes's face. He answered, "If I were you, I would agitate to be moved to my brother Mycroft's department. Although he doesn't undertake the level of deductive reasoning that I do, he is much more adept at the art than I, and would be a worthy case study for someone in a position such as yourself."

Holmes held out his hand and shook Jones's before continuing, "If I might ask one favour of you: Could you have one of the barrels of black powder delivered to my abode this afternoon. I'd like to examine the barrel further. I believe it will assist in my deductions."

"Of course," Jones said, beaming widely, "Anything to help." He turned, shook my hand, and quickly disappeared back inside.

"A young lad full of admirable qualities, I think," I said.

"Yes, Watson, indeed," Holmes agreed. "I do hope he finds his mark before that place strips him of all ambition."

***

True to his word, young Godfrey Jones arranged for one of the barrels to be delivered to Baker Street later that same day. Holmes was elated and carried it to his chemical corner and then set about his work. I relied on the initial fact that the black powder had been heavily mixed with sand to allay any fears that Holmes's investigations would lead to an explosive result. With that in mind, I decided to leave him to his experimentation and occupy myself elsewhere. He wasn't home when I returned later that evening.

It was late the next morning, whilst I was enjoying some morning tea, that Holmes emerged from his bedroom, looking refreshed and exhilarated.

"Good news?" I asked.

He stretched his arms, smiled and said, "Why, yes, thoroughly good news." He sat down and helped himself to coffee and biscuits.

"Well?" I asked with a touch of impatience.

He smiled, took a sip of coffee and began to explain. "I have found out many interesting facts," he began. "The black powder, as I surmised is a mix of gun powder, sand, and ground charcoal. It will burn, but it isn't explosive in any way. Its purpose was to give the illusion of being an explosive, rather than having any destructive power." He took another sip of coffee, then continued. "The powder itself is interesting. It's the type that was used by the British military up until a couple of years ago, when they changed all formulations to cordite, which isn't as explosive but diffuses much more gas-per-

86

weight, thereby creating a greater propellant effect. The original gunpowder burnt too hot and caused damage to the barrels and firing chambers of many of our guns."

He placed his cup down, rose, and walked over to our sitting chairs. He rooted around the discarded newspapers for a moment and brought out the object of his attention. "A-ha, here it is," he said, brandishing the article that I had spied on the day young Godfrey Jones had come to our door. Holmes read aloud: "'*Two weeks ago, there was a break-in at the Royal Artillery Barracks in Woolwich. The stores were raided, but all that was stolen were twenty barrels of gunpowder destined for destruction. The Army has advised the local constabulary in case any local criminal gangs were involved.*'"

He looked up at me and smiled.

"Sounds as if we may have found the source of the black powder," he said, placing the paper down and re-joining me at the dining table, "although the quantity stolen doesn't equate with the amounts that would be in the barrels found under Parliament. I would estimate that only about two barrels-worth of powder was mixed across those we discovered." "Now, the next question I needed to answer was about the barrels themselves."

"They aren't the same barrels?" I asked.

"No, surprisingly not. The stolen powder kegs themselves would have been much smaller, around nine inches tall and seven inches across, plus the strapping bands would have been made of reed or rope to avoid sparks."

I turned and spied the barrel sitting on Holmes's workbench. It was a hefty size, around two feet tall and one foot across, with distinctly metal banding.

"Yes, exactly, Watson. Those barrels are not the originals. In fact, they were built by a cooper down at the Port of London. I wired him last night and confirmed an order by an unknown buyer two weeks ago. Sadly, he only dealt with the delivery driver, whom he described as a balding man of about forty. He said that he'd never seen the man before, and believed that he would never see him again. I suppose that's the problem with cash payments. A businessman is only concerned with the money, not the details of the transaction."

"Where does that leave us?" I asked.

He took a final sip of coffee, placed his cup down, and looked at me over steepled fingers ."Well, we still have eighteen unused barrels of black powder. We are led to believe that a Sudanese organisation is behind all of this, but the powder was stolen on British soil and the perpetrators procured items from a London-based business and used a local to undertake the exchange. I dropped in on Lestrade to see if there had been any known activity amongst the local Sudanese population, but according to Scotland Yard, the only known Sudanese in London are a single-family that lives in Canning Town. They've been monitored since before the war in the Sudan started and, according to Lestrade, are simple dockworkers who escaped from Northern Africa in the early 1880s."

"It's all a front then?" I said.

"Yes," said Holmes, "And – "

We were suddenly disturbed by an insistent thumping on the front door downstairs. Soon, we heard Mrs. Hudson unlatching the door before letting out a surprised cry. Loud footfalls proceeded up the stairwell, causing us both to stand in readiness.

The door to our apartments was flung open and there stood a very flustered Godfrey Jones. He took one look at the both of us and, through a series of strained inhalations, gasped, "Please come quickly. There's been a horrible accident."

***

Jones remained tight-lipped throughout our trip in the hansom. I could see he was fidgety and extremely anxious. I tried on numerous occasions to talk to him, but he fobbed me off with mumblings about secrecy.

It was as we pulled out of Pall Mall and into Carlton Gardens that I realised we were heading towards the secretarial residences. The Crown owned several properties in the area which were made available to members of the Cabinet whilst they were in London. The Home Secretary's address was amongst them.

My concerns grew grave as we passed through a small police cordon that blocked off the end of the street. Inspector Lestrade stood by a young constable and peered into the hansom. "Mr. Holmes?

What the devil is going on? I have orders to let you and only you through," he said.

"All will become clear, Inspector," Holmes answered. "I will inform you as soon as I have finished my investigations."

"Blast!" Lestrade said as the hansom pulled away.

I was still wondering which Secretary was involved when we pulled up outside of Number Three. As I looked out of the cab I became shocked. Holmes even made a small murmur when he viewed the devastation. We quickly exited the hansom to survey the scene.

Carlton Gardens are generally a wonderfully kept set of Georgian Terraced apartments. Each is four stories high, and my understanding is that they contain several bedrooms for residents and staff, with a full-sized catering kitchen, a large dining room for state affairs, and everything that Cabinet ministers might require. They back onto St. James Gardens so that even families with young children had ample room for play and exercise.

On this day, however, the outside of Number Three was a sight of utter desolation. The entrance-way appeared to have been blown apart from below. The front door was missing and the short staircase leading up to the door was simply a smouldering hole with broken masonry and brickwork strewn in a wide arc around the front of the building.

"Good Lord," I said.

"Indeed," said Holmes. "I think we have found the rest of our missing gunpowder – or what remains of it anyway,"

Once the hansom had driven off, Godfrey Jones joined us and simply stared at the hole in the ground at the front of the residence.

"They told me what happened," he said, "but I didn't think it would be this bad."

I turned to him and asked, "Can you tell us which Cabinet minister's residence this is?"

"Yes, it's Sir Nigel's house. The explosion occurred only an hour ago. I was at work at Parliament when I was commanded to fetch you and bring you here," he said.

"The Secretary? Is he . . . ?" I hesitated to finish the question.

Jones shook his head. "No, he's fine," he said.

"I'm afraid that can't be said for some other poor unfortunate," said Holmes from a few feet away.

I looked around. He was looking at some dark stains on the cobbles. I knew straight away what those stains meant.

"Oh, my," I said and turned back to Jones. "Who was it?"

His face bore a look of shock. He stared for a moment then dropped his head. "It was Parsons."

"Parsons? Why in blazes was he here?" Then I realised. He came on our insistence to check up on the members of the cabinet.

Holmes had wandered over to the very front of the house and was peering down into the void left by the explosion. I joined him to gain a better view. The house had a lower basement level, where I presumed the help lived. A small courtyard was visible below the street, probably available to the staff for their use. Previously it would have been a cosy place to sit and possibly smoke or take tea. Now all the furniture was destroyed, and the plants burnt to cinders.

Holmes stood at the edge of the courtyard wall and was peering with great intent at the blackened vegetation below. "Hmm," he said, "I need to gain access to the courtyard." He turned to Jones. "Is there a way that we can enter the house?"

A voice answered from within the house itself. "Yes, Mr. Holmes. Yes, there is," it said.

We turned to find Sir Nigel standing in the ruins of his entranceway wearing a smoking jacket over a pair of silk pyjamas. A stern look crossed his face. "I will give you all the help you need to find this culprit," he said.

***

Sir Nigel met us at the rear door of the property. His sombre mood persisted, and he quietly led us through to the front of the house where a small staircase led down to the servants' quarters. He remained behind with Godfrey Jones as Holmes and I made our way down the stairs and out into the small courtyard.

It looked more of a mess up close than before. Holmes immediately set about viewing the entire scene and taking in as many minute details as he could. I watched as he surveyed the wreckage, dropped to his knee from time to time, and pulled out his glass to examine the clews, such as they were.

I scanned the area myself. The two longer walls consisted of the front of the house, with two windows that looked into the servants' sitting room and the solid retaining wall that lined the street side. At one end, a small under-croft appeared to lie beneath the front staircase. It must have been in there that the barrels of powder had been placed. The explosion brought down the staircase and virtually buried the evidence from view. At the other end, two trees had been planted amidst a once-lovely garden bed. A line of planter boxes bordered the bed which had a small sitting area in the centre, the furniture now blasted into pieces. The far wall had a gate that led into the neighbouring courtyard. The gate had been blown off its hinges and could be seen lying beyond.

As I walked over to the garden bed to lessen my view of the devastation, I noticed something completely out of place. More dark stains were spread out across the grass that had been protected from the brunt of the blast by the planter boxes. The bloodstains radiated away from the blast and towards the small gate.

"Holmes, I think I've found something," I said over my shoulder. As I turned, I found him standing right behind me, holding a small item of interest in his hand. It was the stub end of a cigar. Burnt – but still relatively whole.

"Parson?" I asked.

He nodded then said, "What have you found then, Watson?"

I pointed to the bloodstains and suggested we follow them into the next yard. He agreed, and I led the way.

I was astonished at what we found, but I believe Holmes had already deduced this eventuality. Lying just inside the courtyard and hidden from view was a body. He was covered in blood and had received horrendous burns from the explosion. I checked his pulse and found that he was well and truly dead. I managed to turn him over and we discovered that he was a balding man about forty years of age. The evidence suggested that he was the delivery man that had bought the barrels from the cooper.

"Our culprit?" I asked.

"I would think so," said Holmes, "The evidence is adding up." He returned to the adjoining courtyard and studied the scene once more.

I joined him and asked, "Do you know what happened yet?"

"I can surmise from the existence of the dead man and this cigar, that our poor Mr. Parsons, by pure accident, thwarted the plan to kill Sir Nigel, and inadvertently took his place." He pointed to the staircase. "I presume that Mr. Parsons came to the house early this morning, smoking a cigar as was his habit. He stopped on the entrance stairs to finish it off and casually tossed the remnants into the courtyard rather than the street."

He stepped over to where he found the cigar and pointed out the undercroft and then the line of planter boxes. "Mr. Parsons just happened along at the same moment that our assailant had managed to set up his explosives and was waiting for an opportune time to ignite them. He may have known that Sir Nigel likes to retrieve the daily papers himself of a morning."

I interjected at that point, "How do you know that?" Then I promptly answered my own question in my head just as Holmes confirmed it.

"I had Sir Nigel watched," he said. "Now, Parsons tossed his cigar into the courtyard and was most unfortunate to have it land on the line of gunpowder that our assailant had laid down to act as a fuse."

He pointed to a smudged line of dark black powder which I had taken to be ash or charred detritus from the blast. "The fuse lit and quickly raced towards the black powder. The result is evident." He pointed to the planter boxes. "Our bomber was hiding behind those planters, which are good and heavy and would have provided adequate protection. When he heard the fuse ignite, however, he stood in surprise, thereby becoming the second victim in this little fiasco."

"The fool," I said.

"Quite so," agreed Holmes.

"Who was he then?" I asked.

"For that, I think it is time to head inside. There is a little more to this story, yet."

***

We found Godfrey and Sir Nigel seated around a small table in the parlour. Coffee had been served for all four of us, and the two of them had poured for themselves while they awaited our return. Sir Nigel was the first to see us and placed his cup down in preparation for our arrival.

"Gentlemen, I ordered some refreshments – although I'll admit, at the moment, I don't quite have the stomach for food. Devilish time," he said.

"Thank you, Sir Nigel," said Holmes in a rather stern voice, "but I think it best if we move forward as quickly as possible,"

I was taken aback by Holmes's mood. He seemed annoyed at the events that had occurred, and I was a little afraid that he would overstep the mark and damage the relationship we'd built with the Home Secretary.

I assumed he was about to rebuke Sir Nigel for something, but he spoke to Godfrey Jones instead.

"We have found the body of a poor unfortunate in the neighbouring courtyard. The police must have missed it on their first investigation. Sloppy if you ask me, but it does me no good to dwell on it. Would you be so kind as to go out and inform the constables outside, so they can deal with it? Tell them I have investigated and will update Inspector Lestrade in due time," he said.

Jones put down his own cup and rose. "Of course, Mr. Holmes. Do you think it was the man we are after or just an innocent victim?"

"I'm still trying to determine that, but with Sir Nigel's help, I believe I will have a solution before you return," he said.

"Very good," Jones said and rushed off.

Once he was gone and out of earshot, Holmes turned to Sir Nigel. "That was mostly for your benefit," he said. "I think it would be prudent to bring Mrs. Button out so that we can put this despicable affair to bed, so to speak."

Sir Nigel's face dropped in shock for a moment but relaxed into a slight grin. "How the devil did you know?"

"Well, to be honest," he replied, "there was no deduction necessary. I had an inkling as to what has been going on and asked a few discrete questions. My informant apprised me of the affair. Don't worry," he added, "Your secret is safe with me for as long as you require it to be. That was the main reason I sent young Jones away."

Sir Nigel rose and said, "Very good. I thank you for your discretion."

After Sir Nigel left, I turned to Holmes as I just had to ask: "Who is Mrs. Button?"

"Ah, yes. I used some of that time away from Baker Street last night to initiate further investigations. Plus, I called on the services of my irregulars to conduct low-level surveillance, not only of Sir Nigel but his personal assistant, one Mrs. Angela Button," he said. "You know her as Miss Plumb."

"Why would you need to have his secretary observed? What does she have to do with all of this?" I asked.

Holmes smiled. "Oh, I think we'll find that she has everything to do with this," he said in that slightly irritating but knowledgeable way of his.

It was at that point that Sir Nigel returned and stood aside to let the young lady in question into the room. We both nodded in deference to her.

"Mr. Holmes, you wished to see me," she said retaining as much dignity as she could muster, given her presence in Sir Nigel's home.

"Mrs. Button," Holmes began.

She cut him off by saying, "Angela, if you please," a hint of aversion at the use of her married name crossing her face.

"Firstly," Holmes continued, "let me apologise to both yourself and Sir Nigel, but I employed the use of my associates to have you followed last night."

Both began to protest, but Holmes held up his hands. "I also had my people follow the Chancellor, the Defence Secretary, and both of their assistants as well. The main object was to detect if there were any agents of foreign interest doing the same."

Mrs. Button found some inner courage and spoke up, "I know what you see before you must seem like some sordid little affair, but you would be wrong. Sir Nigel and I have a simple platonic friendship, that's all. I've been his assistant for over ten years, well

94

before I was married, and well before he held the position of Home Secretary. I came to him late last night after David, my husband, and I had a row. He was drunk again and accused me of all manner of ills. Frankly, I'd had enough, and stormed out. At that time of night, I had nowhere to turn but here."

Holmes paused for a moment to gather his thoughts before continuing, "Now, Mrs. – ah – Angela, could you describe your husband to us."

A slight look of surprise flitted across her face before she spoke. "A typical Englishman if you like. Just turned forty years old. Keeps his hair very short, in fact, shaves it bald on occasions. Tall. Has started to become a little stocky due to the drink. Why?" she asked.

As the description continued, my face dropped in realisation. I looked across at Holmes who remained stoic. "I was a little afraid of that," he said.

"What do you mean, sir?" asked Sir Nigel, "What does Angela's husband have to do with any of this?"

"Sadly, everything," said Holmes. He indicated the settee and continued, "Madam I think it would be best if you were to take a seat. My explanation may be a little long and, for you, a little disturbing."

Mrs. Button sat down with Sir Nigel standing behind her. Both retained concerned looks on their faces.

Holmes waited until they were settled, and for a little dramatic effect, before he began. "I'm afraid that your husband, ex-Corporal David Button, was the sole perpetrator behind this whole affair. My inquiries have indicated that he served at the Royal Artillery Depot at Woolwich up until six months ago when he was dishonourably discharged for theft."

Tears formed in Angela's eyes and she dropped her head forward. "He wanted to set us up in a little country estate. I was ashamed of his actions, but we'd just married and I've always been told to support your husband no matter what. Foolish man." She looked up, a trail of tears running down each cheek. "I pleaded with Sir Nigel to help out, and he managed to have the charges dropped, but they had to discharge him as a matter of protocol."

Sir Nigel nodded. His face showed sorrow. I wasn't sure if it was for Angela or for himself.

"I managed to get him a job on the cleaning staff not long afterwards, but he showed up intoxicated on several occasions, and even I couldn't protect him," he said.

Mrs. Button nodded, turned, and looked up into Sir Nigel's eyes. He patted her shoulder and she placed a hand on his for a moment before turning back to Holmes.

"David kept blaming me for all his troubles. He said I was having an affair. He said I was making him less of a man because I kept working. Last night was the first time I became scared. He threatened to kill Sir Nigel, and then he threatened me," she said.

"The black powder was from a robbery at the Woolwich depot," explained Holmes. "Several barrels of old stock. The fake bomb under the House of Commons was probably an attempt to scare you, Sir Nigel. It was never going to work, but he must have used what he learned from his cleaning job to get back into the House and plant the bomb. I found a disused cleaner's trolley nearby. Last night, I presume, a combination of drink and his temper caused him to act. He must have arrived very early this morning and brought the powder in via the next-door courtyard."

"Yes," said Sir Nigel, "That's the Foreign Secretary's residence. He lives in Newcastle when Parliament is in recess. A caretaker comes in a couple of times a week."

"Quite so. Now, I am surmising that Mr. Button finished his work. Placed a trail of powder to the barrels in the under-croft to act as a fuse, then waited behind the row of planter boxes for Sir Nigel to retrieve the morning paper. He fell asleep instead and the unfortunate Mr. Parsons arrived early, looked around the front of the house, and lit up a morning cigar. Once finished, he was either about to leave or to knock on the door to ensure all was fine. He flicked the remains of his cigar into the courtyard, where it ignited the trail of powder. Mr. Button awoke to see the powder alight. He stood up just at the same time as the barrels ignited and exploded," Holmes said.

Mrs. Button reacted in surprise. "How do you know he was down in the courtyard?" she asked.

We all realised that she was the only one who didn't know about the body. "Oh, I'm so sorry dear," said Sir Nigel, "I afraid that Mr. Holmes and Dr. Watson found a dead body in the garden next door."

"And it fits the description that you gave of your husband," said Holmes.

A hand shot up to her face as she gasped, her face a mask of horror.

"I am so sorry to break it to you like this," Holmes said. "In your husband's defence, there's no indication that he intended to light the fuse. I believe it may have still been a ruse to scare Sir Nigel away from you."

"No. I loved my husband," Mrs. Button replied, "but of late his delirium over our supposed affair has escalated. The last thing he said as I fled from our house was that he was going to kill Sir Nigel and he had the means to do it. At the time, I took it as another set of his drunken ravings, but it seems . . . ."

She stopped abruptly as tears streamed from her eyes.

I took that moment to begin our excuses. "I don't know if there's much more we can achieve here," I said as I stood.

Sir Nigel nodded as he reached down and comforted the sobbing woman.

We quickly found ourselves out in the street and were approached by Inspector Lestrade, his face a mass of questions. "What is going on, Mr. Holmes?" he asked. "I have a bomb going off in a Government minister's residence. I have two dead bodies, and I've been kept away from the scene of the crime all morning."

Holmes held up a hand to quieten the policeman. "All will be explained, Inspector, I assure you. At this stage, you have the perpetrator, a Mr. David Button, the second corpse found on the scene. What started out as an act against the Houses of Parliament – " Lestrade's face dropped in shock at this revelation. " – has turned out to be a domestic issue with tragic results. For now, please be so kind as to allow Sir Nigel and his houseguest a little privacy for a couple of hours. They have had a major shock. I still need to tidy up one or two loose ends myself, but I assure you I will come by later and explain the full details to you."

Lestrade huffed and stormed off. Waiting was not one of his favourite hobbies.

Holmes took a deep breath and stared up into the clear blue sky.

"Do you think Angela will be alright?" I asked.

Holmes smiled and turned towards me, "I think that after the shock of this tragedy subsides, Mrs. Button may end up acquiring a new wedding ring that she will be more than proud to display, and a new title that will allow her to cease her duties in the civil service for good."

I smiled at his assumptions. "But she said that there was nothing to Button's insinuation of their affair," I said.

"Ah, yes," he said, "but the affairs of the heart aren't always so easy to deduce, even for those directly involved."

He looked down the street towards the devastation in front of the Home Secretary's residence. "I won't be holding my breath waiting for our wedding invitations, but I think it will be a nice surprise when they arrive," he said.

I chuckled to myself and we walked off to fetch a hansom back to Baker Street.

The Body at the Ritz

Life in the late nineteenth century was an active time in the annals of human history, especially in London. Man's intelligence had always set us apart from the greater animal population, but with James Watt's improvements on Thomas Newcomen's original designs for the steam engine having been put in place half a century ago, man's ingenuity had only been slightly outstripped by his imagination.

I sat on the balcony, with my breakfast coffee and looked out across the wide region that is greater London and smiled at the commotion at play as the populace went about their daily lives.

Horseless carriages, belching puffs of steam along with wisps of black coal smoke, trundled along the byways below. Dirigibles, large and small, ferried goods and people through the airways thick with clouds. Great zeppelins ploughed their way through the upper atmosphere connecting countries like never before and opening up new horizons and bringing new peoples into the modern world.

Wars were almost a thing of the past as technological improvements eradicated the ever-present need to gain resources or land from neighbours.

Sadly, though, one element was always present within any society and led to the need for men such as myself and my erstwhile companion, Mr. Sherlock Holmes.

Crime.

Be it theft. Be it murder. Or any of the multitude of variations that the human mind can muster. There will always be a need for a constabulary to investigate and solve the crimes of men, and when the officials are at the end of their tethers, they call upon outside help such as only we can lend.

I finished my coffee and withdrew back inside.

There I found Holmes in an accustomed position. He sat in an easy chair, resplendent in a silk smoking jacket, a pipe in mouth, poring over the daily paper.

He looked up as I entered and smiled.

"A lovely, quiet day, eh Watson?"

I placed my cup on the tea tray nearby as I answered.

"Yes, yes, it is Holmes. A wonderful time to be alive."

He grinned.

"A bit dull though. I've had nothing to perplex my brain for a good week."

I hadn't realised this and became wary. When Holmes was unoccupied his mind slipped into a state of ennui and could have dire consequences as he sought out other means to temper his boredom.

"Don't worry Watson, I'm not going to embark on any drug-fuelled fervour any time soon. I was just remarking that there seems to be a paucity of crime at the moment. Well, crime that requires my attention anyway," he said.

I sighed with relief but made a mental note to monitor my friend's movements in case of any obvious deviations from the norm that would indicate some chemical abuse.

"I was thinking of going to the Diogenes later for luncheon. Mycroft mentioned that he would be there today. It might be good to catch up with him. You never know he may let slip some little snippet of information that leads to an entertaining case," he said.

I agreed and packed up the tea tray and cups to take down to Mrs. Hudson, more for something to do than anything else, though I do like to help our landlady out when the opportunity arises.

As I reached the doorway a *shoomp* noise echoed up the stairway. Holmes looked up and grinned again. I knew the noise to mean the arrival of something in the sealed vacuum tube messaging system.

Moments later, the sound of footsteps on the stairs greeted us and the door opened to reveal Mrs. Hudson holding a rolled-up parchment. She handed the note to me and took away the tea tray.

"Thank you, Doctor, but you needn't have minded, I'm quite able to clear the dishes away," she said with a grin as she bustled off.

I blanched at the slight rebuke, then looked down at the note. It was addressed to Holmes, so I gave it straight to him and waited, curiosity writ large on my face.

Holmes read quietly to himself, then looked up and smiled.

"The game is afoot," he said.

On our ascent to the rooftop, Holmes stopped by and handed a note of reply to Mrs. Hudson.

"See this is delivered immediately, and thank you," he said to her.

I was still mystified as to the nature of the original message and intrigued about what faced us.

Once outside, I triggered the cab request lever and immediately a hidden mechanism fired up, filled a small balloon with compressed hydrogen then released it on a long line. The balloon ascended above 221B Baker Street and floated into the sky lanes to be spied by the floating network of viewfinders operated by the Greater London Cab company.

Within a few minutes, we noticed a black dirigible deviate from the throng of others of its kind passing overhead and move in our direction.

I triggered the reverse switch on the mechanism and the balloon retracted to avoid entanglement with the vehicle as it approached.

I finally asked Holmes what the note was about.

He replied, "Lestrade has found a body."

"Nothing unusual in that," I said.

"True, but this one was found in a small alleyway off of Piccadilly."

"Again, nothing unusual."

Holmes smiled.

"Outside of the Ritz," he said.

"Oh," I said, "we've been called on the insistence of Sir Rupert, then?"

Holmes nodded and looked up as the dirigible finished its descent. Its landing claw reached out and grasped the edge of the roof platform letting out a mechanical *clank*.

We bade the pilot a good day and boarded. Whilst Holmes gave him our destination, I sat in one of the front seats so as to distribute the weight evenly. Holmes joined me, and we heard the motors whirr and felt the aircraft begin to rise. With a slight bump, as the claw detached, we were away.

The pilot ascended to join the other airships and craft flying along in the sky lanes and headed south towards St. James's Park. I craned to my right and took much pleasure in viewing the landscape below.

Within moments we were crossing Marylebone and drifting within sight of the lush greenery of Hyde Park. Soon, the architecture changed from the simple Georgian and Victorian terraces of Marylebone to towering neo-Gothic structures clad with shiny bronze scales and plates.

This style of building had only come into play in the last ten years or so and was more a reflection of the tastes of the nouveau riche than for any structural or functional purposes.

The pilot turned the airship and began his approach to the landing platform at the top of the Ritz Hotel.

I viewed the building with a slight amount of awe. The current owner, Sir Rupert Linklatter, had taken the once elegant five-story Georgian hotel and added another five stories all clad in brightly shining brass plating with several glass elevators that traversed the exterior overlooking Piccadilly. At night, the hotel was lit up like a beacon with electric lights playing across the façade, reflecting off the myriad bronze plates and shining back across the roadway below and buildings opposite. It was quite a spectacle, one that I had watched on a few occasions but had never been overly enamoured with.

Sir Rupert had made his fortune from coal mining in the Newcastle region, controlling much of the fuel that drove the new industrial age and reaping the benefits. The Ritz was his domain in London. It provided both a high-cost hotel to the rich and famous and a luxurious inner London sanctum for Sir Rupert and his family.

As could be expected, Sir Rupert's status attracted a high level of protection from those in the upper echelons of the political power base. Holmes had enamoured himself to Sir Rupert a few years back when he helped to discover the true nature of the disappearance of the Countess Bruckheimer from within her suite at the Ritz. Holmes managed to solve the case quietly and quickly without drawing any adverse attention upon the Ritz and Sir Rupert. Henceforth, on orders from those in power, the local constabulary often played second fiddle to Holmes when any crimes were discovered in the general area of the Ritz.

The pilot brought us in to dock at the landing platform built out from the roof of the Ritz. I paid the man and followed Holmes from the craft. A well-dressed couple in their sixties entered the airship and were away before we had even crossed the roof to the Hotel's entrance, such was the pace of modern life.

As we approached the main doors, I saw Holmes nod towards the footman and receive a knowing look in return. I assumed this was one of Holmes's informants and wondered if he would prove useful to us later.

The footman opened the doors for us to reveal a tall, lanky man dressed in a dinner suit, waiting inside. He bowed and introduced himself as Allaister Croan, Sir Rupert's assistant. He shook our hands and led us through the hotel at a cracking pace. I struggled to keep up, but Holmes, being almost as tall, had no trouble.

"Sir Rupert expresses his gratitude, in advance, of you solving this little dilemma," Croan said.

"But the body was found outside, surely that bears no problem for the Hotel," I said.

Croan stopped and turned to face me. His face took on a very serious tone.

"Sir Rupert has a very exclusive clientele. The mere presence of the constabulary fills him with dread, and he would appreciate all avenues being taken to keep the details of this matter private and away from the day-to-day operations of the hotel," he said.

To punctuate his sentence further and to stress the importance to Sir Rupert, he continued with, "And the Prime Minister is evidently aware as well."

He turned and moved on. Holmes dropped back to walk beside me. I could see a familiar grin on his face. Holmes has never been one for power players. To him, a crime is a crime, whether it involves a Prince or a pauper.

As we walked, my eyes strayed to the lush pile of the carpet we traversed. Most hotel carpets consist of a short, hardy pile, but this was long and thick, probably woollen and of an extremely high quality. The swirling black, grey and white pattern that repeated every ten feet or so, was intricate and would have added more to the cost.

Finally, we were shown to a side door that opened out into the alleyway beyond.

Lestrade stood with his arms crossed waiting in impatient anticipation for our arrival. As we stepped into the alley, he unfolded his arms and relaxed slightly. He stepped to his right and unveiled the object of our attention.

Slumped, with his back against the wall was the lonely figure of the victim. His head hung down with his hands folded in his lap and legs jutting straight out from the wall.

He wore a long red velvet frock coat, which was bunched beneath him and soaking up the water from an early morning shower.

Beneath the coat, he sported a beige waistcoat, white collarless shirt and a dark brown cravat. His dark brown tweed pants were tucked into knee-high leather boots. All his clothing was of exquisite taste and smacked of expense. On first observations, this was a well to do man about town. One that would fit into the exclusivity of the Ritz seamlessly.

Holmes approached the scene and circled around to the front of the body, carefully avoiding any clues that may lay in the immediate area.

He scanned the ground, bending down from time to time to observe some ephemera. Satisfied that there was nothing of interest he moved in closer to the body.

"Male, Caucasian, approximately thirty to thirty-five years of age," Holmes said.

He stepped back for a moment, scanning the man's entire body.

"Approximately, five foot ten inches in height, about one hundred and seventy pounds. So not overweight, but not overly athletic," he said.

I piped up with an observation of my own, "There's no hat. The current style for one wearing a frock coat and boots is to accompany it with a top hat, is it not? There are none laying around the immediate area either."

Holmes looked towards me and smiled.

"Very good Watson, very good. What does it tell you?"

"That he either lost it before entering the alleyway or it was taken from him," I replied.

Holmes nodded then reached into his inner coat pocket and extracted his goggles. He placed them over his eyes and turned a small side screw that pushed the lenses away from his face, enabling him to zoom in and magnify some minor details that were invisible to the naked eye. He pulled on a pair of fine kid gloves and for the first time reached in to touch the victim's body.

He gently picked up each of the man's hands, in turn, and examined the palms and especially the fingertips. Murmuring to himself as he did so. He bent down and sniffed the man's palms, which I found a little strange, even for Holmes, but chose to ignore it in the interests of the investigation.

Holmes placed the man's hands back in his lap and turned to Lestrade, addressing the Inspector for the first time since our arrival.

"I assume you have already searched him for identification?"

Lestrade looked affronted.

"I have my orders to leave everything alone and wait for you. I wouldn't want to get Sir Rupert offside now, would I?" Lestrade replied with a heavy dose of sarcasm.

Holmes smiled widely, knowing full well what Lestrade meant.

"Found nothing then?"

Lestrade nodded.

"Nothing at all?" asked Holmes with a hint of surprise.

"Absolutely nothing. Clean as a new bought suit," Lestrade replied.

Holmes murmured to himself.

"Why Holmes?" I asked.

"Because Watson, what we have here is a scene depicting a robbery that has gone a little wrong, resulting in a dead body."

"Yes."

"But if you had just accidentally, or even purposely, killed someone you would take the most obvious things, wallet, watch, maybe keys, and leave quickly. This man has been picked clean, including his hat and possibly glasses or goggles."

He stood and scanned around the area again, then took off his right glove, reached down and felt the collar of the man's frock coat.

"Dry," he said.

"It rained this morning," said Lestrade, "Around seven o'clock."

"Well, that gives us our estimated time of death. Sometime after seven o'clock," I said.

Holmes didn't seem convinced.

"Unless," he said.

He hunkered down and pushed his finger into the man's cheek. There was considerable resistance. He returned his attention to the man's hands and prodded the thenar eminence, the fleshy part beneath the thumb, with his finger. The indentation stayed put for quite a while.

"Rigor mortis is quite pronounced," he said.

"Yes. In this weather I would put the time of death closer to four to six hours ago, not two," I said.

"Precisely," said Holmes as he stood up, "I believe this man was killed elsewhere and dumped here. Why? I have no idea and still need more facts to prove my assumption."

He reached into his coat and extracted a strange tool. It was a long wand-shaped brass cylinder, with a clear crystal at one end and a small crank handle towards the middle.

Holmes turned the handle which caused the device to emit a whirring noise as some unseen engine within began to turn. As the crystal started to glow with an inner luminescence, Holmes moved it towards the dead man's coat.

The crystal cast a faint blue light over the red material, causing several small specs on the coat to glow white with a slight purple tinge.

Holmes stopped and peered closely at a small spec on the man's coat. He again reached into his coat and pulled out a small pouch of tools. Opening it, he extracted a pair of tweezers then picked the spec out from the fabric of the man's coat. He stared at the item more closely, turning it to gain a better look.

"What have you there, Holmes?" I asked.

"A sliver of glass," he said.

Holmes put the sliver aside, then returned to examine the man, murmuring as he moved the wand across the man's coat, hovering over a bright spot on the left lapel. He opened the man's coat and waved the wand across his vest and shirt. No more spots showed up which must have confused Holmes as he let out a surprised little murmur.

He shifted his attention to the man's legs and moved the wand down his trouser legs. He looked at the man's boots and with the tweezers pulled out another clue. He held it up to the light and adjusted his lenses to magnify the object.

"What have you there, Holmes?" I asked.

"A woollen thread. Carpet. Dark grey. Similar to something we saw not long ago," he said.

"The carpet in the hallway of the Ritz," I said.

Holmes nodded and turned the man's legs out to check the backs as best he could. I noticed a scuff mark on the back of one beautifully polished boot. Another nod of the head told me Holmes considered this to be a clue. I decided to let him continue without distraction.

He pulled back and wound the little device's handle again.

Turning to Lestrade, he said, "Inspector, if you would be so kind, can you tilt the body forward so that I can examine his back?"

Lestrade, happy to be useful, leapt at the opportunity and gently tilted the man forward.

Holmes ran his wand across the man's back and let out an exclamation. I moved to a position where I could see his find.

The light now showed several large bright white spots that ran down the man's back from the collar. The spots were ill-defined and appeared to be smudged.

"What the Devil?" I asked.

Holmes said, "Blood, Watson, blood. This little device contains an yttrium crystal, which emits ultraviolet light when stimulated by static electricity. The little crank turns a small leather band inside which charges the crystal. Bloodstains always show up under ultraviolet light, no matter how well you try to clean them. As we have just seen."

He reached in with the pair of tweezers again and pulled out a small spike of glass.

"And more glass," he said placing it to the side.

He brought his hand up to the man's shirt collar and pulled the cravat away. We all immediately saw a small puncture mark at the base of the man's skull just below his hairline.

"Good Lord," said Lestrade, "That wasn't done by some Johnny on the street, that was done by a professional. It almost looks like an ice-pick or needle wound."

"Very true, Inspector," said Holmes, "Very true."

He stood up and Lestrade returned the body to the wall. I piped up as a small memory came to the fore.

"That wound is very reminiscent of the one we found on Professor Bhargava who was visiting Durham University from Paris two years ago," I said.

Holmes nodded; his face becoming stern.

"Yes…Yes it is, Watson. We never found the assailant, but my inquiries led me back to the Vishkanya, a league of assassins for hire operating out of India many years ago."

He stared at the body for a moment then up to the brightly lit upper floors of the Ritz hotel.

"I don't wish to jump to conclusions about the assailant, I don't have enough information for that, but I am sure that this man was killed inside the Ritz and was subsequently moved here. I found a small thread probably from the thick carpet in the hallways. Then there are the specs of glass, and the marks on the back of the man's boots lead me to believe that his demise resulted in a large amount of damage to some furniture."

Holmes looked further down the alleyway, away from the blazing lights of Piccadilly. I followed along, leaving a confused Lestrade with the body.

We quickly came to the corner of the hotel and peered around into another darkened alleyway.

"Aha," said Holmes as he spied something sitting near the wall amongst a pile of similar detritus. He moved over to the pile and grabbed hold of a slender cylinder of wood and pulled the frame of a low wooden table from the pile.

He set the frame upon the three remaining legs. The top was missing but appeared to have been glass as there were shards still attached to the frame mountings on each corner.

"What do you make of it, Holmes?" I asked.

"Not a lot, Watson, but if I was to project a story from what we've seen, I would say that our dead man was attacked from behind and stabbed in the neck. He then staggered back, tripped against the edge of this table and fell through the glass top, shattering it and breaking off one of the legs. He was then cleaned up, removed from the hotel room and deposited in the alleyway beyond. The room was thoroughly cleansed, and the broken table placed here amongst the other refuse from the day-to-day operations of the hotel."

Holmes pulled out his crystal wand and wound the handle once more. He ran the wand around the edges of the table and found another bright spot on some of the glass on one corner.

"Is it the dead man's?" I asked.

Holmes shook his head.

"I don't think so, there were no other wounds on the body. Even the bloodstain on the front of his coat wasn't from him. I believe our assailant cut themselves before rummaging around in the man's pockets," he said.

He stood up, put his wand away and brushed his hands together to remove the dust and grime from the table frame.

"In my mind, it does confirm that the man was murdered inside the hotel. The question remains, did the assailant remove him or the hotel staff themselves?"

"Given Sir Rupert's predilection to protect his hotel's reputation, I would say the latter," I said.

Holmes nodded.

"Quite so, Watson."

We turned back towards the corner and the other alleyway when a voice piped up behind us.

"Oi," it said.

We turned and saw a man standing in the shadows a little further down the alleyway. I could just make out his features and realised it was the doorman from the roof. He shuffled his feet and looked around nervously as if expecting to be found out at any moment.

Holmes strode straight up to him.

"Hello Frankie," he said.

"Mr. 'olmes," he returned, tipping his hat slightly, "Sorry I couldn't say anything upstairs. Mr. Croan scares the bejesus out o' me."

"That's fine, Frankie, what would you like to say?" asked Holmes.

Frankie lifted his chin to indicate the adjacent alleyway.

"The body, round the corner, 'e's been 'ere before."

"News travels fast," I said.

"I keeps me nose to the ground, I do. Mr. 'olmes pays me to do it," he retorted.

"Yes, go on. Do you know who the man is?" Holmes asked.

"Nah, but 'e's been here a few times. Comes in an' meets with another gent and the boss, mostly up on the top floor," he said.

"That would be Sir Rupert's office?"

"Yeah, yeah. And then sometimes 'e stays after. Flashes the cash around. Sometimes brings the ladies 'ere. Mostly ladies of the night, if you know wot I mean," he grinned.

Holmes nodded, "Yes, I know what you mean. When did he come this morning?"

"Well, that was weird. 'e arrived about four o'clock. I was on duty upstairs, 'e brings in a tall, dark 'aired girl. Beautiful she was. Foreign though, but still beautiful. They booked into a suite and I suppose got down to it. Maid came about seven this morning with breakfast, went in and found 'im dead as a doornail on top of the smashed coffee table. Mr. Croan found out, all 'ell broke loose, and then 'e was dumped downstairs."

"I suppose if I asked anybody else, they would deny everything?"

"Yep, word's gone out. Immediate sacking or worse."

He looked around nervously again.

"I gotta go before it's me," he said.

I quickly butted in, "Can I just ask, you mentioned the other gent, who is that?"

Frankie turned to me; his expression showed that he had no idea who I was.

"It's alright, Frankie, this is Doctor Watson, my associate," Holmes said.

Frankie relaxed, "The other gent is the Scots man, Sir Stannis McDonald."

My mouth dropped open at the mention of that name.

"Thank you, Frankie, you've answered a few questions I had. There'll be something extra in your payment this month," Holmes said.

"Oh, fank you, Mr. 'olmes," he said and vanished through a side door.

"Sir Stannis?" I asked, "Head of the Watt Steam company? What would he be doing here?"

Holmes turned, "It's becoming clearer, Watson, but there are still several pieces missing."

***

We found Lestrade leaning against a wall, biding his time but becoming frustrated with inaction. He got to his feet as he saw us enter the alleyway.

"Well?" he asked.

Holmes strode up to the corpse again and indicated for both of us to join him. He hunched down and picked up the man's hands again. He turned them over and revealed numerous callouses on the man's fingers and palms.

They were not the hands of a man that the clothes he wore heralded. This man was a tradesman of sorts and a hardworking one at that. I tried to work out how someone in a trade, no matter how hard he toiled, could afford the lifestyle he seemed to be living.

Holmes noticed both Lestrade's and my confusion at the state of the man's palms. He pulled out a small tool and picked out some black matter from beneath the man's fingernails. He held the hands out.

"Smell his hands," he said.

In turn, Lestrade and I leant forward and sniffed at the proffered hand. We both reared back in revulsion at the horrid chemical smell.

"Good Lord," said Lestrade.

"What say you, Watson?" asked Holmes.

"Some sort of oil or spirit-based chemical. It's not paraffin or alcohol," I said.

"No, it's not," said Holmes as he placed the man's hands down again and stood, "It's a new type of fuel called diesel. It is formed from a fractional distillation of petroleum. The black beneath the man's fingernails is possibly asphalt or alkene, one of the by-products of the process."

"A new fuel?" I asked, "Why would we need a new fuel? Coal is used in everything from cars, airships, heating, manufacturing, electricity. It will never be replaced."

Holmes smiled, "True. We have coal, for now, but what if someone could find an alternative. Cleaner, more efficient, cheaper?"

"The human race would advance even quicker than it has so far?" I said.

"Ever the optimist, Watson, that's one of your traits I do so admire. What about who that discovery might affect?"

I thought for a moment before realising where Holmes was going.

"Good Lord. The coal barons. The steam engine companies," I said.

Holmes smiled widely and nodded.

"Yes. Exactly," he said, "And I think they would pay quite handsomely for any information about the development of such fuel and any engines associated with it."

Lestrade's face was a mass of confusion.

"I have no idea what you two are talking about. Care to fill me in, or should I just take care of the body?" he said.

"I think we will require you for the next chapter in this adventure, Inspector. I believe that there will be a need for the yard's services," he said.

He stared off into the distance for a moment, as if recalling some memory from the great databanks of his mind and finally smiled.

"There is only one place that I know of that would require this type of fuel," he said.

***

Lestrade had a car parked nearby with two uniformed constables within. He directed one to secure the alleyway and wait for the coroner's men to arrive and remove the body.

The other man, Collins, was to drive us to a destination known by Holmes. He gave the address to the man, who then sparked the vehicle into action.

The ground car was a different beast to the airborne dirigible. Collins fired up the coal furnace below the small boiler, ensuring it was stoked with plenty of the black fuel and released the steam into the drive train when ready. The car lurched forward with a jolt as the inner turbine reached the required pressure. This form of transport had replaced the simple horse and carriage many years before and Holmes's idea that there was a simpler, ever more efficient system in the winds played through my mind, but I flicked it away with a healthy level of derision.

We took a brief stop at the nearest Police Station in Belgravia where Lestrade exited and strode into the station to organise some assistance for Constable Brown back at the Ritz. He quickly returned, and Collins had us away.

We headed south to the Thames and drove along the sprawling and bustling river, alive with boats and ships belching great gouts of black coal smoke and pure white steam, as they plied their trade along the river and supplied the great city with its needs.

We turned onto the Albert Bridge and crossed over the river. To our left was the expanse of Battersea Park, alive with people and their pet dogs. Children played in the bright sunshine and mothers sat in groups talking animatedly to each other.

I often forgot that the average person does not deal with the morbid and depressing sides of human nature that crop up in the life shared by Holmes and me. The only way that most of these people would learn of a body found in an alleyway, would be to see it appear in a column of the daily paper. Then most would glance at the article and turn the page to seek more light-hearted entertainment.

We entered a highly industrial area made up of large workhouses and warehouses. The area looked decidedly less salubrious than that which we had left in Piccadilly and Belgravia. The people walking the street eyed us both with envy, at the level of dress displayed by Holmes and myself, and with suspicion, as we were in a police vehicle with two officers.

We pulled in through a large set of wrought iron gates, with the sign "British Diesel Company" emblazoned above them. The three wings of the building formed a natural courtyard, and we parked before what was evidently the main entrance.

As we exited the vehicle, a loud droning noise greeted us from above. I looked up and saw a massive airship slowing down above the compound. It stopped in mid-air and hovered. Several men emerged from the nearby warehouse and stood looking up at the ship. A loud clanking sound followed by a whirring noise heralded the descent of the lower half of the aircraft's gondola.

The dirigible was one of the newer types of transport craft. A large zeppelin attached to a split-level gondola, the top half being used for controls and engines, the bottom being purely for cargo.

As I watched, the cargo deck was lowered on thick steel cables attached to winches, supposedly secreted in the upper deck. Within about a minute the lower level reached the ground. It was covered in large cylindrical drums with "North Sea Oil Company" logos plastered on them.

The men unloaded the barrels and rolled them to the bottom of a long flat roller system covered by a large continuous sheet of some strong material. Another man, standing to the side, turned a crank handle at the base of a strange-looking mechanical device. The contraption let out a few of what seemed to be mechanical coughs then began to run. It belched out huge plumes of black smoke and a deafening roar. My hands shot to my ears to protect them from the din.

The operator moved to a nearby switch, pulled it forward, and the whole belt began to move with a series of screeches and groans.

The other men started to load the barrels onto the belt, and they were ferried off into the bowels of the warehouse.

"Fascinating, isn't it?" Holmes said next to me.

"Loud," I yelled.

"Yes, but the power of that primitive engine is incredible," he said.

I looked incredulously back at the contraption. I then realised this was one of the diesel engines that Holmes had been talking about. I noticed it was a lot smaller than some of the steam engines I was familiar with. Even smaller than the one in the Police vehicle that brought us here.

"Why do you say primitive?" I asked.

"By the looks, it's one of Rudolf Diesel's early prototypes. Nothing goes to waste it seems."

He glanced up and spied the large smokestacks above us, plus another smaller chimney that had a constant flame pouring from it.

"Very impressive," he said.

"What is?"

"They have their own refinery for fractional distillation of the petroleum in those barrels we saw. They produce their own diesel fuel here. Small quantities I imagine, just enough to power their prototypes and inventions," he said.

I gaped at the chimneys myself, never imagining that such an operation existed in London.

It was then that several of the workers turned and noticed us watching them. They in turn stopped and stared at us. Some probably suspicious of the two police officers.

Another man stepped out of the warehouse and headed straight for the inactive men.

"Right, you lot, quit your lollygagging and get this lot unloaded. We can't afford to have that ship sitting here all day," he said.

They all snapped back to work. The foreman turned his attention to us and walked over, a stern look on his face.

"What do you lot want?" his question directed at Lestrade.

Holmes piped up before Lestrade could begin.

"If I may, my good man. We are looking for someone, and you might be just the person to help us. We think that one of your workers had a slight mishap at the Ritz Hotel last night. The Bar Manager was forced to have him thrown out. But before then he was yelling loudly about how he worked for this company and would have the owner come and buy the hotel. Well, you can imagine that Sir Rupert Linklatter was not very impressed when he found out and asked us to come and suggest that the chap stay away from now on."

"Seems a bit strange having the police do that," he said.

"Yes. Well, to be honest, it was either us or Sir Rupert's men."

The foreman's face changed to surprise. He nodded.

"Fair cop. Who was it?"

"We only have a description. Five ten. Brown hair. Dressed like a dandy."

The foreman nodded.

"Bloody Danny Green that would be. Came into some money of late. Big notes himself all the time."

The foreman stood up and yelled at the men unloading the dirigible.

"Oi, any of you lot seen Danny today?"

They all shook their heads. He turned back to Holmes.

"I ain't seen him all day either. He only lives around the corner, 13 Beatty Street. Lives with his Mum, the pillock."

The foreman seemed to think this was the end of the conversation. As luck would have it, the men finished their unloading and the raucous noise of the cargo bay ascending blotted out any hope of immediate conversation.

Holmes waited until the noise abated and the airship began to pull away before pressing the foreman.

"If you would be so kind, I think we should talk to Mrs. Fyord, just to warn her in case Sir Rupert decides to visit unannounced," he said.

The foreman smiled, "It's Miss. Miss Madeline Fyord. She's very particular. But, yeah, follow me, I'll see if she's available."

We headed through the main doors and into a brightly lit reception area. Even though we'd been outside in the sun, the light level within this room was almost disorienting.

The foreman laughed as he saw us shielding our eyes from the bright lights.

"Yeah, it takes a little getting used to," he said, "We generate our own electricity. The Boss likes to show off the capabilities of our engines. You don't get lights this bright with steam turbines."

My eyesight finally adjusted, and I could take in more of the details of the room. It was certainly not typical of the exterior of the buildings. The wood panelling had been painted in a clinical white and lacquered to give it a smooth almost glass-like appearance. Polished brass had been used extensively to accentuate the white.

At a desk in the centre of the room sat a young woman who eyed us off suspiciously before replacing the look with a well-practised but welcoming smile. I looked around and realised the foreman was gone.

"Gentlemen," the receptionist said, "Welcome to the British Diesel Company, can I help you in any way?"

Lestrade took the lead.

"I'm Inspector Lestrade of Her Majesty's Scotland Yard, we would like to see Miss Fyord, if you please," he said.

"Could I ask on what business?" the receptionist asked, her smile fading slightly.

"It's about one of her employees, a Mister Danny Green," he said.

The receptionist pushed a small switch which lit up. She reached for a black polished handset and turned a crank next to it.

Placing the mouthpiece to her lips she said, "Sorry to disturb you Miss, but there are several men from Scotland Yard here to see you."

A small indistinct buzzing came from the earpiece.

The young girl answered, "Yes, it's about Danny Green."

More buzzing and the girl eyed us with a slight tinge of concern on her face. She recovered and indicated the large ornate doors to our left.

"Miss Fyord will see you, please just through those doors."

**

Holmes opened the door to reveal a lavishly decorated office with a large wooden desk in the centre with brass and leather accents.

I noticed a door to the side closing and saw a hint of a long leather boot with a woman's hand sporting black nail polish drawing it shut. I turned towards Holmes and saw that he was apprised of the situation.

We both turned back to the remarkable woman that sat behind the desk. Miss Fyord was more than beautiful. Artists would vie for the chance to carve her in marble just for the chance to gaze upon her face. She sported long tresses of iridescent blonde hair that fell around her alabaster skin. Her piercing blue eyes gazed out below long black eyelashes.

She stood as Holmes approached, and I could see that she was also tall and slim. She wore long leather pants with knee-high boots, and her trim figure was compressed into a tight leather waistcoat over a flowing silk blouse.

She held out one immaculately manicured hand and took Holmes's hand in a firm and lingering handshake.

"I am Madeline Fyord, owner of this little enterprise, and you are?"

"Sherlock Holmes, madam," said Holmes, turning to introduce the rest of us, "My associate Doctor Watson, and this is Inspector Lestrade and Constable Collins of Scotland Yard."

Miss Fyord nodded to each of us in turn then sat down. We looked around for chairs but realised there weren't any. I admired that fact as this presented us in a reverse power game scenario.

"And how can I help you, Mr. Holmes?"

"I'm sorry to say, that we've come about the death of one of your employees. A Mr. Danny Green," he said.

Miss Fyord's expression remained impassive as she seemed to search her memories. Finally, she spoke.

"Green. Yes. Low-level Engineer. Working on the development of a new marine diesel engine prototype. We are hoping to use boats as our first move into the power unit market," she replied then continued after a pause, "Sad. How did he die?"

"He was murdered. Presumably at the Ritz Hotel, but his body was found in the alleyway next door."

"The Ritz, you say, I must revisit how much I'm paying my engineers. That's not an inexpensive establishment. Well thank you for informing me, I will have my receptionist contact his next of kin and pass on my condolences."

She stood again to bid us goodbye.

"I'm sure you need to rush off to apprehend the villain behind this, so I won't hold you further," she said.

All four of us held our places. Miss Fyord looked from face to face. Her stern look melted slightly as she realised we weren't going to leave. She sat down. The atmosphere had turned slightly.

Holmes continued, moving forward so that he towered over the desk and looked down at Miss Fyord.

"Mr. Green, a low-level engineer in your words, had been seen at the Ritz on a number of occasions. He held meetings with Sir Stannis McDonald in the office of Sir Rupert Linklatter."

A smile crossed Miss Fyord's face at the mention of those names.

"You know the gentlemen?" Holmes asked.

"Of course, Sir Stannis is my biggest competitor. The diesel engine we are developing is his biggest threat. We may only be a small company, but we have a mighty product on our hands. As for Sir Rupert, he has the largest controlling interest in the North Sea oil fields. He has been playing us off against British Steam for months. Hedging his bets so to speak."

Her demeanour changed.

"Are you trying to tell me that this Green was selling us out to our competitor?" she asked.

"I cannot say at this point, they may have just been old school friends for all I know," said Holmes, a little too quickly for my like. I recognised it as a tone he took when confronted over a point he could not justify with facts.

"Then what's the problem?" Fyord asked.

"Early this morning, Mr. Green was seen entering the same room as a tall, slender, woman of Indian appearance. The next time he was seen, he was dead in an alleyway with a puncture mark to the back of his neck. The puncture mark is reminiscent of a weapon used by a member of an elite all-female Indian assassin's guild."

Miss Fyord laughed out loud.

"And you think that was me?" she blurted out.

A small grin came to Holmes's face. He shook his head slightly.

"Oh no, madam, I don't think you had anything physically to do with this murder."

He walked across to the door we'd seen close earlier, grabbed the knob and wrenched it open.

Standing inside was a strikingly beautiful Indian woman, almost the same height as Holmes, with a slender, powerfully athletic build. She was dressed in a tight-fitting blue silk blouse, with a black leather bodice and black leather pants. I noticed that there were knife scabbards on the sides of her knee-high boots. I was relieved to find them empty. She also wore a black leather aviator's helmet with thick brass goggles. Her long black hair spilled out of the helmet and cascaded down to her waist.

This was not the look of a simple secretary or office worker. This woman was dressed for business. Bloody business.

"Madam, if you would be so kind, could you join us please," said Holmes.

The Indian woman stood in the small, white-tiled room that acted as Miss Fyord's private bathroom. She had a stern expression on her face with her piercing brown eyes trained on Holmes. She looked ready to pounce.

Her demeanour changed when Miss Fyord piped up.

"Parvinder, please do as Mr. Holmes says," she said, "I think we can clear this up quickly."

"As you wish, Ma'am," she said and walked into the office and took an "at ease" stance that would be the staple of any of the armed services.

"Let me introduce Miss Parvinder Singh, my associate and one of my closest friends. I think in future, Parvinder, it may prove prudent to lock the bathroom door," said Miss Fyord.

Holmes blanched a little with embarrassment at the suggestion he'd interrupted the woman. He recovered quickly. Miss Fyord took up the questioning.

"Parvinder, these gentlemen tell me that you were seen at the Ritz Hotel this morning. That you were meeting up with our Mr. Green from the new engine development team," she said.

The Indian woman turned to look at Miss Fyord with a questioning gaze. The blonde-haired woman looked directly into her eyes and nodded slightly. Holmes saw it all as well.

Parvinder turned her gaze forward and nodded.

"Yes. It is true," she said.

"You've been seeing Mr. Green for quite some time now, haven't you, but keeping it quiet, even from me."

Parvinder nodded again and spoke in a deadpan monotone.

"Yes. Daniel and I were in love. We have been together for several months. I think Daniel was going to propose marriage to me this morning. I was very excited," she said.

I almost burst out laughing at the woman's act. It was preposterous. I'm not even sure she knew who the man was, let alone being hopelessly in love with him.

Holmes simply smiled.

"I'm sure young Daniel would have been overjoyed with such a heartfelt response to his forthcoming proposal. Having you kill him probably came as an incredible surprise as well," he said.

Miss Fyord stood up at this suggestion.

"Kill him? Why would she kill him? It's obvious that she loved him."

Holmes turned towards her, his hand on his chin in contemplation of this strange conversation.

"My belief is that you, Miss Fyord, had your associate or should I say your hired assassin here, kill Mr. Green because he was selling your company's secrets to your competitor. You found out and wanted to make sure he died on the premises of one of your enemy's business partners."

"And what proof do you have?"

"For one, we have witnesses that place them both in the same location. We have reason to believe that my suggestion of industrial espionage is true. I will have to approach Sir Stannis to confirm it. He may not be happy, but the truth will come out. And one last piece of evidence would be …"

He turned and grabbed the Indian woman's right hand and turned it over. She sported a large bandage that covered the palm. Fresh blood had soaked through since the bandage had last been changed.

"The assailant cut herself on a glass-topped table, before reaching for Mr. Green's coat and taking whatever information he carried, plus the contents of his pockets."

Holmes turned towards Lestrade.

"Is this enough evidence to at least take Miss Singh here to the station house for further questioning?"

Lestrade nodded in agreement. Suddenly, his eyes grew wide, and he thrust a hand inside his coat. He pulled it out holding his pistol and trained it on Miss Singh.

I watched in shock as the tall woman stepped up behind Holmes, wrapped her injured arm around his chest and pulled her left hand out from behind her back.

She held what looked like a small brass pistol in her left hand and pressed the barrel against Holmes's neck. I looked closely and saw the plunger had been withdrawn and was cocked ready to fire.

I copied Lestrade and reached into my coat and withdrew my pistol. I noticed Collins standing nearby looking a little lost. Constables were only issued with nightsticks, not pistols. He drew his truncheon from his belt and held it at the ready.

"Ma'am, you have two guns pointing at you. We only want to ask you more questions to ascertain the truth. Let's not make this any harder than necessary," said Lestrade.

Holmes remained calm and spoke slowly with just enough volume for the Indian woman to hear.

"Hmmm, from the feel of it that would be a Bharat S13 Spring operated needle pistol, developed for the Bengal Infantry and used for close fighting and assassinations. Well that certainly confirms your origins, Miss Singh," said Holmes.

The Indian girl remained quiet. Miss Fyord broke the silence.

"What origins? Mr. Holmes?" she asked.

"Miss Singh here is a member of the Vishkanya. A secretive guild of female assassins operating out of India, primarily in the Punjab and Bengal areas," he said.

Miss Fyord laughed out loud.

"Nonsense. Parvinder's family has lived in England for decades. She was born in London and lived around the corner from my Grandfather's house. We have been friends for most of our lives," she said.

"Indeed," said Holmes.

"Is that true, Miss Singh?" I asked.

The woman's face remained impassive. Her hand tightened on the gun as she answered.

"Yes. I have lived in England all my life. Madeline is my best friend. We went to school and University together. I have worked with her company since I left school," she said in a dead monotonic voice.

I could see Holmes wasn't convinced. His face showed a slight tinge of anger at what he thought were obvious lies.

"Then perhaps, Miss Fyord, you could convince Miss Singh to unhand me and accompany the Inspector to the station so that this matter can be laid to rest. If Miss Singh was so in love with Mr. Green, then even a policeman of Inspector Lestrade's experience and expertise could not possibly charge her with Mr. Green's murder."

"Yes," said Miss Fyord standing up, "I think this has gone on long enough."

She raised her voice and directed her next sentence at the Indian woman.

"Parvinder, the time has come. You know what to do," she said.

I noticed a flash of confusion and incredulity race across the tall woman's face. She turned to Miss Fyord bowed her head slightly, then turned her face forward. Her face regained its impassive expression again.

"Yes. It will be done," she said.

Parvinder stared off into space and released Holmes who staggered away. He turned back to address the woman just in time to see her bring the needle gun up to her temple and squeeze the trigger.

The gun let out a stifled ringing noise and what sounded like something punching into meat.

The Indian woman's eyes rolled back into their sockets and she collapsed in an unceremonious heap on the floor. The gun slid away from her and stopped near Holmes.

I looked down at the gun and saw a long brass needle sticking out of the end. It was mottled with red blood.

I looked back at the woman and saw a small puncture in her left temple like the wound on Green's neck. A dribble of blood ran out of the hole and dripped onto the floor.

I couldn't help myself but blurted out, "Good Lord."

Holmes looked at the dead woman then turned to face Miss Fyord. The company owner was calm as if this was an expected occurrence.

Holmes cocked his head and spoke.

"Well, that was unexpected," he said, "Wasn't it, Miss Fyord?"

She turned and looked into Holmes's eyes, her face unmoved.

"Shocking, I would say," she said.

"You don't seem very upset," I said.

Miss Fyord turned to face me; a flash of anger ran across her features.

"My best friend just killed herself, in my office. I will not give you intruders the pleasure of seeing my distress," she said standing up and moving around to the front of her desk.

"Now, if you'll excuse me, I will go home so that I may mourn alone," she finished.

She turned to Lestrade and said, "I assume you will need a statement or something from me. I will remain at home for the next day or two. My receptionist can give you my address."

With that, she turned and walked through her office doors and into the reception area before anybody thought of stopping her.

I was flustered. I looked at the retreating figure, then to Holmes and Lestrade.

"What is going on?" I asked keeping my voice from rising to a shrill cry.

Holmes turned from watching Miss Fyord leave, a small sardonic grin on his face.

"What do you mean, Watson?"

"You're letting her go. You said all along that this was a case of espionage. That Green was killed because of what he knew and what he was selling to Sir Stannis," I said.

"Ah, yes, but I don't have any actual evidence. Only conjecture," he answered before turning to Lestrade, "I assume that you are content with the case at hand, Inspector?"

Lestrade looked at the body and then back at Holmes and me. He nodded.

"Sadly, yeah, I agree with Holmes. We've got enough evidence to put this down to a lovers' tiff or something, but not enough to lay any other charges."

He turned to Collins.

"Constable, can you go and organise a coroner's wagon to pick this unfortunate up? There's not much else to investigate at the moment."

"Yes sir, but…?" Collins said.

"I'm sure Mr. Holmes will be continuing the investigation from here on, but as far as the Yard is concerned, it's closed," Lestrade said.

He winked at Holmes, "Isn't that right?"

Holmes nodded.

"Yes. And to allay your fears Watson, I will indeed be looking further afield. There is a lot more to this, and it involves very powerful people, so care is needed at every turn."

He thought for a moment with a finger extended on his chin.

"I may have to consult with Mycroft."

He looked back at the open doorway into the receptionist area and smiled.

"I think, in Miss Madeline Fyord, we have a very intelligent and incredibly shrewd adversary. One that is not above hiring assassins whose code is one of complete loyalty, even unto death. One that is prepared to take on the most powerful men in the country without a drop of fear or doubt, and one that may involve us in many adventures to come. A truly formidable woman," he said.

I stared at the expression on Holmes's face. I shuddered a little as it was one, I hadn't seen since we first met a lady that he always referred to as "The Woman", a Miss Irene Adler.

The Adventure of the Sugar Merchant

It was early one cold autumn morning that Holmes and I were dragged into one of our strangest cases ever, an adventure involving Haitian voodoo and, of all things, zombies.

I was in the sitting room of 221b Baker Street on that cold morning, the fire ablaze to strip the chill from the air. I had finished off a wonderful breakfast provided by our landlady, Mrs. Hudson, and was relaxing with a second cup of coffee and the morning papers when I came across a late article, slotted in between the international affairs and finance sections. It detailed the account of a fire in a warehouse down in Canary Wharf. Many of the city's fire brigades were called, but their efforts were to no avail. The warehouse succumbed and crumbled under its own weight in the late hours of the previous evening. The article had been included so late that there was no more than the scarcest of details.

It was at that point that my erstwhile associate Sherlock Holmes arose from his slumber and sauntered into the sitting room, resplendent in a smoking jacket and looking quite awake for one who had arrived home in the early hours.

"Ah, Holmes," I said, "finally joining the living, I see."

Holmes smiled and helped himself to a coffee. "Obviously you are aware that I was home late."

I nodded.

"I was on the trail of someone that I had presumed to be involved in the affair of the disappearance of the eldest son of Lord Langley. Sadly, the trail went cold sometime in the wee hours of the morning. I returned home to re-invigorate myself for another long night ahead."

"A shame," I said. "Any other clews?"

He looked off into the distance through the window and absent-mindedly replied, "A few, but nothing substantial. The boy has simply disappeared from the face of the Earth."

He sipped his coffee and turned. Spying the open newspaper, he asked, "Anything exciting to relieve my mind of my disappointment?"

"A warehouse fire in Canary Wharf. Scant details. Could be arson. Could be an accident. Could be nothing really."

Holmes harrumphed, pursed his lips, sipped his coffee, and sat down in his easy chair. "Then I will cogitate further over the Lord's son." He placed the cup down, clasped his hands on his chest, and sat back, eyes closed. This was a natural meditative pose for him, or as I soon noticed, a comfortable pose where he could quickly drift off to sleep.

I smiled to myself and quietly finished the paper.

* * *

I snapped awake as the doorbell downstairs rang. I glanced across and saw that Holmes had left his chair and was nowhere to be seen. The clock on the mantel told me it had been an hour since I watched Holmes fall asleep.

I started to rise when Mrs. Hudson appeared at the doorway with Inspector Lestrade in tow. I shook the inspector's hand and thanked Mrs. Hudson. I also asked if she'd seen Holmes at all. She denied any knowledge of his leaving, so I hoped he was still on the premises. I led Lestrade into the sitting room, where it was a tad warmer. He shed his overcoat and gloves and placed them over the back of a chair.

"What brings you on this miserably cold day," I asked.

He looked a little embarrassed but went on with his request. "There's been a fire," he started.

"The warehouse?" I asked.

His eyes opened wide in surprise. I indicated the discarded paper on the settee. "There was a brief article in *The Times* this morning," I said, a wry smile on my lips.

"Ah, that would explain it," he said.

"What about the fire requires Holmes's involvement?" I queried, just as the man himself entered the room.

"Did I hear something about a fire?" he asked, "Not the warehouse fire that you mentioned, Watson?"

I nodded. "Seems to be."

Holmes indicated the seats and took his favourite chair. He sat back and looked at Lestrade across his steepled fingers. Lestrade sat and I made my way to the door to call down for coffee from Mrs.

Hudson. I returned just as Lestrade began and sat down myself, a little flush of excitement within me. I always hoped that Lestrade would bring some case that piqued Holmes's interest.

He began to relate the events of the previous night. "You're quite right, it was a warehouse fire – a big one, down in Canary Wharf. Arson as far as we can tell. It burnt the entire place to the ground. The brigade got it under control quickly. We were lucky it didn't spread any further."

"Any suspects," I asked.

"Just one."

"Oh, well do you need us to help track him down?"

"No," he said. "No need for that."

"Why?" I responded.

"He's dead. They found him in the fire."

"Oh."

Holmes unsteepled his fingers as a question formed on his lips. "What makes him so remarkable that you needed to come here?"

Lestrade wiped his brow with a handkerchief. "It's two things. The first is we know he was the arsonist because the flint box he used to light the fire was lying nearby."

"How very strange," I said.

"The other thing is, the Coroner reckons he's been dead for at least three days."

***

Lestrade's final comment urged the three of us to travel to the city morgue. There we found the coroner, Smithers, working away on the desiccated corpse of the poor unfortunate that had been found in the burnt-out warehouse. The poor man's hair had all but burnt off, and his face was blackened and slightly blistered. His hands were blackened, but the rest of his body was virtually untouched. From this observation, I assumed his clothing had taken the brunt of the flames.

The smell was horrendous, but Smithers had tried to temper it by placing small piles of rose petals around the room to release their fragrance. Holmes held any disgust at the smell in check and began to examine the corpse. He moved in a complete circle around the body, viewing it without touching. He hummed and murmured to himself, an indication that he was finding interesting observations.

"What's your opinion, Smithers?" he asked.

The coroner stood upright and thought for a moment. "He was in here three days ago," he said. "Same body, at the time he was in good condition, but now he's as you see him."

"How do you know it was the same body?" I asked.

Smithers moved around to the head. He pointed at a few wisps of unburned hair. "It's a male. The hair colour is the same. The height is the same. Weight is about the same, give or take what the fire took with it." He pointed at the corpse's mouth. A gold tooth gleamed dully from within the rictus grin. "Second upper pre-molar on the left has a gold cap. Not rare, but given the other features, it points to the same man." He nodded to a pile of scorched and burnt clothing on a nearby chair. "He's was also wearing the same clothing that he was when previously here."

Holmes was impressed. He peered at the gold tooth and the hair. "If this body was here three days ago, how did it get up and leave?"

Smithers turned to face him, his eyes glancing across to Lestrade who had obviously already asked this question. "He didn't. He wasn't here at the time. He was found down at the river's edge last Tuesday. The constables that brought him in said he was just another homeless person. His clothing said as much too. He was part of a group of men all found dead. Four in all. It was a very busy night."

He folded his arms and leaned against the autopsy table. "We've had recent instructions from the Health Ministry and Scotland Yard to process any vagrants as quickly as possible. The cold weather has started to run through the city's homeless population like the plague. Those in charge are worried that we don't have the resources to spend time on each homeless death."

His face grew grim. "I'm neither impressed nor in favour of such actions, but I have my orders." He waved a hand over the dead man. "I performed a cursory examination – heartbeat, temperature, and ligature resistance – to make sure I could pronounce him dead. He was then taken to a local funeral parlour in preparation for cremation. How he was taken from there is a matter for them to explain."

"And you have no reason to suspect the man was still alive?" I asked.

Smithers gave me a withering look. "Doctor, you as well as anybody should know that someone presenting with no heartbeat, a sixty-degree body temperature, and *post mortem* ligature stiffness shows all the hallmarks of a dead man."

Holmes smiled. "I think he has you there, Watson."

I kept my mouth shut at the rebuke.

Holmes continued. "I think your assessment is quite correct, Smithers, and I must commend you for it. The man is obviously dead now. Whether he was dead previously is down to your observations and, given we were not present, we must accept them." He moved around the corpse, his hand on his chin as he contemplated. "The main problem is that I believe this man to be Dominic Langley, the son of Lord Byron Langley, fourth Earl of Northbridge."

"Good God!" I exclaimed. "How do you come to that?" I knew that Holmes had been on the trail of Dominic Langley for a number of days and had been frustrated at every turn.

"Same height, weight, hair, and eye colour. The evidence of the gold tooth seals the deal. Plus . . . ." He moved over to the pile of charred clothing and leafed through the items. "Dominic Langley had a strange compunction to eschew the trappings of his wealth and station and to seek the excitement of the lower classes. He would often wear the clothes of the street and reside amongst the vagrants down at the river bank."

Holmes turned back to stare at the corpse. "Though there is something that troubles me," he said. "Do you object, Smithers, if I conduct my own examination?"

Smithers turned towards Lestrade who nodded. "Not if the inspector doesn't mind," he replied.

Holmes moved around the body and gently picked up its right hand. He bent down and sniffed it. His nose wrinkled at whatever odour wafted from the digits. He repeated with the left hand then placed both at the body's side. He then moved across to a nearby table covered with instruments and picked up two pairs of forceps, a pair of cotton swabs, and a small ceramic bowl. He moved back to the corpse's head and gently prized the man's jaw apart. A sickening cracking sound issued. I assumed it was the tendons stretching beyond their current capabilities.

Holmes placed a swab between the tines of the forceps and pushed it deep into the poor man's mouth. He moved it about then pulled it out again. He withdrew his magnifying glass and examined the swab. "Hmm," he murmured. "Most interesting."

I moved over and stared through the glass at the swab. It was relatively clean, except for the last vestiges of saliva from the corpse. "Clean?" I posited.

"Yes. I had half-expected it to have traces of ash and soot on it."

"A natural assumption if the man was still alive during the blaze," he said. "He would have inhaled the soot as he drew his final breaths."

"Exactly, but there is no evidence."

"So he *was* dead?"

"One would presume such, but I smelt traces of turpentine on his fingers – a powerful accelerant used recently in other cases of arson around the city."

"Perhaps the arsonist was sending a message. Trying to lay blame on the dead man."

"That is one line of thought. There's also this." Holmes pointed out some more observations to me. "Watson, if you would notice: The skin that was covered by clothing is virtually untouched. A little dirty, probably from the fire, but not burnt or scorched in any meaningful way."

He picked up the other swab, dipped it in some water, and ran it across the corpse's cheek. It left a bright area of unblemished skin. "The skin on the man's face is likewise relatively untouched by the fire. There is a little blistering on his scalp where, I assume, burning embers settled to ignite some of his hair, but the rest was only discoloured by the falling ash." He picked up the corpse's right hand and examined the fingertips, murmuring to himself as well.

"What does it all mean?" I asked.

"His fingertips are damaged and scorched, as well as smelling of turpentine, but the rest of him is relatively unharmed. In my opinion, this man, Dominic Langley, simply set fire to part of the warehouse, then lay down in a clear area of the floor and awaited his fate."

I was taken aback. "But he was supposedly dead. How, and why, would anybody in their right mind do such a thing?"

"That is what we need to find out. It is sad to think that young Langley died in this way, and I feel that there is something more to his fate. He was a healthy young man, not one prone to die of exposure, so why did he present as dead in the first place? And then why was his body stolen from the crematory, if indeed he didn't walk out on his own? Then, how did he end up in the middle of a burning warehouse? I am perplexed, and these questions pose the next part of the mystery that we shall address," he finished.

***

The carriage dropped Holmes, Lestrade, and me outside of a wonderfully appointed four-storey Georgian mansion nestled in a quiet street near Grosvenor Square in Mayfair. Holmes made his way to the front door while I paid the cabbie. Lestrade looked a little out of sorts at the opulence of the area. I admit I felt a little awkward as well.

A well-dressed butler in full formal dress answered. Holmes murmured something that I failed to hear, and we were shown into the immaculately presented main foyer where the man took our hats and coats. He showed us into a nearby reception room to wait until our introductions were made to the master of the house. I moved around the room, relishing the richness of the furnishings and decorations.

"Remarkable," said Holmes looking over my shoulder, "how much wealth a simple thing as sugar can produce, isn't it?"

"What do you mean?"

"Lord Byron Langley is the single largest importer of sugar to the United Kingdom. His father, the third Earl of Northbridge, was ambassador to Jamaica during Lord Byron's childhood. He grew up amongst the rich West Indian culture and decided to stay once his father returned to England. He married Myra, a missionary's daughter, who sadly died during the birth of Dominic Langley."

"How sad," I remarked.

"Yes. Dominic was sent to England to be educated while Lord Byron grew the industry that his grandfather had bought into, and expanded it to include the importation of sugar to the United Kingdom. He returned only a couple of years ago. My understanding is that was to be with his son during his final years of college, with the intent that Dominic would eventually take over the business. All this will be a bit of a shock to him, I imagine," he added.

As I was about to ask further questions, the butler returned and spoke. "Lord Byron will see you now. If you would follow me."

All three of us duly followed and were let into an ornately furnished study, with bookshelves lining all four walls and a massive oak desk in the centre. Lord Byron was a rather tall and rotund man, with a large beard and the look of someone that enjoyed life to the fullest. He walked around his desk and took Holmes's hand in both of his own.

"Mr. Holmes!" he said. "Welcome, welcome," He turned towards Lestrade and me. "And these gentlemen would be?"

Holmes introduced the both of us, then his face turned grave. "I suggest you take a seat, Lord Byron," he said. "I do not bring pleasant news."

Lord Byron's face dropped, a touch of fear flashed across his visage. "It's Dominic, isn't it?" he asked as he took a seat.

Holmes nodded. "Yes, I'm afraid it is," he said. "Very early this morning, your son was found in the remains of a burnt-out warehouse. I'm afraid that he had passed."

Lord Byron's face turned to shock and dismay. "Oh, my," he said. "How?"

"We are unsure at this stage, but it appears to be smoke inhalation from the fire."

Lord Byron looked off into the distance for a moment and murmured to himself. "Silly boy," he murmured. "What have you been up to?"

"I beg your pardon, sir," Holmes asked. "I didn't quite catch the question."

Lord Byron looked up in surprise. "Sorry. Nothing. Just thinking out loud. Do you have any clews as to why he was there?"

"None. I was hoping you might know, but didn't want to press, as I assumed the news would be upsetting enough for you."

Lord Byron took a deep breath to calm himself. He let it out in a relaxed and controlled way before speaking. "I won't lie. It is distressing, though part of me believed that Dominic's wild behaviour might result in such an eventuality." He stood up and strode around the room, waving his arms as he spoke. "I gave him everything. The best schools. The riches of Croesus. He has never wanted for anything, but he preferred to turn his back on all that at times to live with the down-and-outs in the slums. To learn what it was like to have naught, he would tell me."

He looked out a side window for a moment, gathering his thoughts. "I had assumed it would be in one of these slums that he would meet his end. Was it at the waterfront down Southwark way?" he said, turning back to face us and pressing up against the desk.

"No," Holmes said. "Actually, it was a warehouse in Canary Wharf."

Lord Byron's eyes lit up. "Where in Canary Wharf, exactly?"

Lestrade pulled out a small pad of paper. "20 Bank Street, on the South Dock."

Lord Byron's face dropped in shock. He sat heavily in his seat, deflated as if he had been struck in the face.

Holmes stood and moved to the desk. "Lord Byron?" he asked. "Is something wrong?"

"That's *my* warehouse," he replied.

***

Lord Byron insisted on joining our little excursion to his destroyed warehouse, explaining that he would have already gone there sooner, except that he was awaiting word about his son. He ordered his own carriage brought around, and within several minutes his driver had us wending our way through the centre of London, Whitechapel, Shadwell, and finally Canary Wharf. The driver pulled up before the awful sight of the devastated warehouse. We exited the cab and Lord Byron's face fell in a shock greater than the news of the death of his son.

The warehouse was beyond salvage. Three sides had been gutted, the wooden walls burnt to the ground. Only the fourth wall, made primarily of red brick, had survived. The contents, large bales filled

135

with refined sugar, had been reduced to large puddles of thick, black sludge. The location of Dominic's body was evident from the lighter-coloured patch in the middle of the scorched cobbled floor. Holmes went straight towards it and began examining the area.

The remains of a wooden fire-lighting kit lay nearby. He bent down and ran a finger over the stones next to it and rubbed two fingers together. He scanned the rest of the area and stood as something in the far corner piqued his interest. He walked to the corner and bent down again. A small lumpy object lay in the soot. Holmes picked it up to examine it. He sniffed, and then pulled away in disgust.

"Something, Holmes?" I asked.

"I think I've found the source of the blaze," he said holding up the object. It appeared to be glass or ceramic but was blackened by the fire. "This was once a small glass vessel and held turpentine. Whoever set the fire, and sadly I believe it to have been Dominic, lit it near this part of the wall. As the liquid burned and became hotter, the surrounding wall ignited and the glass eventually melted. The rest is fairly obvious." He stood and wiped his hands on a handkerchief pulled from his coat pocket.

Lord Byron was flummoxed. He moved across, peering around the warehouse as he did. "Mr. Holmes, you said that you think Dominic lit this fire."

Holmes nodded.

"But why? Why would he do this? This was part of his legacy."

Holmes nodded again. "I must admit, Lord Byron, that I am at a loss as to the reason behind his possible actions. You mentioned he eschewed the high life to spend time with the lower levels of society. Perhaps that clouded his mind and led to this. He may have also fallen in with the wrong crowd, one that sees you as an enemy of society and convinced him to act in this way. At this stage, I have no evidence, and no clews, so I have only conjecture."

Lord Byron dropped his head in defeat. He made his way back to the carriage, turning back before entering. "I thank you for your service, Mr. Holmes. Please forward a letter of request to my accountant with your fee attached. You did as asked and found my son. His state of being was not part of the bargain. I will retire back to my residence for now and make the arrangements for his burial. Again, I thank you."

I could tell that he was on the verge of a breakdown and understood fully. In one fell swoop, he had not only lost his son but had found out that he had betrayed him and destroyed one of his greatest assets.

Holmes walked quickly to the carriage and placed a hand on Lord Byron's shoulder. "I will find out the reason, your Lordship. Until then, I would not even consider any recompense. There is something here that does not make sense, so I am just as invested in finding the solution as you are. I promise I will not let you, or the memory of your son, down."

Lord Byron patted Holmes's hand and nodded. "Thank you, sir. You are a true gentleman."

I noticed his Lordship stare off into the distance over Holmes's right shoulder for a moment before he turned and boarded the carriage. A moment later, with a snap of the reigns, the driver led them away from the desolation.

Holmes watched them go, and then he turned back and walked towards Lestrade and me. I was about to ask him whether he had noticed the Lord's last action, but he swept past the both of us and continued on in the direction of Lord Byron's gaze. I followed in his wake, intrigued as always.

On the far side of the warehouse, in a corner near the brick wall, was a large set of crates. They were scorched, but relatively unscathed from the fire. The contents not so much, however. They held a large collection of small glass vials with cork stoppers. The majority had cracked from the heat and spilled their contents, which had vaporised in the heat. Holmes reached out and moved the top crate aside, spilling a mass of broken glass and residual liquid. I noticed immediately a strong sweet odour wafting up from the spilt fluid.

Holmes found that the contents of the crate below were in much better condition and extracted an unmarked vial. He held it up to the light and showed that it contained a pale, clear yellow liquid. He popped the cork and sniffed at the contents.

"Any idea, Holmes?"

"Yes, Watson, some idea. It's certainly not sugar, that's for sure." He placed the vial into a pocket inside his coat and turned away from the crates, a look of excitement had crossed his face. "I will need to return to Baker Street. I have a long night ahead."

***

That evening I was called out on a late emergency and didn't return until the wee hours of the morning. I went straight to bed and awoke later that day. Still slightly bleary-eyed, I stumbled into the sitting room to find Holmes busily working away at some chemistry experiment. Coloured liquids boiled in beakers and piped up through a series of distillation tubes.

I stepped closer and spied a beaker of fresh blood sitting on the end of the table. "I'm sure you could ask Mrs. Hudson to fix you something more suited to sustaining yourself," I said pointing at it.

Holmes looked at the beaker and then at me. A wry smile came to his face. "How very droll, Watson," he said, "but regardless of what you think, I'm not a vampire. That is our young Dominic Langley's blood. I stopped by the morgue early this morning and convinced Smithers to withdraw some for me. I believe it may contain some vital answers."

"Have you managed to determine what the yellow, fragrant liquid is?"

He stopped. A look of excitement came across his face. He motioned to the bench and a large volume on botany. I read the entry aloud:

"Chrysopogon zizanioides, *or common* vetiver. *A long-stemmed grass that produces a fragrant oil when crushed in quantity.*"

"Yes," said Holmes. "It is used widely in perfumes and cosmetics. The liquid we found is the oil of the plant. On the current market, a single vial of one fluid ounce would be worth the same as about ten tons of sugar."

"A very valuable commodity, then," I said. "I thought that Lord Byron was purely an importer of sugar."

Holmes smiled. "Like any good entrepreneur, he has a diverse range of investments and means to derive profit. It seems, as my research has yielded, that two years ago, Lord Byron bought out a vetiver plantation and refining plant in the southwestern region of Haiti."

"Haiti?" I asked.

"Yes. It makes sense. The vetiver can be extracted, packaged, and shipped quite simply and quickly from Haiti to Lord Byron's sugar refining factory in Jamaica, and from there to be transported to the United Kingdom or Europe along with the sugar."

"All right, a good investment then. What of it?"

He held up the vial with the remains of the liquid inside. "At this stage, not much, but given Lord Byron's distant look in its direction yesterday, I think this means a great deal to him."

"What of the blood, then?"

Holmes placed the vial down and put on some thick leather gloves. He picked up a beaker full of a cloudy yellow liquid that had been heating over a Bunsen burner. He placed it down on an asbestos mat and, pulling off the gloves, withdrew a small dropper from a glass bottle. "Let's hope this works," he said, displaying the huge grin on his face that I had seen so often when some experiment had piqued his fascination for obscure chemistry.

He gently squeezed the dispenser's bulb and two drops of a transparent liquid fell into the beaker. The result was immediate. The cloudy liquid went completely clear. "Fascinating."

I leaned in closer to the beaker. He placed a hand on my chest. "Probably not a good idea, Watson. Best to stay a little back."

I stood up and moved back. Holmes wasn't usually the most careful man during his chemistry experiments, so anything that had him cautious was obviously far more dangerous than desired.

"What is it, Holmes?" I asked.

"*Tetrodotoxin*," he replied. "Rather quite deadly."

I was shocked. This was even more reckless than normal for Holmes. "Why in blue blazes are you messing around with that?"

The poison was a highly potent neurotoxin, occurring naturally in several deadly species of fish. It would attack the central nervous system and paralyse any person or animal that came in contact with it, within moments. "I found it in young Dominic Langley's blood."

"Is that what killed him?"

"It's incredibly potent. A tiny amount can disable, and larger amounts can kill. I can't reliably tell what concentration he had in his body, but there's a good chance it was the cause of death."

"Good Lord!" I said.

"And that's not all, Watson. I also found that our Dominic had a large dose of a hallucinogenic drug or a deliriant in his bloodstream. I haven't isolated it as yet, but it seems to be akin to that extracted from the common Devil's Trumpet, or datura plant."

"Strange," I said. "Where would that have come from?"

"Well, funny enough, the datura plant is quite common across Central America and the West Indies."

"Haiti?"

"Possibly."

Holmes paused in thought for a moment, his hand beneath his chin, his forefinger braced against this cheek. Finally, he moved towards his room. "I believe," said Holmes, "that we need to visit the last known location for young Dominic – the riverfront."

***

A hansom dropped us off on the high street in Shadwell. I paid the driver, who had eyed us with suspicion from the moment he had picked us up. I couldn't blame him really. Holmes had delved into his extensive collection of costumes and was dressed in the manner of a common street beggar, complete with makeup.

I didn't have the same level of costumery available to me. I sported my oldest pair of pants, complete with several small tears, a stained shirt and vest, plus my oldest coat. I found some dust, a remarkable feat given Mrs. Hudson's predilection for cleanliness, and mussed up the shoulders a little. I located an old pair of boots and dirtied them up in a small mud puddle on Baker Street.

As we made our way towards the riverbank, I felt very self-conscious, but Holmes took it in his stride. He slumped his shoulders to affect the caricature of an elderly street denizen. I tried to follow suit but felt even more uncomfortable. We reached a small alleyway that led to the river and my hackles were raised straight away. It felt very much like a perfect place for an ambush, and soon enough shadows appeared at both ends of the lane.

A tall man shuffled towards us. The light filtering through showed me his scarred face and a sneer full of blackened teeth. "What do we have here?" he asked. "If you want to use this pathway, you have to pay the tax."

I began to speak, but Holmes shut me up. "I'm looking for Snivellin' Pete," he said in his best East End accent.

"Who?" the man returned.

"Snivellin' Pete. 'E controls this area, I'm told. An 'e don't like it when others try to take over."

The man's face grew red with anger. He stepped forward, grabbed Holmes by the shirt front, and pushed him against the wall. "I'm in charge now," he said. "This Snivelling Pete is gone. Dead."

I went to move, but Holmes was much quicker. He grabbed the man's arms, twisted to one side, stepped forward, and slammed the taller man to the ground. All but one of the other shadows disappeared.

Holmes stared down at the man and spoke in his normal voice. "Are you telling me that Snivelling Pete is dead? How would you know that?" he asked.

The man stared up with incredulous eyes. It was obvious he hadn't been bested in this way for quite a while.

"I . . . I . . . ." he stammered.

A quieter voice piped up from behind us. "Is that you, Mr. 'Olmes?"

I turned and saw a diminutive little man. He stared wide-eyed in disbelief. Holmes looked up and smiled. "Tommy the Rat, isn't it?"

"Yes, Mr. 'Olmes, yes. I know what 'appened to Pete, I does."

Holmes looked down at the man on the ground. "If I were you, I'd find another area of the river to command, or else I might be forced to come back another day. Are we clear?"

The taller man, his eyes still wide in fear, nodded. Without looking back, Holmes stepped away and the man scampered to his feet and disappeared around the corner. Holmes turned to Tommy. "Let's get out of here in case he decides to disobey my advice."

141

***

We retired to The White Swan, two streets over, where our clothing and appearance fit, and we knew we were on neutral ground in case of any reprisals. It turned out that Tommy the Rat was a long-time cohort of Snivelling Pete, whom Holmes confessed was both the local tough who controlled this part of Shadwell, and, by chance, was also a member of the Baker Street Irregulars. Holmes had hoped to catch up with him to see if he had any information about Dominic Langley's demise. He had co-opted Pete into keeping an eye out for Langley two weeks earlier.

I brought three pints of local ale back to the table. Tommy took his and downed half of it without taking a breath. I sat, mildly amused, and took a draw from my own. Holmes waited until Tommy paused before asking him about Pete's disappearance. "You mentioned that you knew what happened to Snivelling Pete."

"That I do, Mr. 'Olmes, that I do," he said taking another sip of beer.

"Well?" I asked, growing a little impatient.

"Oh, yes, sorry. Is good beer this," he said. "It all happened about three nights ago. We was just 'angin' around down at the bank. There'd been a rumour of some roughs coming down from Whitby and trying to muscle into Pete's territory. 'E was going over a plan to find them and teach 'em a lesson." He stopped and took another sip of beer.

"Was there a young man in your group that didn't quite fit?" Holmes asked.

"The toff?" Tommy countered.

"I assume, yes," Holmes answered.

"Yeah. Pete 'ad brought 'im along a week before. Said 'e would be useful to us. I didn't like 'im one bit. Seemed a bit soft if you ask me."

"Fair call. What happened to Pete and the toff?"

"Right. Well, on that night, we was making plans and getting ready for a bit of a rumble, if it came to that, an then it all goes to 'ell."

"How?"

"Pete's standing there, talking away, 'is 'and goes to 'is neck and 'e collapses. Pretty soon the other three, including the toff do the same."

"How is it that you escaped?"

"I was in the shadows, like always. I don't like the spotlight, me. Anyways, I waits for a bit then creeps out to check on 'em. I couldn't find no breath. They was dead as doornails. I got outta there as quick as like. Next day I comes back and they's gone. Don't know if the plods got 'em or what."

"You didn't take long to find another gang to run with," I said.

"It's a dog-eat-dog world out there. Man's got to do what a man's got to do."

"Quite so," said Holmes.

***

The next morning, I was awakened by Holmes rapping on the door to my bedroom. "Come, Watson," he said. "Time is wasting. We have far to go today."

Moments later I shuffled down to the sitting room, dressed and ready for the day. Holmes was already at the door, waiting to depart. My stomach rumbled, but I spied a basket of fresh scones that Mrs. Hudson had made on Holmes's orders. I loaded some into a tea towel and hurried after him. "What in blazes is the rush?" I asked as we stepped into a waiting hansom.

"Our first stop," he said, "will be at the funeral parlour, the use of which has been seconded by the coroner. I wish to ask the proprietor some questions, and your presence will help in two areas: One to provide a numerical advantage, and two because of your medical knowledge."

I munched on a scone, spilling crumbs across my front, and pondered his words. I hated to admit it, but on a number of occasions Holmes's medical knowledge had outshone my own, but I hoped for my own sake that I could help.

We stopped outside of a building with *"Richard's Funeral Parlour"* emblazoned above the door. I brushed a good number of scone crumbs to the street and shook out the flour dust from the tea towel before pocketing it. I made a mental note to return it to Mrs. Hudson when we arrived home.

Meanwhile, Holmes was examining a small window to the side of the double doors. There was a crack extending across the length of it. As I joined him, he reached out towards the doors and turned the handles. Even at this early hour, the business was open. We let ourselves into a small but well-adorned reception area. A sideboard held a jug of water and several glasses. I shrugged off my manners and headed for the water. The three scones that I had ingested had left my mouth rather dry.

As I drank, I watched Holmes examine the door through which we had just entered. I was about to ask why when a rather tall and gaunt man appeared in a doorway leading to a service room. He had a surprised but inquisitive look on his face.

"Gentlemen, I am Mr. Richard," he said, "the owner of this establishment. My condolences to you at this time."

Holmes smiled. "Oh, that won't be necessary. We aren't customers. My name is Sherlock Holmes, and this is my associate, Dr. John Watson. I am a consulting detective in the employ of Lord Byron Langley. We merely have some questions regarding a recent visitor to your establishment."

Richard's face changed slightly to suspicion. "Yes?"

"We are under the impression that you have been receiving the bodies of unidentified street denizens who have succumbed to the cold during this unseasonal weather. One such victim arrived three days ago, but we believe he may have not been disposed of properly and was taken away once more."

Mr. Richard look surprised at that last statement. "I assure you, all unfortunates that arrive here are accounted for on receipt, through to their final destination."

"In fact, it was only three nights ago," Holmes added. "The person in whom we are interested arrived at the city morgue with three others. They were quickly dispatched to your establishment."

"We tend to prepare the victims very quickly," said Richard. "He must have been cremated later that day. I could check the files if you like."

He turned to leave, but Holmes stopped him. "That won't be necessary, as we know that the man we are interested in was not cremated. He turned up at the city morgue again, yesterday morning."

Mr. Richard turned, a shocked look on his face. "Impossible. A theft of a body from this establishment has never happened. Not in the hundred years that my family has been running it."

"And I believe that to be the case. However, some evidence may contradict your assertion. If I may be so bold, where were you, exactly, last Tuesday evening?"

Without thought, Richard's hand rose to a small bandage on his neck as he thought up an answer. "I was here," he said. "All night."

"I believe you," said Holmes.

"What?" I asked.

"Quite so, Watson. I believe that Mr. Richard is telling the truth. He was here all night last Thursday. In body, but perhaps not in spirit."

"I don't follow," said Mr. Richard.

"That wound on your neck," questioned Holmes. "Have you had it since Tuesday evening?"

Richard was shocked. He nodded dumbly.

"Perhaps, you were leaving last week and felt a sharp pain in your neck? The last thing you probably remember before waking up the next morning?"

He nodded.

"How?"

"The pane of glass outside the main doors is cracked," he said. "I propose that you stumbled, put your hand out to brace yourself, and broke the glass." Richard raised his right hand. A small cut was visible on the edge of his hand.

"I believe that you were actually attacked as you left," Holmes said. "Where did you wake up?"

"In here," Richards replied, "but I have no idea how. I had locked the doors."

"And the lock," said Holmes, "as I observed earlier, has been broken, but from the inside."

Richard again nodded in agreement.

"From the inside?" I asked.

"Yes," Holmes said.

"By whom?" I was feeling very frustrated.

"Possibly by Dominic Langley. Possibly by Snivelling Pete. Possibly by one of the bodies brought here," said Holmes.

"But," I countered, "but, they were dead."

"And that is the pertinent fact, isn't it?"

***

That afternoon, we bought tickets and departed Paddington on the train to Windsor. Holmes had explained that we had an appointment at Lord Byron Langley's country residence. He had gone there to prepare for Dominic's funeral. I felt that there was something that Lord Byron was keeping from us. Holmes was of the same opinion, although I believed that he knew more than he was letting on. I hoped that he did. The whole question about corpses walking out of funeral homes was causing my doctor's brain to have palpitations.

We disembarked and found a hansom to take us out to Dorney Court, a beautifully presented Tudor house about seven miles from Windsor Station. Holmes remarked that Lord Byron had purchased the manor house before he returned from Jamaica.

"I'm flabbergasted," I said. "I didn't think that the importation of sugar could be so lucrative."

"I think it might be that, and also the other investments that Lord Byron has made over the years – especially the one located in Haiti."

"Haiti?" I asked. "There's that country again. You mentioned Haiti the other day. What about it?"

Holmes smiled. "This is one of the reasons we need to meet with Lord Byron again."

We stepped out of the hansom, crunching gravel underfoot as we made our way to the main doors. I looked up as we walked and noticed the sun setting in the west. The night was going to be clear and I presumed very cold. I was glad I'd worn one of my thickest coats. The same butler met our knocking and, after taking our coats and hats, showed us the way to Lord Byron's study.

The sugar merchant was seated behind an enormous carved oak desk with a pile of paperwork to one side. The desk sat in front of a large window that showed the last vestiges of light as the evening intruded onto the day. Lord Byron's face was grave. I put it down to the arrangements he was undertaking to bury his son. We took seats before his desk and I sat back in the comfortable folds of the well-padded chair. Holmes looked at Lord Byron through his steepled fingers.

"Again," Holmes said, "we are very sorry to intrude on you in your time of grief, but we have come across some very troubling clews and I believe that I need more information from you before I can make sense of everything that has happened."

"Anything at my disposal is yours," said the Lord as he leaned forward, "I just wish to bring the culprits for my son's demise to justice."

"Thank you. Many of the avenues of our inquiry seem to stem from the small Caribbean nation of Haiti."

At the mention of that country, Lord Byron stiffened. Holmes stood and moved across to a nearby cabinet displaying a variety of artefacts. He picked out one and studied it as he began to speak. It seemed to be a bottle made of translucent glass with a small cork stopper. It seemed old, and an inner feeling intruded on my consciousness that urged Holmes to put it back lest it be dropped and broken.

"Your son was in fact killed by a poison called *Tetrodotoxin* – a very rare chemical in this country, but one which is extracted from the common pufferfish found across the world – including the waters of the Caribbean. Another substance was found in his bloodstream that also seemed very curious, a hallucinogen or deliriant derived from the datura plant, or what you may know from your previous homeland as The Devil's Trumpet. Incredibly rare in England, and only a few specimens exist within the hothouse of the botanical gardens in London. The presence of the datura deliriant once again brings up the name of that West Indian country, Haiti. The plant occurs in abundance on the entire island."

"How would my son come into contact with such chemicals here in Britain?" Lord Byron asked.

Holmes turned and smiled at him. "Indeed. A very valid question that I have been pondering for some time."

He uncorked the little bottle and brought it up to his nose. Lord Byron's eyes grew wide. Holmes took the bottle away and studied it. "This is a very old artefact," he said as he turned to look back at Lord Byron. "I place it as mid-eighteenth century, by the looks of it. A perfume bottle I would say, possibly used by a lady of some standing. Perhaps it was one of your ancestors. Your mother, or even your grandmother perhaps? Your grandparents were residents of Jamaica well before your father became the High Commissioner. Isn't that right?"

"Yes. Yes. That is right. My family resided in Jamaica for well over a hundred years. We established the sugar plantations in the central hinterlands at that time and have been importing sugar to Britain and Europe since. How does that have anything to do with all this?"

Holmes put the bottle back then turned and moved closer to the desk. "It's not the sugar that is the primary matter in this case. It's the perfume."

Now I was confused, but then Holmes brought out the glass vial he had found at the warehouse. He held it up. Lord Byron's face went pale.

"You recently procured a plantation on the island of Haiti, did you not?" Holmes asked. "Just before you returned to England."

"Yes," Lord Byron replied. "What of it?"

"The plantation," he said, "grows a special type of grass called *Chrysopogon zizanioides*, commonly called *vetiver*. The plant's oil can be extracted and used in perfumes. From what I understand, the value of the oil is over one hundred times that of sugar by weight. For someone in the export business, this would have been worth its weight in gold. I also understand that in a short time, you have set up a very lucrative arrangement with Yardley and Statham here in London and *Houbigant Parfum* in Paris."

Lord Byron sat staring at Holmes. His face had become impassive as he listened to Holmes explain. "As you said, I'm a businessman. It was a great opportunity, so I jumped at the chance."

Holmes moved a step forward and placed his hands on the edge of the desk. His imposing height allowed him to stare down into Lord Byron's eyes with an intensity that I had always found quite disturbing. "How great was the opportunity?" he asked. "How far were you willing to go to complete the deal?"

Holmes let the question hang. The room became suddenly very quiet. The evening outside was incredibly still with no hint of wind or breeze.

Lord Byron finally broke eye contact with Holmes. He rose unsteadily to his feet and turned away to look through the window, out at the darkening night. "I only did it to ensure the future of my business and safeguard my legacy for Dominic," he said turning back to face Holmes, "The damned Government set up the British Sugar Company four years ago. They grow beets of all things and extract the sugar that way. It was becoming cheaper than importing the real thing. I had to find a way of expanding my operations. When I became aware of the plantation on Haiti, I acted on it."

"But something went wrong, didn't it?" asked Holmes.

Lord Byron's face went grim. "Yes. The local farmers weren't willing to sell. They revered the vetiver plants for some reason. They only farmed what they needed. Had no concept of industrial farming. Something about their heathen religion. I employed local militia to take over and expand the plantations. I offered recompense to the local chieftains, but there was trouble," he said as he turned back to look out the window letting the last statement hang. His head dropped as he fought his conscience.

"Trouble?" I prompted.

He peered back then dropped his eyes. Even a man this resolute in his station in life was disturbed by what he was about to say. "The militia that I employed overplayed their hand," he explained. "They virtually wiped out a local town. Killed the chieftains and members of the council. Any men that took up arms were killed."

He turned back to us. Tears had formed and run down his cheeks. He was truly distressed by the events undertaken in his name. "By the time I found out, it was too late," he said, "I had travelled to the plantation and made what restitution I could with the locals. I dismissed the militia and employed as many of the townsfolk that would work for me. I tried – honestly I did – but they had lost all hope. Their men were dead. Their women left as widows, their children orphans. I returned to Jamaica and started preparations to leave. My heart wasn't in it anymore. I left a manager to continue the operation, but I decided it was time to retire. I vowed to bring Dominic in to take over."

He was weeping profusely by now. "I was almost too late. One night they attacked."

"Who?" Holmes asked.

"*Zombies!*" Lord Byron whispered his face now a wasteland of fear and trepidation.

"Zombies?" I blurted out in disbelief, "Dead people? Re-animated?"

He nodded slowly. "Yes. The townsfolk on Haiti had employed a *caplata*. A dark witch of the Voodoo religion. Capable of raising the dead to do her bidding. That last night, before I set sail, the plantation was attacked. My staff were slaughtered where they stood. My only saving grace was that I was in Kingston awaiting the ship that brought me back to London. I found out after I arrived. That was two years ago. I haven't returned."

He pulled out a handkerchief and blotted the tears from his eyes. A strange resolve seemed to come over him. I'm still not sure if it was an acceptance of fate or a shimmer of courage to face the unknown. He stood to his full height and spoke one last time.

"I feel that she's here," he said. "I now believe that she killed my son, turned him into a zombie and bade him to set fire to the warehouse. I know that I cannot fight her plague of dead men, but I will not go down meekly. I ran before, but now I must face my accuser and plead my case."

I was impressed but confused at his stance. He was, of course, guilty of the deaths of many people, if not by his word at least by his deed.

Suddenly, Lord Byron's guilt was no longer a factor in this case. I started to form a question on my lips when all hell broke loose, and it was forever forgotten in the maelstrom that followed.

A scream issued from deep in the house. All heads turned towards the cry. The sound of glass breaking made Holmes and me turn back to face the sugar merchant.

Several panes on the window behind him imploded inwards. Pairs of arms reached in through the broken glass. My doctor's mind noticed the long gashes form down their length as the jagged glass shards bit deep into their flesh. Blood flowed as they reached for Lord Byron. He screamed as he was grabbed by many hands and wrenched off his feet.

I remarked in my mind's eye that the owners of the arms were incredibly strong, as Lord Byron was by no means a small man. He was dragged bodily through the broken window and disappeared, leaving only a scream hanging in the tumult.

I sprang to my feet, ready to run to Lord Byron's aid. Holmes had already vaulted the desk and was peering into the gloom beyond the window.

"What in blazes happened?" escaped my lips as I ran. Holmes continued to peer into the dark grounds outside.

"Zombies, it seems, Watson," he said, matter-of-factly.

"What?" I asked.

Before he could answer, the door into the study burst open. We both turned.

Standing in the doorway was a black woman. She wore richly coloured robes and had strange designs painted across her face in light colours. She stepped into the room and was followed by two slack-jawed men. They stood well over six feet tall, their arms hung by their sides and their eyes were glazed and unable to focus.

As I turned to look at Holmes, something struck my neck. It stung like an insect bite. I raised my hand and pulled the offending item from my throat. It was a small feathered dart.

My mind became clouded, my vision blurred. I managed to turn and stare at the woman once more. She held a long hollow tube to her mouth. A small sound of expelled air followed. Something flew past my face and the tiny grunt I heard could only have been Holmes.

Darkness began to cover my eyes. I fought to maintain control, but gravity won, and I fell to my knees. The wooden floor was the last thing that I saw before the shadows drew a close to my consciousness.

***

My eyes blinked open and drew focus on a white tiled ceiling. I lay for a moment gathering my thoughts and trying to determine where I was when a figure passed into my view. He wore a blood-stained white coat and mask and held a pair of forceps in one hand and a scalpel in the other. As the scalpel hand came closer, I thrust up my right hand up and stopped its descent.

He yelped and jumped back slightly. "Good Lord! Dr. Watson – You're alive!" he said, dragging the mask from his face.

I immediately recognised Smithers. I tried to sit up. Smithers aided me, and I realised I was sitting on an autopsy table in the morgue.

I looked around and saw Holmes lying on the table next to me. Thankfully he hadn't been the object of Smithers's occupation yet. The table beyond held a larger body, covered in a blood-soaked sheet.

Smithers noticed where I was looking.

"Lord Byron Langley," he said. "The constables said he was mauled by a wild animal or . . . something. I'm still trying to determine by what."

"Holmes?" I managed to croak.

"Dead. Like you – " he said, before rushing over to where Holmes lay.

He bent down and listened. He then stood and lightly slapped Holmes on the cheeks. A harder slap brought a groan from the recumbent form of my associate. His eyes flickered and opened. Within moments he sat up and looked around. The fog lifting quickly from his drugged mind. He focused on me and a wry smile came to his face.

"We survived," he said. "She mustn't have wanted us to join her zombie army."

"What?" Smithers and I both asked.

"The *caplata*," said Holmes. I sat staring at him with a confused expression.

"The *caplata*. The black woman. A female voodoo witch hired by the townsfolk in Haiti. It all makes sense now."

I didn't share his feeling of completion. "In what way?"

He took a deep breath, closed his eyes for a moment then continued. "Dominic Langley was hunted down and turned into a zombie by a voodoo priestess. Under the influence of *datari*, she was able to coerce him into lighting a fire in Lord Byron's warehouse. Not only did she want him dead, but she wanted to destroy his life as well. Very vindictive, but I suppose it sent a message. In the end, she led her zombies to Lord Byron's estate and finished what she had been employed to do."

I was still confused but had to know. "What about us?"

He smiled. "We were poisoned with *tetrodotoxin*. Not enough to kill, just enough to disable us. We were lucky. Any more poison and Smithers here would have needed to conduct real autopsies. As it is, we survive to fight another day."

"The zombies?" I asked, "What about the zombies?"

"Ah, similar to us, I suppose," he said, looking around the morgue. "The *caplata* poisons them with enough to disable and incapacitate. They appear to be dead but are in reality alive. She then administers the *datari* and bends their will to do her bidding. I wouldn't be surprised if Smithers receives several more clients over the next couple of days as the zombies are found. They will either recover or to cover her tracks, the *caplata* will probably administer more poison to finish the job."

I contemplated what Holmes had said, but one question remained. "Dominic Langley," I said. "He was dead *before* he entered the warehouse. You established that as there was no soot in his throat."

"Yes?"

"So . . . how did he set fire to the place?"

Holmes stared at me blankly as his mind tried to determine the answer.

The Adventure of the Disappearing Debutante

It was late spring in 1882 when a knock at the front door of 221b Baker Street presented my good friend Sherlock Holmes with an unexpected opportunity.

The caller was a simple messenger boy who delivered an expensively embossed invitation to Holmes on behalf of his old university friend, Roderick St. John-Smythe. I was the one to answer the door, partly to relieve our landlady, Mrs. Hudson, of the chore, and also because of a slight case of boredom.

I brought the envelope to Holmes, who proceeded to withdraw the card within, accompanied by a single-page handwritten letter. He began to smile a little as he read to himself, before explaining the details to me.

"It's from Roderick. It seems that we have been asked to attend a coming-out ceremony."

I was a little surprised, as it didn't seem the type of occasion in which Roderick or Holmes would have shown an interest.

"Any idea why?"

"No. There's no mention of a reason. I believe that Roderick may be trying to introduce me into polite society, or perhaps to pair us up with young ladies to take us away from this bachelor life of ours."

"That may be worthwhile then," I said. "I don't intend to stay single all my life."

"And good for you, Watson. I myself would need to meet someone extremely special before I shrug off my bachelor ways."

"Indeed," I answered with as healthy a dose of cynicism as one word could allow.

"Regardless of the bevy of young ladies on display, I believe that the event may prove useful from another front altogether."

"Such as?"

"There will no doubt be many affluent gentlemen at this event. Some there to display their eligible daughters, others there to examine the goods on offer."

I was a little put out by Holmes's graphic description of such a time-honoured event as a debutante ball.

"That's a little harsh, isn't it?"

He noticed my expression and smiled.

"I do apologise, but I find these sorts of evenings little more than a few steps above a slave auction in medieval Arabia. But I'll still go. It may be amusing. It may even be beneficial. I hope to make the acquaintance of some of the gentlemen there and, when next they are in need of services such as I can provide," he finished, "my name will spring to mind."

Three nights later, I stood in our sitting room, dressed in my finest black-tie ensemble. I was a little put-out, as I'd hoped to be allowed to wear my dress uniform and show off my medals. Ladies of all stations have always been drawn to the trappings of service, but Roderick's invitation and a follow-up telegram stated that the men must be attired in simple black-tie. Something about not taking the attention away from the debutantes, and especially the guest of honour. Who this guest was to be was a question to which I would seek an answer on arrival.

Holmes stepped out of his rooms resplendent in his own ensemble and immediately I felt rather frumpy. The long black suit highlighted the tall, slim stature of my friend, and even accentuated his aquiline features so that he appeared even more devilishly handsome than usual.

"Ready then, Watson?" he asked.

"Er, yes. Ready."

"Good, good. Let's be on our way then, shall we?"

Downstairs, we found that the night had set in, as the invitation was for nine o'clock, well after the dinner hour. Luckily, Mrs. Hudson had provided a sumptuous feast to keep us going. She had hinted it was to forestall any effects of the champagne that would certainly be on offer.

A hansom sat outside, ready to whisk us to our destination. We didn't have to travel far, as after a quick trot through Marylebone and Mayfair we arrived at St. James's Square. Before us stood Cleveland

House, the London townhouse of our host for the evening, Harry Powlett, the fourth Duke of Cleveland.

Cleveland House is a lovely four-storey Georgian mansion overlooking St. James's Park. My understanding is that it was used only rarely on such occasions, as the Duke spent most of his time in County Durham, at the family home of Raby Castle.

Our hansom was greeted by a footman and we followed the red carpet to the front door, where we handed our invitation to a doorman who announced us as Mr. Sherlock Holmes and Dr. John Watson.

A few heads amongst the assembled guests turned towards us, but failing recognition returned to their own conversations.

We stood on the small landing for a moment, peering across the assembled guests. I noticed a lovely melody creeping across the room from a string quartet nestled on a balcony above the main ballroom.

As Holmes and I stepped into the throng of people, one well-presented guest made his way over. I thrust my hand out to greet Roderick.

"Thank you ever so much for inviting us," I said.

"My pleasure. It was mostly as a favour to the Duke. He had asked for an assemblage of the most eligible bachelors in London."

"And you think we are included in that group," asked Holmes.

"I didn't really care. You two just happened to come to mind."

Roderick stopped talking as a tall, elegant man in full dress uniform, complete with feathered headdress, a line of medals, a ceremonial sword, and a blood-red sash across his chest stepped into the room. I was a little miffed at seeing the man, as I would have liked the chance to wear my own uniform.

The doorman announced, "Presenting his grace, Baron Sebastian Von Steurer of Bavaria."

"A German," I retorted out loud, receiving a slightly reproachful look from Roderick.

He waited until the Baron and his coterie had moved away before answering. "Yes. Another reason the Duke wanted so many eligible bachelors here," he said, "All will become clear in a few minutes."

I kept an eye on the Baron as he made his way through the crowd, stopping from time to time to make the acquaintance of someone he obviously knew. I had never heard of him, but admit it was probably due to the fact I rarely circulated in these sorts of social circles.

Eventually, the Baron stopped before an older but very proud and upright man who sported a healthy shock of silver-grey hair and an impressive lion's mane beard with no moustache. He was dressed in a tail suit, with a single pin on his left lapel showing three swords leaning in with their points almost touching. I assumed it was the family crest or arms.

Roderick noticed my fascination and spoke up. "Ah, you've spied our host then," he said.

I was a little taken aback. "That's the Duke?" I asked.

"Yes. This entire affair is to introduce his young daughter, Elizabeth, into noble society."

I then noticed a woman standing demurely behind the Duke. She was small and a little diminutive, but attractive. She appeared to be around twenty years younger than the Duke.

"The woman is his wife, Lady Catherine Stanhope. They married late, as the Duke was engaged with his business affairs abroad for much of his early life. The child was a surprise to both of them, I think, but now the Duke wants only the best for her."

"To a point," Holmes piped up. "She has been promised to the Baron, has she not? Not something I would prefer for my own child if I had one."

Roderick harrumphed under his breath.

"Well, yes. That is partly why I am here, after all. The engagement was coordinated by the Home Office, along with the blessing of the Duke, who will benefit remarkably from the business opportunities between the two countries that this match will bring about."

I was flabbergasted. "You mean to tell me that poor young girl is just a pawn in some diplomatic and business coup?"

"Well, if you put it that way," said Roderick, "yes. It's not any different to the proposals made between Royal families of old. It will be of great benefit to her family and to the country as a whole. The British and German governments have been negotiating a trading pact for some time now. The Baron here is a senior member of the

Emperor's cabinet. We wished to open up channels of communication between our two countries. The Baron will receive a one-off payment of fifty-thousand pounds, and the marriage between himself and Lady Elizabeth seals the deal."

It was my turn to harrumph. Holmes simply smiled. "Fear not, Watson," he said. "Some things have a way of working themselves out,"

A loud voice rang out from across the room. We all turned to find a footman in full Georgian dress standing before a doorway and reading from an unfurled scroll of parchment.

"My ladies and gentlemen, if you would give me your attention please."

I realised this was the moment that the debutantes were to be introduced, and joined the group around me in forming a small open circular area for them to enter and parade around.

The Duke and the Baron were accommodated with positions at the front of their group.

Two doormen opened a pair of ornate brass doors and a line of beautifully attired young ladies could be seen stretching off down the corridor. Each was attended by a maidservant, making final touches to their hair, makeup, and dress.

The footman began, "May I present Lady Josephine Swann."

A tall, slightly gangly girl strode into the room. She appeared quite embarrassed, probably because she was the first to be introduced. She found her confidence and made her way past the assembled guests, her eyes meeting each in turn and stopping on one fellow across the circle from myself. I imagined this was her particular favourite and would be afforded the first dance in short time.

The footman continued and presently announced the arrival of ten other girls who followed the tall girl into the room and milled around in the circle under the calculating gaze of all and sundry.

I noticed the footman peer over at the doorway as he was about to announce another name. The lack of a further debutante stopped him short. He strode across and checked with the doormen. They both shook their heads. One marched down the hallway but returned quickly shaking his head and speaking in hushed tones to the footman.

The footman's face flushed red and sweat popped out on his forehead. He resumed his position and addressed the gathering one last time.

"My ladies and gentlemen, the band will now strike up for the first dance," he said, peering up at the band leader, who nodded to the footman and then to the other instrumentalists. Soon a lilting melody filtered over the crowd and young men approached each of the debutantes, in turn, to ask for their hand in a dance.

The rest of the crowd withdrew to the edges of the room to allow the courtship ritual to continue.

I noticed a new commotion erupt near the entrance-way and caught sight of the Baron and Duke in animated conversation. The Duke's face was flushed red – possibly with anger, probably with embarrassment.

I realised that his daughter was not among the young girls introduced previously and that this was the cause of the Baron's protestations. I continued to watch as they both made their way from the room, through the debutantes' entrance.

I turned back towards Holmes and Roderick to see a young man approach from a side doorway. He stepped up to Roderick and whispered in his ear. Roderick nodded several times and waved the man away. He closed in on Holmes and me and spoke.

"If you would both be so kind to accompany me, I think your services would be of valuable assistance," he said.

We followed the young man and quickly made our way out of the ballroom and down a nearby corridor. He stopped outside of another doorway and indicated for the three of us to enter.

Inside, we found the red-faced Duke and the even redder-faced Baron, still embroiled in a heated conversation.

"I do not understand why you would embarrass me in such a way," the Baron said, his voice thick with a German accent.

The Duke was obviously trying to defuse the situation but failing miserably. He held his hands out in placation, but the Baron did not seem to want any consolation.

"Sebastian, I have no idea what Elizabeth is up to. I don't know what could have happened but can only think of the worst. Do you think I would expend so much money on this event if it was only to embarrass you?"

The Baron looked long at hard into the Duke's eyes and a slight hint of calm crossed his face.

"No. Not unless you wish to do yourself an injury. What do you intend to do about it, then?"

The Duke looked across at Roderick and sighed in relief. "Roderick, thank goodness," he said and indicated the three of us to the Baron.

"Yes, I know this Roderick," said the Baron then continued. "These two," as he indicated Holmes and myself, "I do not know."

Roderick quickly introduced the two of us and added, "I invited them along tonight simply as they are eligible bachelors, but Sherlock Holmes is also a renowned consulting detective and, by chance, can add a level of investigation that would be problematic due to my position within Her Majesty's government."

Holmes quickly took the lead, turning to the Duke and saying, "Can you please explain what has happened, from the start, and do not leave out any details, no matter how small."

The Duke pursed his lips and regarded him for a moment before starting. "My daughter, Elizabeth, has recently come of age. A pivotal time in any woman's life, but more so for Elizabeth, as it makes her eligible for wedlock. In this case, I negotiated her hand in marriage to the Baron."

The Baron stood prouder and puffed out his chest slightly, no doubt assuming to affect more of a presence. Personally, I was unimpressed and hopefully hid my views from those around me.

"And in return . . . ?" prompted Holmes.

"In return, there would be a discreet change in the way Bavaria exchanged business with my companies – a benefit to both my family and to England as a whole."

"The reason that Roderick was involved," he said.

"Yes, precisely," said the Duke.

160

"Was your daughter accepting of this arrangement?" Holmes asked.

"What does that have to do with anything?" the Duke replied. "She is of noble stock, and that has been an expected part of her future – to accept the contract of marriage as negotiated by myself."

I could hold my tongue no longer. "But surely in these enlightened times, such a forced proposal would be rejected by the younger members of even the most noblest of families."

The Duke blanched at my suggestion. A tiny smile crossed Holmes's lips.

"That is immaterial," he answered. "The arrangement was made. It is Elizabeth's duty to accede to it."

"That may well be so," Holmes countered, "but we should investigate all facets of this mystery. There is the *why*, plus the *how*, the *when*, and naturally the *where* to determine before we can close this case. Also," he added, "the *who*."

"The *who*?" I asked.

"Yes. *Who* stands to benefit from Lady Elizabeth's disappearance? *Who* does it most affect? *Who* could be responsible? Even *who* is the root cause?"

I nodded.

"I don't understand," said the Baron.

"Well, sir, we simply must establish various facts," Holmes continued. "Was this a kidnapping?" The Duke's face dropped in shock. "Is it an attempt at ransom? Or is it simply a sign of cold feet on behalf of the young woman? All ideas are relevant until we dismiss them one by one."

Holmes stepped towards the entrance to the parlour and then turned back. "First, shall we retrace young Elizabeth's steps?"

***

The Baron followed us for a while but decided to return to his lodgings. It turned out that he had been offered rooms within Cleveland House as a guest of the Duke, a fact that I found interesting in itself, and I noticed that it also piqued Holmes's curiosity.

161

The Duke led us to the first-floor bedrooms, and we stopped outside of Elizabeth's room. Holmes turned back to the Duke. "Do you know if anyone has examined this room?" he asked.

"I have no idea," he said. "I can only assume that one of my servants came here to confirm that my daughter was missing."

Holmes actually smiled. "Good," he replied. "That means it should remain almost exactly as it was when Lady Elizabeth left it."

He opened the door and peered in. The gaslight was still burning, casting a yellow pallor. It was a large double room with a free-standing four-poster bed along the centre of one wall. A wardrobe and tallboy sat opposite, with a dressing area complete with a mirror beside it. Nestled against the opposite wall sat a small dressing table and writing desk.

Holmes entered and glanced around. I followed close behind, not wanting to miss any of his investigative techniques. However, I purposely stopped in the doorway to restrict entry by the others in our party. A harrumph from the Duke greeted my actions. I stood my ground until he spoke. "I say, Doctor if you wouldn't mind moving aside so I may enter," he said.

Holmes spun and held up a hand. "If you would be so kind and please do not enter until I have finished my initial investigation."

This was greeted with another harrumph and an audible sigh. Holmes ignored both and continued to peer around, not touching anything while he perused the scene in its entirety. Finally, he moved across to the writing desk and peered down. I noticed a folded piece of parchment sitting in the middle of the desk.

Holmes reached for a small pencil and gently pushed the folded page open until he was able to read it. His expression was one of intense interest. I noticed a small smile play on his lips for a moment before being replaced by a more serious look.

He dropped the pencil onto the desk and reached inside his pocket for a kerchief. He used the small square of cloth to smooth open the parchment, then picked it up and brought it across to the doorway.

"What have you there?" asked Roderick.

"The first clew in this mystery," Holmes said, "though it may be all that is required for now."

Roderick withdrew a pair of gloves from his jacket and took the proffered note in hand. He read aloud for the benefit of the rest of us.

"*To the Duke of Cleveland*," he said. "*We have your daughter. There will be no marriage between a Bavarian prince and the non-Teutonic spawn of the Englander.*" Then he added, "It is signed by The Sons of Bavaria."

He handed the note back to Holmes before turning to the Duke. "I am so sorry, your Grace," he said. "It would seem that your daughter has indeed been kidnapped, and by some German resistance group. I've never even heard of these 'Sons of Bavaria'."

The Duke's face was a mesh of anger and fear and glowed bright red with it. "We must talk to the Baron, immediately," he said, "And have the local constabulary search high and low. My daughter must be found."

The Duke, Roderick, and the Duke's valet left at high speed, leaving Holmes and me alone. I was slightly mystified. It was then I heard Holmes chuckling to himself. I turned to find a grin across his face.

"You find the kidnapping of this young girl funny?" I asked.

Holmes opened the note which was the first chance I'd had to have a good look. The writing was a delicate flowing script. It occurred to me straight away that this was a woman's handwriting. When he saw that I'd finished, Holmes moved back to the writing desk and began to search the drawers. He finally found the object of his search and straightened up, holding a small diary. He opened to the first page and read the name inscribed there.

"Lady Elizabeth's journal," he said.

He placed it on the desk and opened to a random page full of a similar flowing script. He put the note above and compared the two writing styles.

He let out a little sigh of anguish as I noticed that the two scripts didn't match as he would have first imagined. He flipped through several pages until one particular passage stuck out from the rest. The writing on this page was almost identical to that of the note.

"What do you surmise?" I asked.

"Well the diary is most certainly Elizabeth's – it has her name on the first page. I assume that the lighter, more-delicate script is hers. The single passage that matches the note must have been made by another."

He flipped through the diary and found two more passages in the same style. "I would say these were written by a very close confidant of Miss Elizabeth. A close friend or . . . ."

He stood up and smiled at me.

"Or?" I asked. "A maidservant. Somebody that would be as close as a friend and always be with Lady Elizabeth."

He read one of the passages and another laconic smile grew on his face. "Yes. This passage follows on from the previous one, but that was written in Elizabeth's hand. I would say that it was dictated to somebody whilst she was predisposed, possibly while she was in the bath."

He checked the pages closely and then showed it to me. His finger pointed to two small discoloured circles at the top of the page. "Water droplets," he said.

"Extraordinary," I replied. "But what does it mean?"

"Our young Elizabeth has either staged her own kidnapping, or this maid-servant was responsible."

"That seems unlikely."

"Indeed," he said. "I would think that there is something more that has triggered Lady Elizabeth's actions. We must ensure that she left of her own free will, and then determine why."

"Should we tell the Duke or Roderick?" I asked.

Holmes grinned. "Why would we do that? They have their investigation to pursue, and it will keep them busy and out of our hair long enough that we might even solve this case without them."

I nodded in agreement.

Holmes moved across to the wardrobe and opened it. The wardrobe was half full, with several bare hangers dangling from the rack. A couple had fallen to the base and lay abandoned. The remaining clothing was of a very high quality, suited to a woman of

Elizabeth's station in life. Satin and silk dresses for formal occasions, plus several cotton dresses for day-wear.

Holmes closed the door and moved to the tallboy. He opened and examined several drawers, finding a similar result with two of them being only half-filled with clothing and essentials. There was a drawer dedicated to Elizabeth's smalls, which I was a bit embarrassed that we were investigating, but Holmes in his wisdom simply opened it to check its emptiness before closing it once more.

Another held several exquisite silk scarves, neatly rolled up. Again, several were missing, not something that would require laundering all at once.

He closed the last drawer and stared at the four hat stands arrayed on the top. Only three held hats, and those were of the delicate type used for formal occasions.

"What do you think, Watson?" he asked.

"Someone has packed for a trip, perhaps," I replied, "or it's washing day, though given that there are scarves and a hat missing, I would be surprised if those items are located in the scullery."

One of Holmes's eyebrows raised. He moved across to a small wicker basket and glanced inside. I checked as well. It was empty.

"Could still be washing day, I suppose," Holmes said as he headed for the doorway.

"Where to next?"

"The laundry, of course. Not just to check on the young lady's clothing, but below-stairs is always a good place for gossip and hearsay."

**

As we descended the stairs to the basement, the noise of suppressed conversation was palpable. It was obvious that word of Lady Elizabeth's disappearance had reached the underground world of Cleveland House.

As we stepped out of the stairwell shadow and into the dimly lit passageway, two maids, engaged in a deep conversation, immediately straightened up, almost dropping their loads of plates and towels. They scurried off before we could even apologise.

We made our way down the long passageway towards the bowels of the basement. Tiny snatches of conversation ceased as soon as we were in eyesight of the speakers.

Finally, we reached the kitchen and stepped through into the scullery. A large, formidable-looking woman was busily running a tablecloth across a washboard. A large red stain spoiled the appearance of the normally crisp white linen and seemed to be drawing its own ire from the woman.

After a moment of patient waiting, Holmes let out a small cough. The woman jumped and dropped the cloth into the bucket in her fright. She turned around a hint of anger on her face which disappeared as soon as she saw us.

Immediately she stepped down from her stool and wiped her sudsy hands against her apron. "My word," she asked. "Are you two gentlemen lost?"

"Not at all," replied Holmes. "We seem to have found the person we were seeking."

"Me?" she asked. "Why?"

"If I am not mistaken, you would be the person most skilled in the laundering of this household's clothing."

Her chest puffed up at the slight compliment. "Why yes, that would be me," she said. "What can I do for you then? Have you soiled your lovely suits?"

Holmes smiled. "No, nothing like that, but thank you for offering. We are investigating the location of the Duke's young daughter."

The woman's face dropped. "That poor dear. If those Germans harm one hair on her head, then they'll have to deal with me."

I felt that I wouldn't want to be in the kidnappers' shoes – if there were kidnappers.

"And that is a sentiment shared by me and my associate here, Dr. John Watson."

"Oh, a doctor, aye. Well, I'm Mrs. Havsham, if you have a mind to know. Been in this house for nigh on twenty years. Seen that lovely lass grow up, and would never wish any harm to her."

"Quite so," said Holmes, "You are the perfect person then to help our inquiries. Would you know if young Elizabeth has any clothing that has been brought here for laundering?"

"That's a very personal question," she said, tensing a little before smiling, "But you seem to be a lovely gentleman, so I will tell you. No. I'm surprised, but there's naught been brought down here for a day or so."

"Interesting," said Holmes.

Mrs. Havsham was about to speak when a very loud voice cut through from the folding room next door. We turned to see an attractive flame-haired young woman dressed in a kitchen hand's uniform float down the stairway into the room carrying an armload of tablecloths. She directed her speech to a straight-backed man who stood at the shoe bench, polishing a pair of knee-high boots.

"Hello, Fritz," she said. "What's up with your master this evening? I haven't seen him since before luncheon."

The man stopped working, a look of intense hatred bordering on fury crossing his face. "My name is Friedrich, not Fritz," he said in a very thick German accent before diverting his attention back to the boots.

"Doris," said Mrs. Havsham. "Leave the Baron's man alone and get those over here."

Doris smiled, walked into the scullery, and across to the washing barrel. She dumped the tablecloths onto the ground and clapped her hands together, releasing a cloud of white powder.

"Don't know why they needs me to go up and get these. Those maids upstairs are just lazy good-for-nothings."

Mrs. Havsham face showed a look of indignation. Her reply was a little sharp. "The maids have guest rooms to prepare and beds to turn down. You were asked to help out, so there should be no argument."

"I have pastries to bake for the morning," she said, turning around and heading back to the kitchen.

Mrs. Havsham shook her head. "Don't know what gets into their heads nowadays."

We bid her a good evening and Holmes stepped into the folding room, with me close behind. Friedrich was busy with his boots and ignored us. He was wearing a starched white shirt with a dark tie with a vest, matching his black trousers. I noticed a small red-and-white pin in the lapel of his vest. It had the look of a pin given for having been in military service.

Meanwhile, Holmes was scrutinizing a nearby pile of laundry, topped by a jacket that clearly belonged to the Baron. He leaned in and pulled a long red hair from the shoulder. It was then I noticed a small smear of white powder on the arm. My eyes grew wide.

"Can I help you?" came Friedrich's voice from behind us.

Holmes turned towards the valet and studied him for a moment. The valet began to become very agitated before Holmes spoke to him in German. "*Sie sind der Mann des Barons?*" he asked. (You are the Baron's man?)

Friedrich straightened. I spied a military background just by his posture. "*Ja. Seit vielen Jahren bin ich mit ihm zusammen,*" he said. ("Yes. For many years I have been with him.")

Holmes returned to English, much to my happiness, and continued. "Ah, born in Saxony, I think?"

Friedrich's eyes opened wide as if he had seen Holmes perform an unexpected magic trick. I was growing used to the way that Holmes could pick apart a person's life solely through observation.

"Yes, but how?"

"And from your posture, I would say Army – First Royal Saxon Corps, perhaps?"

Friedrich's face softened slightly. He appeared intrigued by Holmes's remarks. "Yes, but – ?"

Holmes cut him off. "Is this your first time in England?"

"No. Ve have come here a number of times. The Baron has interests in this country. He keeps a close eye on them."

"And the Duke?" Holmes asked.

"Yes. The Duke and the Baron have long known each other. The Duke has companies that deal vith the Baron's as vell."

"Interesting. And the Lady Elizabeth? She has known the Baron for a while?"

"Not really." He stopped and put the boot brush down. An exasperated look appeared on his face, and he looked like one under some internal torment. He stared off into space and began to speak more to himself than to us. "It's these Englanders. They have changed the Baron. He vas never interested in politics, just business. Then they arrange this marriage to the young Lady Elizabeth. The Baron has always liked the ladies. Especially the young ones. He has never vanted just one, so I don't understand it. It does not make any of the sense."

He suddenly caught himself and realised what he'd been saying. He remembered his chores, picked up the boot brush, and began polishing the boots once more. "If you'll excuse me, I am the busy," he said.

Holmes turned and moved back into the scullery. He stepped up to Mrs. Havsham again.

"I beg your pardon again, madam," he said.

Mrs. Havsham stopped her washing, happy to have Holmes's attention once again, and dried her hands on her apron. "Not a problem, sir."

"The young Lady Elizabeth, and the Baron?" he asked.

Mrs. Havsham's face went very serious. She checked on Friedrich, then looked from side to side before leaning in closer to us.

"All arranged without young Elizabeth's consent. The Duke has sold her off to further his business interests, and that old lech just wants to get his hands on a young filly, if you know what I mean. He's never been able to keep his hands off them since he's been coming here."

She stopped herself when she realised what she'd said. She started to turn, but Holmes asked one more question. "Lady Elizabeth would have needed a maidservant, would she not?"

Mrs. Havsham nodded, "Yes, that would be Caitlin. Caitlin Brown."

"Where could I find her?"

"She should be around unless she's gone for the day. She has family over in Lambeth. Since we've come back to London, she's been going home regularly to see them. Check with Mrs. Scunthorpe, the housekeeper, just down the hall," she said pointing off down the corridor.

Holmes smiled and said, "Thank you, Mrs. Havsham. Sorry to have taken your time."

"It's all right," came her reply as she turned her attention back to the washing.

Holmes took my arm and led me away. We moved through the kitchen where Doris was busy making pies, her arms dusted in flour up to the elbows. She noticed us and smiled coyly. I nodded in reply as we moved on.

***

Luckily for us, Mrs. Scunthorpe was in her room, readying herself for the servants' evening meal. Our appearance brought an interested look to her face. "Are you gentlemen lost?" she asked. "The party is still going upstairs. I can take you back if you wish."

"No, that will be quite alright, Mrs. Scunthorpe. I am Sherlock Holmes, and this is my associate, Dr. John Watson. We are assisting with determining the location of young Elizabeth, and were hoping that you could help us."

Mrs. Scunthorpe sat down heavily, almost in a faint. She put a hand to her forehead in anguish. "Oh, my, this has been a night. I think we've kept it from most of the guests, but it won't be long. I'm happy to provide any help to find that young girl, and soon."

"I understand that her maid's name is Caitlin Brown," Holmes said.

"Yes."

"She would probably have been the last person to have seen Elizabeth, and presumably would have been helping to ready her before the introductions. Has she been around since then?"

Mrs. Scunthorpe thought for a moment, a quizzical look on her face, and then shook her head. "No. I haven't seen her since earlier. The guests finished dinner around seven o'clock, and the young ladies went back to their rooms to prepare for the ball. Elizabeth and Caitlin went past me as I was coming upstairs to supervise the removal of all the dinner dishes, but since then I haven't seen hide nor hair of her." She sat bolt upright. "You don't think that she was kidnapped as well, do you? Or worse, that *she's* the kidnapper?"

Holmes held his hands up to calm the housekeeper. "No, no, nothing like that, I assure you. We just need to retrace Elizabeth's steps and talk to Caitlin. Could you give us her home address?"

"Certainly," she said and quickly pulled out a piece of paper and a pencil, jotting down a Lambeth address.

Holmes smiled and took the paper.

Mrs. Scunthorpe looked up at him, her eyes full of anguish. "Please find our young Elizabeth. She's a good girl. She doesn't deserve any of this."

"You mean the kidnapping?" Holmes asked.

"Oh, and that as well," she said, his question drawing a look of surprise.

***

As we climbed the stairs back to the ground floor, I had to ask Holmes a question. "The First Royal Saxon Corps? It was the pin on Friedrich's vest's lapel, wasn't it?"

"Why, yes, it was. Well done."

"Is that how you determined his accent?"

Holmes smiled. "Actually, no. I met a fellow student at University who was born and raised in Leipzig. I polished my very basic German by conversing with him from time to time. Some of his pronunciation was vastly different to what I'd learned, and we decided that it was because of the local dialect influences."

"Outstanding," I said. "Where to next?"

"Well, I believe a short trip is in order," he said, holding the small scrap of paper in his hand. "I feel that the current occupants of this address will reveal a lot more about this mystery than anything else."

We walked a short distance down the corridor before hearing stern voices coming from a room nearby. We stopped and crept up to the doorway. They belonged to the Duke, the Baron, and Roderick. From the tone and volume, the Baron was enraged.

"This disappearance is a ruse! You are just trying to humiliate me. What more do you want? More money? More business contacts? I'm very close to forgetting everything and returning home. The Emperor will not be amused."

Roderick piped up, "I assure you, your Grace, there has been no intent by either the British Government or by the Duke himself to undermine this deal. For all we know, Lady Elizabeth has been kidnapped and is in great danger as we speak."

"The police have been informed," said the Duke. "The Government has dispatched agents to search as well. I am at my wit's end. This is my only daughter we are speaking of here. I can only assume that we will receive a ransom note soon. I will pay whatever they ask to get Elizabeth back."

"That may be so," said the Baron, "But what if the Lady Elizabeth is soured by this experience? What if she returns damaged? I was promised a young beauty. If that is no longer the case, then where is my recompense? In fact, I may simply walk away from this deal altogether. It seems very slovenly for the British Government to have let these brigands snatch the Lady from under their noses."

We could hear the Duke simply bristling in rage. "See here! That's my daughter you're talking about!" he said, his voice rising in volume along with his anger.

Roderick stepped up and diffused the situation. "I'm sure that Her Majesty's Government was not responsible for this act, and I'm also sure they would be happy to provide compensation, or indeed improve your situation, should anything untoward arise."

"Very well," said the Baron. He suddenly appeared at the doorway, causing us both to jump back in surprise. He had a wry smile on his face which didn't fade when he came upon the two of us. He quickly looked each of us in the eye and continued on down the corridor. I felt that he would have been quite happy to whistle a jaunty tune as he did. I started to have severe doubts about his innocence in all this.

Roderick appeared at the door. "There you are. Anything new?" he asked. "We need to find this lass as soon as possible. The favourability of this deal for the Government is degrading by the minute."

Holmes replied, "I understand your concern, but there was nothing new in her room. We questioned a few of the staff and nothing either. I plan to journey home and contact my Irregulars. They have an ear to the street and may have come across these so-called 'Sons of Bavaria'."

Roderick thought for a moment and then nodded. "Agreed. I have men working on it as we speak, but they don't have as close an insight into the criminal underbelly as your urchins do." He pulled out a pocket watch and we realised it was well past eleven o'clock. "Hmm. I daresay there will not be much sleep gained in this house tonight, but that will only lead to more anger and indecision. Meet us back here in the early morning – say eight o'clock. Hopefully, there will be more information by then. With any real hope, we may have even found the Lady Elizabeth."

"Indeed," said Holmes.

With that, Roderick went back into the room to inform the Duke. We turned on our heels and proceeded to the front door.

***

As we alighted from the hansom that dropped us in front of 221b Baker Street, Holmes stepped to the side of the footpath and spied up and down the street. He focused on a shadowy spot a couple of houses away, held up his hand, and clicked his fingers. I swore that the shadows dissolved and a figure moved quickly away.

The hansom drew away and I turned to enter our house just as a young boy in filthy clothes ran up to Holmes. "Wiggins," Holmes said.

The boy, Wiggins, removed his flat cap and addressed Holmes. "'Ello Mr. 'Olmes. Sorry, I took so long. What can we do for you this fine evening?"

"Small job for you. I need someone to keep a watch on Cleveland House at St. James Square. Pay particular attention to a German called Baron Von Steurer – tall, fifty, grey hair, moustache. I want to know what his movements are." He turned towards me, "Watson, do you have a crown on you?"

I fished around in my purse, drew forth a silver coin, and dropped it into Holmes's hand. He turned and gave it to Wiggins. It disappeared into a pocket as quickly as it appeared in his hand.

"Here, this should cover any expenses you'll have. Whoever goes will be there all night. Stay out of sight and send word if the Baron leaves"

"Is the prize on offer?" Wiggins asked.

Holmes smiled, "Naturally. Anyone who brings me a vital clew will receive a guinea, as always."

Wiggins gave a mock salute, placed his hat on his head, and said, "Right you are Mr. 'Olmes. We are on the case." He turned and hightailed it down the way he'd come with increased speed.

"I'd hate to say it," I commented, "but I think that the police will still be putting their boots on by the time your Irregulars have come up with solid clews."

"Quite so. It's amazing what can be achieved with an eager force of invisible urchins and a little cash incentive. Now let's change. We have another address to visit before this night is out."

***

By the time the hansom dropped us outside the Lambeth address supplied by Mrs. Scunthorpe, it was well into the wee hours of the morning.

There was a light still burning in the front parlour window – a good sign for us and one that bode well for a quick conclusion to our search.

Holmes stepped up to the door and rapped lightly with the knocker, trying hard not to cause too much ruckus for the neighbours.

For a moment there was an immediate hive of activity inside the terraced house before a shuffling could be heard just inside, and the bolts were drawn on the entrance door.

A grey-haired, stoop-backed man opened it and peered up at Holmes's tall imposing figure through watery eyes.

"Yes?" he asked, "Do you know what time it is?"

"I do apologise, sir. I assume that you are Mr. Brown? Father of Caitlin?" Holmes said.

"Grandfather actually," the old man said.

"Ah, good. I am Sherlock Holmes, and this is my associate, Dr. John Watson," Holmes said.

The old man looked Holmes up and down then repeated the gesture with me. "What's that to me?" he asked.

"Well, your granddaughter was in the company of Lady Elizabeth Powell, the daughter of the Duke of Cleveland, earlier this evening, and now both have disappeared. We have been tasked with ascertaining their whereabouts," Holmes added.

The old man looked us both up and down again. He seemed very determined to stop us from entering his house.

Suddenly, a softer voice came from within. "Father, let those gentlemen in. It's cold and you'll pay for it tomorrow, I tell you."

The old man turned for a moment and then looked back at us. He shuffled backwards to allow us to enter.

It was much warmer inside. While we divested ourselves of coats and scarves, The man wandered back into a nearby sitting room. I looked for somewhere to hang my coat and noticed that there were no free hooks. All four were taken up with coats, all of which had scarves draped over them as well.

In the end, Holmes and I simply folded our coats over our free arms and stepped into the parlour.

A woman of about forty years of age sat in the warmth of the little room. A cooling pot of tea was in the middle of the room on a small table. A quick scan showed a total of four teacups distributed on either the middle table or the two other side tables.

Holmes sauntered up to the woman. "Mrs. Brown, I assume? As I mentioned, I am Sherlock Holmes, and this is my associate, Dr. John Watson."

"Yes," she said. "I'm afraid that you've wasted your time, Mr. Holmes, Caitlin hasn't been home for weeks. We are so proud of her. She's fallen on her feet with Lady Elizabeth. The two are inseparable."

"That is my understanding as well," said Holmes, "So much so that in such a time as this, when young Elizabeth has been driven to her wit's end, she seeks solace in the only other place available."

Mrs. Brown's face creased up in confusion. "Where would that be?" she asked.

"Why, *here*," said Holmes, "Amongst the family of her closest friend."

"But I just told you, Caitlin is not here, and Lady Elizabeth has never visited before."

"I admire your audacity in protecting the young lady," he said, "as well as your daughter, but we both know full well that they are within,"

Mrs. Brown's face showed a distinct flash of anger. "I said they aren't here," she said, her voice rising in volume. "This is my house, and you should believe what I say."

Holmes paused to let the irritation in the air dissipate for a moment, before continuing. "And that would be fair, except for the evidence."

"What evidence?" said Mrs. Brown.

"Four coats hanging in the entranceway – one with an exquisitely expensive-looking silk scarf. No offence to you or your father, but I would think such an item to be quite an indulgent addition to your wardrobe. Plus there's the matter of the four teacups scattered around this room," he said.

Mrs. Brown looked deflated by the simple logic. "Come in here, Caitlin," she said, not even needing to raise her voice.

A door at the other end of the room opened and two shamefaced girls in their late teens entered the parlour. Elizabeth was immediately recognisable by her more opulent attire.

"Sit," said Mrs. Brown.

Holmes and I shifted around to allow the two to take their seats.

Lady Elizabeth sat straight-backed and stared up into Holmes's eyes. "I do not think we've had the pleasure, sir."

Holmes bowed slightly and said, "No, we haven't, Lady Elizabeth. I am Sherlock Holmes, and this is my associate Dr. John Watson. You may have met Roderick St. John-Smythe. He works for Her Majesty's Government and has been assisting your father broker the deal with the Baron regarding your hand in marriage."

At the mention of the Baron, Elizabeth stiffened and drew in a sharp breath. "Something that brings you concern, it seems," Holmes added.

Elizabeth was close to tears, Caitlin, sitting next to her, took her hand and tried to console her. Elizabeth regained her composure before continuing, her voice slightly shaky. "Are you here to take me back?" she asked, her tone tingling with nervousness.

"I believe that you are of age. Therefore I, and no other person in authority has any right to do so. I am also happy to keep your secret until you are prepared to return. I would say, however, that your father is extremely worried. They believe the story that you and Caitlin fabricated regarding your presumed kidnapping."

"But you didn't," she said. "Otherwise you wouldn't be here."

"True. I generally look beyond the obvious. My purpose here is to establish *why*. Why would you steel yourself away at the instant of, perhaps, the most important moment of your life so far?"

At this Elizabeth lost her control. Tears flowed freely down her cheeks as Caitlin pulled Elizabeth's head to her shoulder and allowed her friend to weep. She turned her head towards Holmes and spoke, her accent much broader than the gentle speech of Elizabeth.

"It's all because of that rotter, and that red-haired tart," she said.

Holmes smiled at the descriptions. "The Baron and – I presume – Doris, the kitchen hand?"

Caitlin nodded. "Yes. She's been gettin' above her station with the Baron. It started with a little flirtin', and then suddenly she goes missing late at night and slopes in just before dawn. I knows she ain't been out the house. You can talk to Friedrich – he knows all about it. Poor lad. He has to keep a lid on it. And then she parades around like she owns the place. Sayin' she's gonna move to Germany and work in the Baron's house and all that." She turned back and patted Elizabeth's head, cooing softly to her.

With her head still buried in Caitlin's shoulder, Elizabeth sobbed. Caitlin patted her head and continued, "I takes her back to her bedroom and we worked out a way for Elizabeth to disappear."

"Did you plan to go back at any stage?" Holmes asked.

"We hadn't thought that far ahead," she said.

Holmes turned towards me and spoke. "Watson, I think we can leave these people in peace. We shall retire for the night and return to Cleveland House in the morning." He turned back to face Elizabeth and Caitlin. "Lady Elizabeth, I will not reveal your whereabouts until I have resolved this matter. I feel that there is a lot more to the Baron's activities than a simple tryst with a servant girl. I wish you luck with the future, but I feel by nine o'clock tomorrow everything will be in order."

We bid *adieu* to the four, replaced our coats, and stepped out of the house, closing the door behind. Moments later the bolts were drawn.

***

On Holmes's instructions, I made my own way back to Cleveland House the next morning. He said he would be leaving early and would meet me there.

As I stood outside the grand mansion, another hansom arrived, depositing Holmes and Roderick to the footpath beside me. Roderick was in a less-than-hospitable mood but contained it behind his normally stoic façade.

Holmes greeted me and we made our way into the house. We were shown into the drawing-room where the Duke and Baron were having a stern conversation. It finished as soon as we entered, and the atmosphere remained business-like. I then noticed Friedrich standing to one side, not far from the Duke's own valet.

Roderick withdrew two sets of papers from his satchel and placed them on the desk, along with a beautifully crafted fountain pen, laid at the head of each contract. The Duke and Baron immediately set about poring over the documents. The Baron then turned towards Holmes and Roderick. "No word on my beautiful Elizabeth?" he asked.

Holmes and Roderick shook their heads and dropped their gaze.

I noticed a slight smile cross the Baron's face before he removed it. He turned his attention back to the contract. "One-hundred thousand," he said. "Well, this should more than compensate my broken heart for the loss it feels." He picked up the pen, signed both contracts and pocketed the pen in one fell swoop.

He turned to Friedrich and spoke in German. "*Mach die Taschen fertig,*" he said. "*Je eher wir uns von diesen Engländern und ihren blöden Frauen trennen, desto besser.*" ("Get the bags ready. The sooner we get away from these Englanders and their stupid women the better.")

Friedrich looked shocked at the Baron's words. He shot a furtive glance towards Holmes, knowing full well his grasp of German. Holmes simply smiled back and nodded. Friedrich's eyes grew wide and he quickly left the room.

The Baron was oblivious to everything and hovered over the Duke, waiting for him to sign.

"If I may be so bold, your Grace, you may wish to read the contract a second time to be clear on the terms," said Roderick. The Duke regarded him for a moment and went back over the details of the contract.

Suddenly a shrill voice entered the room from the doorway. "You pigeon-livered flapdoodle!" it cried.

We all turned to find Doris, her angry face almost the same colour as her flaming hair. Her eyes stared daggers at the Baron. He stood up straight and was taken aback by the vitriolic delivery of the young kitchen maid.

She stepped into the room and headed straight for him. "You used me! All that sweet talk about taking me with you was just bollocks!"

She walked up to the Baron and slapped him hard across the cheek. He was left stunned and unsure how to continue, his hand going to his jaw.

She continued to yell into his face, punctuating each word with a finger jab to the chest, "I'm not just some common strumpet looking for some well-heeled johnny to sweep me off my feet! I got talents, I do, and I'm not gonna waste 'em on some foozler like you!"

She stared deep into his face for a moment before letting out an enraged howl and storming from the room.

The Baron stood, stunned. The Duke placed his pen on the unsigned contract, turned towards the Baron and asked, "Would you care to explain?"

The Baron stammered for a moment before Holmes interrupted. "I believe the Baron is trying to apologise. It seems that ever since this deal began to be brokered, he has been playing the field, as it is called, with your staff. The primary reason has been to undermine his relationship with your daughter."

The Baron began to grow angry. "How dare you!"

Holmes ignored him and continued, "The unfortunate Doris there was just the main player. My informants, who were watching the Baron, saw him leave your presence with a young blonde girl late last night. She was wearing simple brown street clothes with a brown bonnet. Her hair was quite long, braided into in a single plait.

The Duke's eyes lit up. "That sounds like Audrey, my chambermaid," he said. He threw a stern look at the Baron. "How could you, sir? She is barely sixteen!"

A voice with a thick German accent came from the doorway. "I know how."

We turned to find Friedrich standing there. He stepped into the room and spoke. "It vas always his plan. The young ladies who consented vere a bonus, but he only vanted to make the young Lady Elizabeth grow jealous and enraged so that she might do something silly and help the Baron change the deal in his favour."

"What are you doing?" yelled the Baron, stepping up to his valet and staring straight into his eyes.

"I am fed up vith this charade. I was born a man of honour. I am a Saxon. I vas an army officer. I cannot condone vat you had planned, and I vill not be a part of it. You bring dishonour to my country, and all for a little money. Your bags are packed. I quit."

The Baron's rage knew no bounds. He seethed at his valet and brought his hand up in a fist ready to lash out at the younger man.

The Baron's fist flew, but Friedrich simply stepped aside and the Baron tumbled to the floor. Friedrich looked down at him and shook his head.

"Baron, you really are a petty little man. I vish I had never come into your service."

The Duke stepped up to him and placed a hand on his shoulder. "You will always be welcome in my employ, dear boy. Go back to your room and I will find you later. We can discuss it then."

Friedrich nodded, said, "Thank you, your Grace," and left.

The Duke looked down at the Baron and shook his head in dismay, he then peered across at Roderick.

"Why didn't you know about this charlatan?" he asked.

"I do apologise, your Grace, I will be sending out some severe reprimands when I return to my office."

The Duke turned back to the desk, picked up both contracts, and tore them to shreds. He threw them at the Baron as he picked himself up and tried to regain his dignity.

"To think I almost let my daughter marry you," he said. "Get out of my house!" He turned on his heel and left the room.

The Baron started to move from the room. "Would you like a hand with your bags?" Holmes asked.

The Baron stared back at him with a steely gaze that could melt ice. He ignored the question and left.

"Obviously not," I said.

***

Back at Baker Street, we enjoyed a mid-morning repast of scones and coffee.

"I think that went quite well," I said.

Holmes took a sip of coffee, a pleased look on his face. "I'm not sure what was better, seeing the Baron's comeuppance, or watching Roderick embarrassed and grovelling to the Duke."

"Don't be too harsh on Roderick," I said, "He obviously doesn't have the quality of informants in his network like you do."

"Perhaps," he said. Then his face changed as he remembered something. "You wouldn't have a guinea on you, would you? I'll need to pay Wiggins for his information."

Grumbling, I reached once again into my purse.

The Adventure of the Edinburgh Professor

After all these years I can truly say that life with Sherlock Holmes never presents a dull moment. Even a simple train trip has the opportunity to turn into a case of life or death.

Such was the situation I once again found myself in as we returned from a trip to Edinburgh on the East Coast express. Though some would argue that the ten-hour journey, with multiple stops along the way, could be called anything but an express route.

The occasion had seen us journey north to visit my cousin, Dr. Patrick Watson, a renowned surgeon who emigrated to Scotland ten years previously. It was there that Holmes and I became embroiled in an investigation of an apparent haunting of a young family. The case was cleared up quickly and as with most supernatural occurrences was explained away, by Holmes, in an utmost rational solution.

We had booked a first-class sleeper, even though we did not envisage needing the beds. It gave us the comfort of knowing we had somewhere safe to store our belongings and seek refuge if the situation required.

The train itself was quite full. It was mid-January, and many Scots sought out the warmer climes of the south of England at that time of year, plus the service only ran once or twice a day, putting immense pressure on the limits of the train. We were very lucky to have retained our sleeper, as we were almost required to postpone the return trip due to the haunting.

All that aside, we managed to enjoy the first half of the journey, spending the majority of our time in the club car after a delightful luncheon. It was there that we met up with Professor Bernard Lumley. A fellow first-class traveller from Edinburgh who was travelling in the sleeper three doors down from our own.

He was a jocular fellow in his early sixties, that thoroughly enjoyed the sound of his own voice. We found that he was an emeritus professor of Eastern European anthropology at the University of

Edinburgh. His work centred on the early Prussian kings and the influence of the last vestiges of Charlemagne's rule on them. He was very coy about the purpose of his journey, but it seemed to involve the transportation of a very important relic to do with his work. He was bringing it to the University College in London as they were undertaking their own studies in that same area.

Holmes was entranced and engaged with the good Professor in a thoroughly detailed conversation about Prussia and Charlemagne. I'll admit that I was completely lost and as time drew on began to grow extremely tired and quite bored. I decided I needed to stretch my legs and possibly take in some of the cool evening air to reinvigorate my senses.

I stood and bid adieu to Holmes and the professor before striding from the carriage. I found the gangway between the club car and first-class sleeper occupied by several smokers. Even though I enjoy the odd pipe and cigar, I didn't wish to partake in their second-hand smoke and pushed through into the sleeper car.

As I rounded the corner, I noticed two gentlemen further down the corridor. One was leaning over, the other seemed to be keeping watch. I ducked back and stood with my shoulder pressed to the wall listening intently.

They spoke German and the coarseness of their hushed tones precluded me from translating anything I could hear. I could, however, hear the rattling of a sleeper door which seemed to indicate that they were struggling to open it. I deduced that they were either breaking into the sleeper or had forgotten their keys. My suspicious mind told me the former.

I decided to play dumb and simply stroll down the corridor to take in as many details as I could.

Upon seeing me they both straightened up and tried to look as innocent as possible. Failing dismally on all accounts.

I genially said, "Good evening," to them as I passed. Taking in the number of the sleeper, and as many details about the two men as I could. They mumbled a similar reply to me and fidgeted about until I was well past.

I noticed that they turned back to the door as I rounded the far corner.

I quickly found the guard at the far end of the next sleeper and told him what I'd seen. It was his duty to move them on, so I made a note to check back with him later.

I soon found myself in the second-class coach. Almost every seat was taken. The racks above were full to overflowing with suitcases and bags, and at either end, several people milled around. These were the poor unfortunates that either didn't manage to book a seat or were left adrift when the earlier train was cancelled.

I made my way down the centre aisle, feeling a little self-conscious as I was wearing my travelling suit which was a more expensive style of dress than most of these passengers could afford.

As I moved along my eyes were drawn to a most lovely face. She was young, in her early twenties, had shortish brown hair and a rather dark and swarthy complexion. Very out of step with the lighter skin tones and reddish-brown hair of the passengers around her.

I also noticed she was reading one of my own treatises of Holmes's cases. A shimmer of pride ran through me to think that a young girl, such as this, would take the time to read my work.

It was at that moment that she looked up and caught my eye. A small smile played across her lips before she took her attention back to the story.

I carried on and eventually found myself in the guards' car at the very rear of the train. I had a quick chat with the guard and said I was just trying to find somewhere to take in some fresh air. I noticed his straight-backed demeanour and managed to prize the name of his regiment and the rank he had held. Upon hearing of my own service, he relaxed, and we quickly swapped a few war stories and remembrances.

At one point, he even pulled out a bottle of whiskey and offered it to me. I thought better of it for a moment, but then the chill made its presence known, so I thankfully took the bottle from him and gleefully downed a short swallow.

It was as I handed the bottle back, that there was an almighty thump from the front of the train.

The carriage swayed dangerously as the driver applied the emergency brakes. I was thrown forward and the bottle slipped from my grasp and broke upon a large steel box hidden in the corner. I landed in an unceremonious heap at the guard's feet. He managed to hold on to one of the railings nearby.

Screams and shouts of dismay could be heard running up and down the carriages. I rolled over and looked up the aisle. Suitcases were strewn all over. Several people had been cast from their seats and lay atop the cases or vice versa.

A few people had suffered small cuts and abrasions either from striking the seats nearby or from the baggage that rained down on them.

When the train finally came to a standstill, I regained my feet with the help of my newfound friend and moved forward to provide any level of assistance that I could.

Luckily, most of the injuries were light and superficial. Most of the passengers were simply in a state of shock. I told those suffering to sit still in their seats and relax themselves until more information arrived. I did not have any supplies to treat the wounds, so told the guard to stay with the injured passengers and I would come back with my medical bag.

I worked my way through the next carriage, attending any unfortunates that I found and telling them to remain seated and relaxed until I could return. In the back of my mind, I started to worry about whether I had enough supplies on hand.

It is my habit, especially when travelling with Holmes, to bring my medical bag, but it is only ever lightly packed with bare essentials for emergencies. This was an emergency, but the scale was probably beyond even my foresight.

I reached our sleeper and unlocked the door. On returning to the corridor, bag in hand, I began to make my way back to the second-class car when a voice called out from behind.

"Watson? Where the devil have you been?" it said.

I turned to find Holmes moving up the corridor towards me.

"I was taking some air with the guard at the back of the train, just before this calamity," I said, "There are injuries to many of the passengers, I was returning to give aid where I could."

"Good man. I wanted to check that you were uninjured then lend a hand outside. This may be a simple problem with the train, but there was a loud thump before we braked that has me puzzled," he said.

"I heard that too, I presumed we'd hit something on the track."

"From the forward compartments it sounded a lot like an explosion," said Holmes, his face becoming stern as the thought of an investigation loomed.

***

I managed to dress the majority of wounds very quickly within the second-class carriages. They were only superficial, and my assistance was more or less comfort to the passengers rather than a medical need.

As I was finishing up with one patient, the head conductor entered the carriage. He addressed the assembled passengers and said that the train had been damaged and would require repairs before there was any chance of proceeding through to London.

He stated that the train had stopped about ten miles north of Grantham, near the small town of Hougham. Two porters had been sent to a nearby farm to procure some horses and ride on to Hougham to organise transport and accommodation.

The conductor said that all passengers would be lodged for the night or could be transferred to Grantham where they could make alternative arrangements.

A passenger raised a hand and asked, "Can we not sleep on the train?"

The conductor said that suggestion had been brought up, but that all the sleeper cars were full of first-class passengers and it was considered unfair to subject others to the inconvenience of sitting for the entire night. He added that there were also standing passengers and did not consider it appropriate that anybody sleep on the floor.

There was a general murmuring and mumbling of voices as the passengers gathered their things and prepared to leave the train.

I quickly tidied up my medical bag and made my way back towards the first-class sleeper carriage. As I stepped into the corridor, the door of the compartment near to ours, opened and a man stepped out. I once again found myself face to face with one of the German gentlemen. He was as surprised as I was and quickly ducked back inside.

I made a note of the compartment number and stopped by my own to retrieve my suitcase in readiness to leave. I noticed that Holmes's case was still present, which seemed odd as he'd had much more time to pack than I.

I decided to find him first so that we could join the procession of passengers together rather than become separated.

As I reached the end of the corridor, I turned back just in time to see both Germans leaving their compartment. They looked around suspiciously then headed towards the second-class carriage. I noted they only had a small valise between them. I thought about calling out to them that the train was being evacuated but they were away before I could gain their attention. I stared after them for a moment before carrying on to seek out Holmes.

***

As I entered the club car, I found the majority of first-class passengers milling around with their belongings. A porter was checking names and allocating people to small groups for the onward journey.

I asked what the current plan was, and he told me that they had managed to acquire two small wagons that were able to transport four passengers at a time on to Hougham. There they had managed to find accommodation in the Inn, and a nearby manor house, for the first-class passengers. The townsfolk had rallied and set up temporary beds in the town hall for the remaining passengers.

I gave my name and Holmes's and we were allocated to a twin room at the Inn. I noticed that the Professor was in the same place. I was a little inwardly disturbed by the prospect of spending an evening talking further about mid-sixteenth century Prussian politics but decided if there was brandy involved then I would be fine.

I pushed on further, searching for Holmes but finding nothing until I came upon the open doorway leading down to the trackside. A chilly breeze wafted in through the doorway, so I pulled my collar up and left the train.

Darkness had well and truly set in, making it very difficult to see anybody outside. A few paraffin lanterns marked a bustle of activity further up the track. Just the sort of thing that would draw Holmes, so I pushed on through the cold to see what was happening.

A group of men milled around the train engine, pointing and waving hand-held lanterns at parts of the train.

From what I could see, the driving mechanism on one of the great steel wheels, located towards the rear of the engine car, had been damaged.

From my rudimentary knowledge of trains, I realised that the pin that held the crank in place was missing. There was just a hole with buckled metal, and the crank itself was bent and broken and lying askew.

It was that crank that drove the wheels, which meant this engine was going nowhere on its own.

"Damnable luck, ay, Watson," came Holmes's voice from behind me.

I turned and saw that he was smoking a cigarette and viewing the broken engine next to me.

"What would have caused something like that?" I asked.

"I can only assume we either hit a rock or tree trunk, or it was poorly maintained and broke from overuse," said Holmes.

I found his explanation a little below his usual enthusiasm for solving the unknown but forgave him as this didn't appear to be anything worthy of his skills.

Then a new voice piped up from the gloom behind us. It had a much higher pitch than either of ours.

"I reckon I know what's happened?" it said.

We both turned to see a young woman sitting on a tree stump in the gloom out of reach of the paraffin lamps. She stood up and stepped towards us.

It was then I realised it was the young lass I'd spied in the second-class car reading one of my pamphlets.

"And what do you think caused this?" Holmes asked, his interest now piqued. I was unsure if it was because of the attractiveness of the woman or from boredom.

"A bomb," she said.

I admit I guffawed out loud at the claim.

Holmes simply smiled and asked, "And why would you say that?"

"Two reasons," she said, "Don't you think there's an interesting smell?"

Holmes leaned in towards the wheel and sniffed.

"Oil, coal smoke," he said and sniffed again. It was then his face changed to surprise.

"That's it," she said.

"What is it, Holmes?" I asked.

Holmes turned and peered at the girl.

"Smells sweet. I'd say it's Nitro-Glycerine, mostly likely from dynamite. They still use it in Scotland. Easy to get," she said.

"And your second reason?" asked Holmes.

"This," she said and brought something out from behind her back.

Holmes reached down and grabbed one of the paraffin lamps to allow us a better look.

The object that the lass held was simply a mess of wires, metal strips and pieces of wood. It looked nothing like any type of bomb that we had ever dealt with before.

"Perhaps it's just some trackside rubbish that fell from a previous train?" I said.

She stared into my eyes with disdain. I immediately felt like retracting my statement just on the piercing derision contained in that stare.

"I think you sell the young lady short, Watson," said Holmes. He handed the lamp to me and took the object from the girl. Then proceeded to study almost every part of the mess.

After a moment he said, "Ingenious."

He looked up at the young woman and said, "Not just this device, but the fact you recognised it as such."

He began to point out parts of the contraption and explain what they did.

"These two flat panels would have been placed over two consecutive pieces of track. When the train wheel ran over both it completed an electrical circuit. The current ran down these wires that would have been inserted into a bundle of dynamite. It would have taken less than a second for detonation to occur. The fact that the main pin on the eccentric crank, which sits on the third to last wheels, was affected explains that. With the pin blown out, the wheels could no longer turn; therefore, the train was disabled. By design not accident."

He leaned in and sniffed the device.

"The same sweet smell as the train wheel. This device was definitely in contact with nitro-glycerine," he said.

He looked at the girl and handed the device back to her.

"Have you told the engineers?"

She nodded, "Yeah, they took one look at me and fobbed me off. I'm a girl. They know better."

She indicated the tree stump behind us.

"I've been sitting there, hoping you two would turn up," she said giving me a scornful look, "Thought you might at least listen."

I dropped my eyes to the ground, a little shameful of my own dismissal of her claims.

"Where did you find that?" Holmes asked nodding towards the device.

She turned her head and looked up the track.

"About seven hundred yards that way," she said, "When that bang went off, I started counting. We came to a standstill around thirty seconds after the bang. One of these trains goes about fifty miles an hour. I did the math."

"Extraordinary," I said.

"Then I walked off seven hundred steps and started looking. Found that about a minute later and hightailed it back here."

I found that I was regarding this young lady in a whole new light. Not only was she rather attractive, she was incredibly intelligent and resourceful.

It was then she held her hand out to Holmes.

"I'm Lois Cayley," she said shaking his hand and smiling.

"Sherlock Holmes," Holmes replied.

"Oh, I know who you two are," she said.

"Really?" I questioned.

"Yeah. I've read all your stories, Dr. Watson. Love them. I couldn't believe my eyes when I saw you walk through the second-class carriage."

She pulled a pamphlet out of her vest pocket and unfolded it. A small drawing of my likeness sat in the centre of the back page. I couldn't even remember sitting for the portrait but was most approving.

She looked at the drawing and said, "The picture doesn't really do you justice Doctor, but when I saw you here with Mr. Holmes, who looks exactly like his drawings, I knew it was you two."

"We are very flattered to have such a public knowledge of our appearance," said Holmes with a reproachful tone to his voice, mostly aimed at me, "But the question remains Why?"

"Why?"

"Yes, why, did someone wish to stop the train? What is their motive? Has there been or will there be a crime? If so what is it?" he said.

***

A group of engineers appeared to take another look at the broken wheel and crank. Holmes showed them the broken device and tried to convince them that the damage was possibly due to a bomb. None of the men seemed to be imbued with any level of humour and refused to even give any credence to the notion. After several moments of interchange between Holmes, Lois and the engineers, the three of us gave up.

Holmes said, "There's nothing more we can really achieve until we determine why someone wanted to stop this train. I think the only avenue open to us is to journey into Hougham with the rest of the passengers and take stock of those present."

"Ask around?" I asked.

"Precisely," he said.

Holmes handed the device back to Lois and said, "Yours I believe."

She simply looked at the mangled mess of wires and metal and tossed it to one side. Its usefulness had passed.

"If you think you're ditching me to take over this investigation, then you've got another thing coming. You're first-class passengers, so I'll meet you at the Inn," she said and walked off into the gloom towards the second-class carriage.

We both watched her leave, then I remarked, "My word, what a remarkable young lady."

Holmes simply watched her leave, a small grin on his face.

"She is that," he said.

We made our way back onto the train and found it remarkably empty. The other passengers had been ferried off to the nearby town whilst we had investigated the damaged train.

We headed back towards our sleeper and as we approached our own room, I noticed the door to the cabin the Germans had occupied was slightly ajar. It shouldn't have been of any interest but being a part of Holmes's life instils a heightened level of curiosity in one's soul.

I stepped up to the doorway and knocked. There was no reply, so I pushed the door open and looked inside. It was empty, the Germans and any luggage long gone.

It was only through sheer luck that I heard a groan as a started to close the door. I pushed my way into the room and noticed the connecting door was open.

From what I had gathered so far, the connecting room was Professor Lumley's room. I ducked in and was stunned at the scene.

The room had been ransacked. The contents of drawers and cupboards were strewn across the place. The professor's suitcases were open, any remaining items tossed aside.

Another groan echoed up from the floor.

There lying amidst the detritus of his suitcases, several items of loose clothing draped across his supine frame, was the professor himself.

I dropped to one knee and examined him. He had a nasty gash on his forehead and bruising around his chin and cheek. I was certain that the poor man had been assaulted.

"Professor?" I said, "It's John Watson. Can you hear me?"

Holmes poked his head into the room and looked around.

"What have you found, Watson?" he asked.

I looked up.

"The professor has been assaulted. My initial reaction is it was those Germans who were using the room you're standing in."

I looked back at the professor and lightly tapped him on the cheek.

"Professor? Professor?"

His eyelids fluttered slightly then opened.

"Professor, thank Lord," I said.

His face showed abject terror. He grasped my arms with his thin, scrawny fingers.

"I didn't tell them where it is. I didn't. It should still be safe."

"What is?" I asked.

He pulled himself towards me.

"You must protect Charlemagne," he said, his eyes wide in fright.

His eyes slowly shut again, he let out a final breath and relaxed his grip on my arms. I eased him back to the floor and gently tapped his cheek once more.

"Professor? Professor?" I asked.

I felt his neck, searching for a pulse or any sign of life. There was nothing. My shoulders slumped.

As I turned away, my knee caught some of the clothing and dragged them off the Professor's body.

"That explains it then," said Holmes.

I peered back and saw a large bloodstain on the professor's midriff. I could see an inch-wide wound, with blood still seeping from it.

"Murder," I muttered under my breath.

193

I turned to Holmes and asked, "But what was he muttering about?"

Holmes simply shook his head. I turned and began another scan of the room.

"The simple answer would lead to the reason the train was stopped," said a voice from behind Holmes.

I looked over Holmes's shoulder and saw Miss Cayley standing behind him. I was stunned that she could have crept up on him without notice.

Holmes pondered for a moment before posing the question.

"What was so important that the poor professor gave his life to protect it? And what was that about Charlemagne?" he asked of no-one in particular.

Miss Lois took that as a request for information and began to speak.

"Well, the professor and I were undertaking a similar journey, I presume. I am transferring from Edinburgh University to Cambridge. The word across campus was that Professor Lumley was taking a leave of absence to undertake some study in London. He was an expert in modern anthropology, specialising in early Prussian monarchy and politics. One of the rumours that has haunted the university, since I joined at least, was the existence of some rare artefact in the anthropology department. Nobody knew what it was, but all the gossip led back to Professor Lumley," she said.

"Well we'll never know now," I said.

"Have you found his journal?" Lois asked.

I turned back towards the comely girl.

"What?" I asked.

She pushed past Holmes and came into the professor's room. I thought it most impertinent of her at the time but was beginning to gather this was her normal attitude.

"His journal? He's a professor of history, surely he would have some form of diary or journal in his possession," she said as she began to rummage through the spilled contents littering the room.

I turned to Holmes, a questioning look on my face. He simply smiled and watched the young woman at work.

"She has a point, Watson," he said.

I spun back just as Miss Cowley stood up with a thick leather-bound volume in her hand.

"I'd say this would be it," she said handing it across to Holmes, "It's locked. I reckon you'd have a better chance of breaking it open than me."

Holmes reached into a pocket and extracted a small set of picklocks. He had the diary open within a matter of moments and flipped straight to the last entries.

All three of us crowded in to see the pages. Holmes flipped backwards and found one that had a rather detailed hand-drawn diagram of an ancient crown. It had none of the delicate beauty of Queen Victoria's crown jewels but was more of a simple affair. There were eight golden panels each in a rectangular shape with a curved top. Each panel was adorned with large, somewhat gaudy jewels. I assumed that the artisans of the day did not possess the quality of implements to cut the gems to a smaller more ornate size. Four of the panels contained pictograms surrounded by jewels, the front was topped with a large golden cross and an arc of gold ran from front to back to strengthen the whole thing.

"The crown of Charlemagne," said Holmes, "Formally used to crown the kings of France and believed to have been lost during the revolution."

"It must be priceless," I said.

"That would be an understatement," said Holmes, "But the monetary value is negligible compared to the intrinsic heritage value to any of the Prussian, German or French states that Charlemagne once ruled over."

"Do you reckon that's what the Professor was bringing to London?" asked Lois.

Holmes flipped to the last entry, read it to himself and nodded.

"That's exactly what he was doing," he said.

"Does it say where he hid it?" Lois asked.

"No, but any person of intelligence would have left it in the safest place possible," he said, "And that would be the strongbox in the guards' carriage."

"You met the professor, didn't you?" asked Lois, "He was very intelligent, just lacked a bit of common sense."

"We can check the baggage car as we go through then," he said.

***

As we exited through the connecting sleeper and into the corridor, Holmes ducked back into our room and moments later returned cradling our guns. We had taken them with us to Edinburgh in case any rum business arose. Thankfully they weren't needed.

He handed mine to me and the weight of the cold metal in my hand brought back a flash of memories from the action I had seen in Afghanistan. I felt the phantom pain from my bullet wound again and winced.

Holmes saw my look and said, "These are just for protection. I don't envisage we will be needing them." He patted me on the shoulder and placed his own gun away. I followed suit and proceeded after him towards the rear of the train.

Lois piped up behind me.

"You don't have a spare do you?" she asked.

I shook my head.

"Damn shame," she said, "I suddenly feel a little vulnerable."

I turned to her and said, "I'm sure that's a new position for you, not something you would feel very often."

"It's a modern world, Dr. Watson, a woman has to have confidence and be prepared to survive in it."

I nodded and smiled. We hurried on after Holmes.

As we made our way through the next first-class carriage, we could hear grunts and muffled curses from ahead. Holmes slowed and eased himself against the wall leading to the gangway between cars.

I could hear the noise of several large suitcases and trunks being tossed around and finally, a curse in German wafted out. The owner of the voice was evidently looking for something as he mumbled to himself, "Wo ist es? Gottverdammt." (Where is it? Goddammit)

The sound of another loud thump against a sidewall announced another suitcase flying across the car. Holmes placed his right hand in his pocket, grasping his gun, and walked out into the gangway. We followed close behind. I had my hand on my gun as well.

"Hello there," he said, "We've just come to see about our bags. I see you're having a little trouble yourself, perhaps we can help?"

We stopped as the tall, ugly faced man, stared at us with intense hatred and pulled a knife from his pocket.

"Niemand wird dir helfen, Englander," he said and launched forward with the knife. (No-one will help you, Englander)

Holmes batted the blade away and stepped to his left. He immediately jabbed at the German's jaw with his left hand and followed through with a right punch.

Dazed, the German reeled back, before refocusing and launching forward with the blade once more. Holmes managed to grab his leading arm and brought it down on his knee. The blade dropped from his hand and skittered across the floor of the baggage car, disappearing under a discarded suitcase.

Holmes and the German squared up and began to trade blows. I pulled my gun and tried to aim at the German. I intended to wing him, but such a shot was difficult to pull off in the circumstances.

The two combatants finally parted, and just as I was about to pull the trigger, Lois stepped in front of me. I cursed under my breath and dropped my gun hand.

The young lady kept moving and it was then I noticed she held a portable fire extinguisher. She hefted the shiny cylinder above her head and waited for the right moment.

Suddenly, the German was forced back towards her from one of Holmes's left crosses and she struck. Lois brought the extinguisher down onto the German's head with a resounding crack. He dropped like a stone and lay still.

Worried that she'd killed him, I dodged around her and knelt to check the man's vitals. I let out a sigh as I realised he still had a pulse.

Holmes said, "Good work young lady, though I would have had him eventually."

"I figured we didn't have time for macho heroics. We need to find the other one and rescue the crown," she said.

Holmes nodded in deference, "Quite, so."

He turned and led the way through the second-class carriage. I sidled up to him and whispered.

"We should have tied him up," I said.

"No time, Watson, plus the young lady is right, we need to get after his friend," he replied.

***

Just as we entered the final second-class carriage, we spied a shadowy figure moving about in the Guards' carriage.

"There," shouted Lois.

I drew my gun, as the three of us hurried our way down the aisle. Holmes managed to outpace both Lois and myself and reached the final car first.

He suddenly turned, a horrified look on his face, and rushed back towards us.

"Back," he cried. I soon knew why.

An explosion in the guards' car rocked the carriage, throwing the three of us backwards. I landed heavily against a row of seats and struck my head. I understand that I passed out and only have the recollections of Holmes and Miss Cayley to piece the rest of my narrative together.

Holmes landed near me and was rendered unconscious also. Lois was the lucky one. She was shielded from the blast by the two of us but was thrown backwards. She landed heavily but remained relatively unscathed.

She got to her feet, her head still a little groggy, and looked towards the guards' car. The shadowy figure crept back into the burning carriage and picked a cube-shaped object from within the ruins of the strongbox. The figure turned and looked once towards her before darting out of the back of the wagon.

Lois picked her way past our reposing forms and hurried towards the rear. As she reached the exit she spied the man running up a nearby pathway towards a waiting horse-drawn cart. She jumped down and gave chase, catching up with the man just as he placed the small box into the rear of the cart and jumped up onto the trap.

In the most unladylike fashion, Lois leapt onto the trap runners, grabbed the man by his lapels and pulled him bodily from the cart. They both landed amongst the dust and stones by the side of the road.

Lois regained her feet first and strode to the cart and pulled out the metal box. She turned to the man and said, "I will return this. It's not your property. It's the property of the University and the Queen herself."

The man began to chuckle as he got to his feet.

"Oh, but there you are right and very wrong, Fraulein. True, it is not my property, but neither is it the property of your Queen. In fact, it is the property of Kaiser Wilhelm, the Emperor of Germany and modern Prussia," he said.

"If that is the case then he should talk to the correct authorities, not send a pair of common thieves to steal it for him," she said, "I'm sure they would listen."

"You are still yet young. The power and prestige possessed by such as that crown, are not given up lightly. Your Queen, your Prime Minister, your Government, would never submit to such a request. We thought it much easier to take matters into our own hands," he said as he brushed dirt from his coat.

"You killed an old man," she said, her voice filled with vitriol.

"He would not cooperate. Damn fool. Gunther overstepped the mark, but," he held out his hands in a plea of innocence, "if the professor had complied he would still be alive."

Lois stared at the German. Her anger simmering and ready to boil. She took a step forward.

"I will take this, and the proper authorities will deal with you," she said.

"I think not, Fraulein," the German said.

Lois stopped when she spied the gun pointed at her.

"Are you going to kill me too?" she said as her anger began to subside, and she tried to maintain her composure.

"I wish not as you are a lovely creature, but you know too much and that could embarrass the Kaiser," he said, "Now please put the Crown back onto the cart. There's a good girl."

"Don't good girl me," Lois screamed, her resolve flooding back in waves.

She hefted the box and threw it towards the German. It struck him in the chest, knocking him slightly backwards. The box continued its journey, falling to the ground with a dull thud.

The German's gun hand rose and aimed at Lois.

"Thank you, Fraulein, and Auf Wiedersehen," he said.

The sound of the gun cocking filled Lois's ears. She turned away in an attempt to avoid the bullet.

The sound of a gunshot rang out into the still night.

After a moment, Lois's eyes opened. Her brain searched through every nerve ending but failed to feel any pain. She straightened in time to see the German's stunned expression as he stared at her, his finger still poised on the trigger of the gun.

He gagged several times, trying to form words but failed. A dark stain spread out across his shirt. His hand relaxed and the gun fell to the ground, no longer a threat to anyone. The German dropped to his knees then fell face-first into the dirt.

Standing behind him, smoke trailing from the barrel of his gun, was Holmes.

***

I awoke to find Holmes kneeling over me, a concerned look on his face. As I blinked my eyes to allow them to focus on his aquiline face, I saw a smile bloom on his mouth.

"How are you, old friend?" he asked, reaching out a hand to help me into a sitting position.

I noticed Lois standing nearby holding a solid-looking metal box.

"Is that?" I asked.

Lois nodded.

Holmes cocked his head and said, "Actually we haven't checked yet."

I managed to regain my feet as Lois placed the box on a nearby seat. The strong padlock on the front proved to be no hurdle for Holmes as he quickly went to work with his picklocks.

The padlock dropped to the floor of the carriage and we all congregated around as Lois slowly opened the lid.

I think all three of us were rather relieved when we saw the circular gold shape within the box. Lois reached in and withdrew the crown. It was almost exactly like the drawing in Professor Lumley's journal.

It was a very chunky and overtly ornate piece of jewellery, but it had a certain regal look about it and I could well imagine it sitting on the head of the once king of all of western Europe.

My thoughts were broken by Lois.

"Good Lord it's ugly," she said.

"It has a certain charm though," said Holmes.

"I believe it would have looked magnificently majestic on top of Charles the Great's head," I said in defence of the crown.

Holmes smiled and said, "I do agree with you there, Watson. Maybe not the style of crown to adorn our own Queen's head, but a ninth-century warrior king? Yes, I believe so."

Lois turned it around to examine every side of the crown, before returning it to the box.

"Well, what do we do with it now?" she asked.

***

We quickly found the chief engineer who was still surveying the damaged engine and consulting with his crew to determine a way of moving the train. After briefing him of the whole affair he located the conductor and left us to it.

As luck would have it the next carriage to Hougham was just leaving, we sent word with them to alert the local sheriff. With nothing more to do we settled into the club car and awaited the arrival of the authorities.

The bar had been vacated, so I fixed some drinks and we sat down to allow Holmes and Lois to run through their version of the evening's events. I pulled out my notepad and took down copious notes, surprised and alarmed by the various actions of my cohorts.

When both stories were finished, I reread and asked questions to garner extra details. I was amazed at the audacity and athleticism of the remarkable young lady. I peeked across at Holmes from time to time while she told her tale and saw a smile and a look of admiration on his face.

"This was probably not the gentle journey you had expected, my dear," said Holmes, "Where will you go to from here?"

Lois took a sip from her gin and tonic and told us how she spent two years at finishing school in Switzerland, before returning and entering University in Edinburgh.

"I'm afraid that I didn't enjoy the courses on offer, so am heading south to Girton College in Cambridge. I hope to finish my course over the next two years," she said.

"Admirable," said Holmes, "What is your desire for career and life?"

Lois thought for a moment, staring off into space as if to gather her thoughts.

"Adventure," she replied, "I think not the dull life of a married woman for me. My father was a soldier, he always told me to take life by the throat and wring as much out of it as possible."

"And good for you," said Holmes, "Too many a good-spirited woman succumbs to a life of servitude. There needs to be more of your ilk in this world."

I thought on the mention of her father for a moment then asked, "Your father. Where did he serve?"

"He was in the Forty-second Highlanders," she said, "Sadly he died in the war with Afghanistan."

"My word," said Watson, "Captain Thomas Cayley."

She cocked her head at the name.

"Why yes," she said.

"One of the bravest men I've ever met," I said. We had crossed paths during the war. It was one of the biggest regrets of my life. I met him several days before his final campaign. So, full of life and a larger character than even his imposing frame could promote. The next time we met he was carried in on a stretcher. His flesh rent by wounds and bleeding profusely. I had neither the skill nor tools to aid him and he passed under my care.

I related this all to Lois whose face dropped, showing a mix of sadness and admiration. She held back tears as she leant forward and took my hand in hers.

"Thank you, Doctor," she said, "He obviously made quite an impression on you in such a short time, and I can only express my gratitude that you tried to save him."

She leant back and took a long draw on her drink. I repeated her actions. I rose and fixed another round. After my little story, I think we all needed it.

After a brief pause, Holmes finally spoke up.

"I think, Miss Cayley, should accompany us to London for the time being. If I understand correctly, the next semester does not start at Cambridge for at least another week," he said.

Lois nodded. Holmes pointed to the metal box.

"We need to see that the cause of all this fuss is taken on to its intended destination. I also believe that my brother should be informed of these events," he said, "And I strongly believe that Miss Cayley here should be rewarded for her part in the recovery of the crown. I will be putting that to Mycroft as well," he said.

He smiled at Lois.

"My brother works for the Government, so I am sure they will be filled with gratitude and can be convinced to convert that gratitude to some form of compensation," he said.

Lois's face lit up with that thought.

"I was only doing what I thought was right, but could always manage better with extra funds," she said.

"Couldn't we all," I remarked.

www.ingramcontent.com/pod-product-compliance
Lightning Source LLC
Chambersburg PA
CBHW070005260626
47159CB00005B/1683